Bailey   c.1
Kitty and Virgil

Vermillion Public Library
18 Church Street
Vermillion, SD 57069
(605) 677-7060

DEMCO

Other titles by Paul Bailey

Fiction
At the Jerusalem (1967)
Trespasses (1970)
A Distant Likeness (1973)
Peter Smart's Confessions (1977)
Old Soldiers (1980)
Gabriel's Lament (1986)
Sugar Cane (1993)

Non-fiction
An English Madam: the Life and Work of Cynthia Paine
(1982)
An Immaculate Mistake (1990, revised 1991)
The Oxford Book of London Ed. (1995)

PAUL BAILEY

THE OVERLOOK PRESS
WOODSTOCK & NEW YORK

First published in the United States in 2000 by
The Overlook Press, Peter Mayer Publishers, Inc.
Lewis Hollow Road
Woodstock, New York 12498
www.overlookpress.com

Extracts from *That's Him* on pages 42 and 82: words by
Ogden Nash © 1985 Chappell and Co., Inc./Kurt Weill
Foundation for Music, Inc./WB Musicorp, USA Warner/
Chappell Music Ltd, London W6 8B5.

Cataloging-in-Publication Data is available from the Library of Congress.

Manufactured in the United States of America
First Edition
1 3 5 7 9 8 6 4 2
ISBN 1-58567-010-3

For the Bartolozzi Family

Contents

Prologue: A Comical Hero

When she learned that Virgil Florescu was gone from her life, Kitty Crozier remembered their first, silent encounter. She had opened her eyes after a long, drug-induced sleep to find a stranger sitting by the side of her hospital bed. He'd risen as soon as she looked at him. She had noticed there was a glint of something like silver in his smile.

Then he took his smile out of the ward, and she surprised and amused herself by thinking, 'I can't have your baby now, even if I wanted to.' Months would pass before she spoke the thought aloud, to the very same man who was its inspiration that October morning.

'I am not easy in English,' said Dinu Psatta, who had come from Paris to bring her the news. 'Not like Virgil.'

She assured him there was no need to apologise. The only Romanian words she understood were the ones Virgil had taught her – about a hundred, if that, in all.

'You might solve a mystery for me, Mr Psatta. If you can.'

'Mystery? Which mystery?'

'Virgil never told me how he escaped from Romania. Do you know how?'

'Yes. The Dunărea. You say the Danube. He crossed the River Danube.'

'In a boat?'

'No, no. With body.'

'He swam?' She pretended to swim – her arms beating a way through imaginary water. 'Virgil swam across the Danube?'

'Yes, yes. From Turnu Severin. God was with him. Many others were shot. Many were caught and shot. Virgil survive.'

He had crawled into the country that once was Yugoslavia, Kitty heard. Somehow – it was quite a miracle, in Dinu Psatta's view – he had got from Kladovo, near the border, to Split, and from there to Ancona in Italy. He had slept in fields, washed in streams, hidden himself in forests, in the manner of the gypsy.

'He had dollars, in a leather bag, for food.'

She tried to picture an heroic Virgil, a man of daring, of extraordinary physical prowess, and could not see him in her stooped, shambling lover.

'It is natural you are distressed, Mrs Kitty. I am not embarrassed. Cry, as you please.'

What was causing her to weep, she wanted to explain, was the fact that she found it almost impossible to believe in Virgil's courageous swim to freedom and felt ashamed at doubting his bravery. Yet it was the God-attended atheist, the miracle worker, who even now was responsible for her being so sceptical, as she recalled his constant references to his puniness ('I am more bone than flesh, Kitty') and his distaste for sport.

'The idea of an athletic Virgil is –' She choked on the word she had in mind.

'Comical, perhaps?' Dinu Psatta offered.

'Yes, comical. Ludicrous. Terribly funny.'

'It is the truth, Mrs Kitty, the comical truth, that Virgil swam, with body, the Dunărea.'

She had no alternative but to answer 'Of course it is,' such was the conviction in his voice. 'I'm sure it is,' she added more emphatically. 'I'm sure it is, Mr Psatta.'

'He talked of his escaping just one time and he laughed.'

'Did he?'

'Yes, yes. He mocked himself. He mocked what he did with his body. For him, as for you, it was funny. Not so serious, not so important, as his poems.'

'That one time, Mr Psatta – when was it?'

'Seven, eight years past. Before he was in England, in London. We met in Rome.'

'Then you escaped, too?'

'No, no. I was lawful, if that is the exact term. I had a post in the embassy. I feared I would be ordered back to Bucharest every day and night. I am a coward.'

'I'm sure you aren't.'

'You cannot be sure, Mrs Kitty, of what you do not know.' It was the gentlest of rebukes, delivered with a smile. 'I truly am a coward.'

'If you insist, Mr Psatta.'

'Please,' he said and nodded. 'I am one of millions upon millions, all frightened. I am no one unique.'

'Oh, but you are' – the phrase came to her spontaneously, but she did not say it. She offered him a drink instead. 'I have nothing stronger than wine.'

'I shall take wine with you. I shall be happy.'

He took most of the bottle, while she lingered over the small amount she had poured for herself. Dinu Psatta regretted he was not so easy in languages as Virgil. He was forced to stumble in English, the words like stones in his path – 'On bad days they are boulders, Mrs Kitty' – but in French he had less trouble. Now that he was living in Paris, his French path was clearer than it had been for him in Romania, with no big stones left to stop him. He could

3

make his way without falling, now that he was the owner of an apartment on rue de Dunkerque.

'Is there a word for small stones, tiny stones, Mrs Kitty?'

'We call them pebbles.'

'Then I have just pebbles to worry me. On my French path.'

She suspected that he might have Italian and German paths, and waited numbly for reports of his progress along them. But he stayed silent.

'Virgil –' he began and stopped.

'Virgil? What of him?'

'There are papers, Mrs Kitty, and some books. There is a letter. They are for you.'

'Where are they? Have you brought them?'

'Yes and no. They are in the hotel, in the hotel's safe. I did not bring them with me today – here I am stumbling, and at your mercy – because of etiquette. I thought it would be discreet to bring first the news, and after the news to bring the books and papers and letter. I did not want you to have a too great shock at once.'

Although she was irritated by his perverse thoughtfulness, she thanked him for showing her consideration.

'I am in London until Wednesday. I can visit you at any hour tomorrow. You will be at home?'

'In the early evening.'

'With your permission, Mrs Kitty, I shall come with the books, the papers and the letter from Virgil.'

'Of course you have my permission,' she almost snapped.

'You will not need to offer me your beautiful wine and delectable biscuits. I shall come and be gone in moments.'

He kissed her hands and bowed his farewell.

'Is one of the books *Miorița*, Mr Psatta?'

'Yes.'

'And is another the *Meditations* of Marcus Aurelius?'

'It is.'

'His old, old copies?'

4

'So old, Mrs Kitty, they are *infirm*.' He smiled at his choice of word, which amounted, he realised, to a conceit. She smiled, too, in appreciation. He could have observed that they were battered or used or much-read, but 'infirm' nicely described the look of them, if not their substance.

'And they were with him when he crossed the Danube?'

'In his leather bag, yes.'

He kissed her hands again. 'Dear Mrs Kitty, they were only made a little wet. He dried them in the sun, with his dollars, in a field near Kladovo.'

Kitty Crozier did not sleep that night. She lay with closed eyes on the bed she had often shared with Virgil Florescu, aching for his bony embrace. She longed to hear him insist that he had to leave before morning, while it was dark outside, with his familiar joke: 'I have no home to go to.' He sometimes added, as bleak decoration, '. . . I must see if it's still there' or '. . . and it's where my heart is'.

She dozed once, briefly, and in those seconds or perhaps minutes she saw her lover wearing the kind of clothes her father wore in his modelling days in America – a bright-green blazer, a yellow shirt, a floral tie; trousers with perfect creases, polished brogues. He seemed comfortable, happy even, in this implausible outfit, for he was smiling the wide smile that revealed his Communist tooth, which glinted like silver.

Soon after his arrival, 'on the dot of the nineteenth hour', Dinu Psatta urged Kitty Crozier to address him by his first name: 'You were the friend of Virgil and I was also his friend.'

'That's a good enough reason, Dinu.'

'Exactly, Mrs Kitty.'

'No, not "Mrs". Relieve me of "Mrs". Let me be Kitty.' She wondered if she would tell Virgil's plump ambassador, his bearer of bad tidings, that she did not merit the title, having been rescued from marriage with Freddy by Freddy's sudden defection to Ethiopia. 'I prefer to be Kitty,' she simply said.

All that Virgil had left her was contained in a bag from Galeries Lafayette. 'I bought him a pullover there,' Dinu Psatta explained. 'For his birthday. It was two sizes too small. I had to drag him to the shop to change it.'

'I didn't know he had a birthday,' she said, then apologised for sounding ridiculous. 'Virgil kept the day of his birth a secret from me.'

'It was the five of May.'

'And the year? It was nineteen forty-six, wasn't it?'

'The same as myself, yes. I am a month behind, in June.'

She took the bag from him and remarked that she wasn't surprised to find it so light.

'It holds his books and his poems, but nothing more, Kitty. His letter for you is also inside.'

'Have you read it?'

'Virgil's letter? No, no, most certainly not. It is private. It is for yourself alone. It is sealed. It is not opened.'

'Forgive me.'

'You must not imagine, Kitty, that because I worked in an embassy I have the habit of reading always the letters of others. I am away from diplomacy for ever. You will trust a music publisher, which I am today, I hope.'

'I trust you, Dinu.'

'You should.'

She persuaded him to break his promise to come and be gone in moments and to share a simple dinner of fish and salad. She assumed that he understood why Virgil had had an abhorrence of meat and made no reference to it. Nevertheless, she asked him, casually, if he was a vegetarian.

'I regret no. I enjoy lamb, Kitty. Lamb is my ultimate weakness in food. But I shall be most happy tonight with your trout.' He hummed the opening bars of Schubert's

6

Piano Quintet in A and laughed. 'Whichever way it is cooked.'

'Plainly, Dinu. Under the grill.'

Dinu Psatta ate everything she set before him with obvious pleasure. Food, for Virgil, had rarely been more than a necessity, except on those occasions – she recalled to herself – when his delight in the world encompassed it. Then, an oatcake or a handful of raisins would be ambrosia; whisky or water, nectar. Then, a glistening dollop of jam on his breakfast plate would be the cause of inexpressible joy.

'I see why you live in Paris, Dinu.'

'I see what you see.' He patted his stomach. 'Yes, alas, yes. I cannot resist the place. I cannot resist this cheese also.'

She took *Miorița* out of the bag, and Marcus Aurelius, and a pocket edition of George Herbert – stained with tea or coffee and annotated with innumerable pencilled comments – that he must have added recently to his portable library.

Virgil had attached to each of his poems his own rendering into English prose.

She opened the letter, cautiously, with a paper knife. It ran to twelve pages, of which she only managed to read the first before the most terrible dismay possessed her. She let out a howl of misery and listened to the silence that followed it.

I

Stainless Steel

Early one summer evening, nine months after the operation she had begun to fear would leave her permanently listless, Kitty Crozier was overcome by the sweet scent of angels' trumpets. She looked about her to find the source of the smell, so familiar from childhood, before she came to understand it was of her own imagining. There were no flowers in the room. There were no datura plants in the garden, or in any of the other gardens along the street. Memory, and memory alone, had brought the loved and hated perfume to her.

She had been thinking of her mother. The dark-haired Eleanor Crozier was taking her two small daughters, Daisy and Kitty, to their new home, their stately home, in the country. 'You have to thank your dear dead grandfather for this,' she told them as they stared in wonder at the grand house. 'I bought it with the money he put in trust for me. The money he made in India.'

(Daisy and Kitty were to believe for years what their mother and grandmother would have them believe – that Kenneth McGregor had died, as many settlers did, of

9

malaria. Daisy Hopkins, visiting Darjeeling in middle age, learned from an elderly missionary how the dedicated tea planter had occupied his last hours on Christmas Day 1938. He had eaten porridge, prepared by his Nepalese cook, for breakfast. He had bathed – the bath drawn by a servant – and dressed. The morning being fine, he had walked to St Andrew's, the Presbyterian church where he and his fellow Scots regularly worshipped. He had joined in the singing of carols and heard the rector warn from the pulpit of the terrible trouble fermenting in Europe. The service over, Kenneth McGregor was given lunch by Gavin and Elsie Anderson, friends of his parents. No meal of Mrs Anderson's was complete without broth, and the broth that day – the missionary remembered, for he had tasted it – was one of her rarities. Mrs Anderson, God rest her, had stored the smoked fish that was its glory in her larder, beneath a muslin food cover that debarred even the smallest insect. When she lifted the lid of the tureen and revealed the precious flakes of haddock, it was as if the four of them – they each remarked on it – were near the faraway North Sea again. The next moment they were laughing at their foolish fancy.

'I do meander,' confessed the missionary. Then, sensing her impatience, he said: 'Your grandfather took his life, Mrs Hopkins. We used to say there were two things that sent white people to their deaths – mosquitoes and misery. Poor Kenneth was afflicted by the latter. He wanted to be with his wife and child, and they weren't here. He wasn't always at his ease on the McGregor plantation. That much I saw in his grey-blue eyes, but never learned from his lips. He was a man of discreet feeling. On that worst of Christmases he drank whisky and sang with us around the piano, and some time that night he went up to a spot on what we used to call Suicide Hill and put a pistol to his head. It was, if I may be flippant, a popular place with the seriously depressed. Indeed no, Mrs Hopkins, he did not die of malaria.')

Kitty Crozier asked her mother why she had bought them a palace to live in, and Eleanor replied that she had always dreamt of living somewhere with great big rooms and with a great big garden, and now her dream had come true. 'You can share it with me, Kitty. And you, Daisy. The three of us are going to have wonderful fun at Alder Court.'

They were standing together, hand in hand, on the back terrace. Kitty, breaking free, saw flowers that looked like bells. She wondered if you could ring them and whether they made a noise.

'They're angels' trumpets, Kitty. They're silent angels' trumpets. I should imagine nobody hears them except angels.'

'I can smell them,' Daisy said. 'Can't you smell them, Kitty?'

'Yes,' she answered, and began to cry. She was suddenly aware that her father was missing, and as the strange smell became more powerful so did her sense of the loss of him increase.

'What's the matter, Kitty? What's wrong?'

'It's him's the matter. I bet it's him,' Daisy ventured.

'It isn't, it isn't.' Kitty glowered at her sister. 'There's no matter. Nothing's wrong.'

Eleanor Crozier praised her lying child for being brave: 'You are my brave girl.' Those five words, lightly and tenderly spoken, caused Kitty's tears to stop, her anger to vanish. Hearing them in London, in her mind, on another July evening, she was struck once more by her own childish percipience, for she had recognised her mother's praise, bestowed upon her at the age of five, as the surest evidence of love.

'It is you.'

The man who called out to Kitty Crozier as she walked

distractedly in Green Park was picking up litter from the grass with a long spike.

'It is you,' he repeated, approaching her.

'Yes, it's me,' she responded. 'Whoever you suppose I am.'

'You are the beautiful woman in the bed. I watched you sleeping.'

'I'm not, and you didn't. You've been watching in someone else's bedroom, not mine.'

'It was a bed in the hospital. I was working there as a porter. I stopped doing my work to look at you. I thought you were beautiful. I still think you are beautiful.'

She remembered him now – as the stranger who had taken his glinting smile out of the ward.

'It pleases me to see you again. I call myself Virgil Florescu.'

He pronounced his first name in a way she hadn't heard before, and she knew at once that she would be using his way of saying it in the weeks, months and, perhaps, years to come. 'Virgil,' she said. 'I'm Kitty. I'm Kitty Crozier.'

'Now I must tell you, Kitty Crozier, what I have to tell you. I wish to be with you. I am sincere. I wish to be with you, if you will allow me, if you will please grant me the honour.'

His words came in a rush. When she was sure they had ceased, she said she couldn't stay and talk to him as she had an appointment to keep. 'Let me give you my address and number. I have a pen, Virgil, but no paper to write on.'

'I have plenty of paper, Kitty Crozier.' He lifted up the spike and picked off the wrapping for a bar of Swiss chocolate. 'Take this. It is large enough.'

(She would see the Lindt wrapper again, after he was gone from her life. It would fall out of his copy of *Miorița*, the little book of songs and ballads that once belonged to his mother. She would resist the urge to tear it into pieces.)

12

'Please, Kitty Crozier, make my back your desk.'

A moment passed before she did so; before she pressed the scrap of paper against his bumpy spine and wrote on it. In that moment, she wondered if she ought to be cautious, sensible, reserved. She decided, instead, on recklessness.

'I will telephone you, Kitty Crozier.'

'Yes,' she replied and added, 'You really must. I'll be at home tomorrow evening, Virgil.'

She imagined her sister admonishing her as she headed towards the gate near the Ritz. She made Daisy remind her that she had been foolish, worse than foolish, all those years ago with that kaftanned creature, Freddy, and now here she was, losing her senses over a stranger from a foreign country, from Romania by the sound of it; a man with no prospects, no future, who was working in the lowliest of jobs. He's a labourer, Kitty, she could hear Daisy insist; a picker-up of other people's rubbish: whatever is possessing you?

'I hope I'll discover,' she answered aloud.

Virgil Florescu phoned Kitty Crozier shortly after six that Tuesday evening and arrived at her house less than an hour later. 'I have seen a man with rings in his ears and rings through his nostrils and a ring on his lip,' he told her excitedly, as she opened the front door. 'On his lip, Kitty Crozier. On his upper lip, on his top one, he wears a ring. Think of him eating, think of him drinking, think of him kissing –' He paused. 'I think, and I am confused. I am in total darkness thinking of a ring in such a spot. I invited him to enlighten me. I asked him why he has the ring on his lip, and he shrugged his shoulders and said "Because". Then he stopped. I repeated my question and got the same response: "Because, because, because." I shall never know his reason, Kitty Crozier – the because he is hiding behind his "because". It was a delightful encounter, though – especially delightful.'

'Come in, Virgil.'

'You could have given me a false address and a false number. But you didn't.'

'No, I didn't. Of course I didn't.'

'I am glad. I was happy to hear it was you when I telephoned. I almost expected to hear the voice of someone else. I almost expected to hear no one at all.'

(He had wholly expected that the numerals would end for him in nothing. Why should he have expected otherwise? He had embarrassed her, and from that embarrassment had come the mythical house in a mythical street with a phantom telephone and, probably, a made-up name for its owner as well. He had doubted that the beautiful woman he had first seen sleeping in the hospital was even called Kitty Crozier. The 'Kitty' and the 'Crozier' had rushed into her head while the madman with the spike was staring at her – of that he had convinced himself as he watched her walk briskly away. It was too much to expect that she had been completely honest with him.)

'You *are* Kitty?' he asked when he was in the hallway.

'Yes, I am Kitty. I was definitely Kitty when I last looked in the mirror.'

'Kitty Crozier?'

'Yes, yes, yes. Yes, and yes, and yes. A thousand times yes, Virgil – if it really is Virgil Florescu I'm trying to convince.'

'I am he.'

'I don't think it actually worries me what your name is. But I do like the sound of Virgil.'

He took her hands and kissed them, and then they embraced. 'I assume we have sorted out our identities,' she said, leading him upstairs. 'Some sad people never seem to.'

She wiped the tears from his face with the edge of a sheet when they had finished making love. He assured her, again and again, that they were tears of gratitude. He was not unhappy. He was thankful.

'Are you hungry, Virgil? Have you eaten today?'

14

'Some fruit. Some biscuits.'

'That's not enough. I shall cook us supper. Do you like steak? Beef steak?'

There was a silence before he answered. 'I cannot.' He shook his head slowly. 'Not beef. Not lamb. Not pork. I cannot eat such meat. I have a reason, Kitty. Perhaps, one day, I will tell it to you. Please do not ask me to do so now, not now that I am happy.'

'I can make you an omelette, Virgil. I can make you a delicious Spanish omelette.'

'That I should prefer. Fish I can eat, and any bird that has flown free. But not those others.'

In the kitchen, she gave him a bottle of Saint Amour to open. She drew his attention to the label and laughed. 'I bought it this afternoon. In anticipation, I suppose.'

He watched her prepare the meal. 'You are serious with food, as my mother was.'

'Was? Is she dead?'

'She is.'

(If he had stated, as he nearly stated, that she had died in life, Kitty would have stopped doing her delicate work with onions, peppers and potatoes, and asked him what he meant. It was best, at present, to say, simply, that yes, she is dead.)

'Will it upset you, Virgil, if I have steak? I'm eating it once a week, on my doctor's instructions.'

'You must do as your doctor commands. You must understand, beautiful Kitty Crozier, it is my problem only.'

'An allergy, is it? An aversion?'

'An aversion. Precisely.'

'When you come here again there won't be any meat. I promise.'

'You wish me to come here again?'

'I do.'

'You are kind to me.'

15

'I'm being kind to myself, I hope, Virgil. I haven't been so kind to myself in ages.'

(Not, she might have said, since the days with Freddy – the days that came to an abrupt end when he decided, against everything she thought she knew of his character, to become a responsible person. He'd left her a note with the message that he'd seen the light and for the good of his soul he had to follow it to north-east Africa.)

'Where are you living in London?'

'In rooms. In lots of rooms. At the moment I am in a room in Hammersmith. The property is owned by Mr Nicos Razelos, an Athenian Greek with a magnificent belly. He calls it his promontory, Kitty, and he laughs when the buttons on his silk shirts give up the struggle of containing it. Last Saturday morning he lost three all at once – pop, pop, pop, they went, like three tiny bullets being fired. He has this vast stomach, this promontory which he strokes and caresses, and yet he moves on his dainty feet with the grace of a ballet dancer. He is a diverting individual.'

'Why *rooms*, Virgil? Why lots of them?'

'I do not care to grow attached to a place. I fear becoming, as you say, *settled*. I fear most the sadness of leaving. That is why I leave each room without anguish, without melancholy. I go on to the next one in a spirit of discovery, though what I discover is not always – which English word shall I use? – inspiring. Inspiring, yes. I am not always inspired when I open the door on the latest room. I am often greeted with nothing to inspire inspiration.' He smiled his full, glinting smile. 'I shall be gone from Hotel Aphrodite very soon.'

'Is it made of silver, Virgil?'

'Silver? Is what made of silver? The hotel?'

'Your tooth. The one that glints when you smile.'

'Silver,' he shouted. 'Silver! Silver, Kitty? You think the dentist worked with silver? You think I have precious silver in my mouth?'

'I wondered if –'

16

'If it was silver. I'm sorry, Kitty, but I must laugh.'

He sniggered to start with, then he began to splutter, then he said 'Silver' to himself and this released the promised laughter. It started deep in his throat, but in an extraordinary moment became almost falsetto. It was the noise of a boy soprano, his voice not yet broken, his laughter high-pitched and pure. Then the noise was a man's noise once more, followed by a man's loud, satisfied sigh.

'I assume that the tooth is not made of silver,' she remarked when he was finally silent.

'You are correct in your assumption, Kitty Crozier. My shining tooth, my Communist tooth, my tooth that is the gift of the kind and merciful state, which is now led by the kind and merciful Conducător, is made of a more lasting metal than silver.'

(The Conducător, whose name Virgil Florescu refused to speak, was to become a presence in her life for two whole years – a familiar, absent presence. He would be the subject of stories, of cautionary tales, of fantasies Virgil insisted were true in every detail. 'I am a truth-teller, Kitty,' her lover would remind her, 'even when I am allowing myself the luxury of a little invention.' The Conducător's lady, the renowned scientist, would be there at her husband's side, offering him on all occasions, public or private, the approving look, the encouraging gesture. The Conducător's consort had also sacrificed her right to a merely human name – a name such as Virgil Florescu, or Kitty Crozier, or that of any person who wasn't the Conducător or the Conducător's wife.)

'A much, much humbler metal than silver. My tooth is composed of steel, Kitty, of stainless steel. Silver stains, but not stainless steel. My other teeth will decay in time, but not this one. It is impregnable. It is stronger than nature. It is resilient, as the dentist told my parents. I shall take it to my grave, and if that grave is opened in a thousand years nothing of me will be visible except my eternal Communist tooth. Let me predict that it will shine forth from the earth.'

'Drink your wine, Virgil.'

'Yes, yes. I have been talking, haven't I? I have been rhapsodising about my tooth.'

'You have. What kind of artist are you?'

'I am an artist at whatever I do. I am an artist when I sweep floors, when I push trolleys in hospitals, when I pick up litter on a spike. I try to be artistic in each of my endeavours, Kitty.'

'Say.'

'I have written poems. I am writing poems. Now I am hungry.'

She awoke in the night to find herself alone. Virgil's clothes were no longer where he had left them, slung across the chair. His socks and shoes weren't on the bedroom floor. There was no sound of him anywhere in the house.

He had written her a note. It was propped up against the empty Saint Amour bottle on the kitchen table.

> Beautiful Kitty Crozier [she read]. I have to return to the Aphrodite. I rise early most days in order to begin my artistic activities in the park as promptly as I can.
>
> Kitty Crozier, you have far too many books.
>
> I will be in touch with you.
>
> Your Virgil.

It was already that terrible hour, she noticed as she slid back into bed, when certain discontented people find themselves denied of sleep; when their minds are alert to nothing but the inadequacies, the failings, of the past. She was one of those people as a rule, but not on this Wednesday morning. The usual crop of nagging memories was in abeyance, was out of mind, and she felt radiant.

She ought to have felt irresponsible, but was unconcerned about it. She had twice made love – and it seemed like love, not just that other matter, sex – with a man whose looks,

18

whose awkward bearing, had immediately attracted her and whose genuineness she had as immediately taken on trust. She felt she knew she was right to have faith in him.

She slept contentedly.

An aversion? Let us keep it an aversion, Kitty, for the sake of politeness. For simplicity's sake, let my private horror – my most particular horror – of slaughtered flesh remain an aversion. An aversion will do. 'Aversion' is a paler word for 'horror'. Let us use the paler word, if we have to.

Virgil Florescu walked slowly down deserted streets. He was in no hurry to reach the Aphrodite. 'You may wonder, Mr Florescu, why I call this place a hotel,' Nicos Razelos had said as he puffed his way up the stairs in front of him. 'I mean to say, the Savoy it isn't. And never will be. No, I call it Hotel Aphrodite because Aphrodite Guest-House and Aphrodite Boarding-House don't sound right. They sound all wrong. You look like a scholar to me, Mr Florescu, and I'm sure I don't have to remind you that Aphrodite was one real classy lady. She was a goddess and ladies don't come classier than that. That's why hotel. Enjoy your stay at the Hotel Aphrodite.'

He would be sharing the second-floor bathroom, Nicos Razelos revealed, with three other gentlemen: Mr O'Brien, Mr Taylor and Mr Khan. They had a system, a rota – first in, first out, second in, second out, and so on and so forth – which prevented unpleasant skirmishes, bangings on the door, any lowering of the tone of the establishment. He would have to fit in with the rota. 'Otherwise pandemonium.'

'Miss Eunice, who occupies the ground-floor suite, is the only tenant with a personal bathroom. Miss Eunice is a very special lady, very special indeed, if you grab my meaning. You look like you're red-blooded to me, Mr Florescu, but I'm sure you won't take offence if I give you a friendly warning. Miss Eunice is a hands-off zone.'

Lucky Mr Razelos, Virgil Florescu thought, to have the world reduced so; to live with the single fear that someone might steal away Miss Eunice, the frightened pet he fed with baklava. Fortunate man, to be so simply and dedicatedly jealous.

A woman with a ruined face – a face, he could see in the half-light, a surgeon had somehow reassembled – slithered out of a shop doorway and asked him for the price of a cup of tea.

'I have only this,' said Virgil Florescu, giving her a fifty-pence coin. 'I am not rich in money.'

The woman grunted in reply and retreated into what he assumed must be her nightly resting place: there was a canvas chair, of the kind film directors are photographed sitting in, and a sleeping bag, and beside it a tall vase of dried flowers. Her home, such as it is; her portable home.

'You do not have a carpet.'

'I did have,' the woman answered. 'It wore away. It wore itself to a frazzle.'

'Explain for me, please, "frazzle".'

'You must be foreign if you haven't come across "frazzle". When we say a thing is frazzled, we mean it's worn-out, it's threadbare, it's frayed. You follow? Kaput, it's kaput.'

'Thank you, madam.'

'My poor little welcome mat had known too many feet.'

He said good night to the woman, who was now seated in her chair, and moved on. He commanded himself not to let the words 'home' and 'carpet' do their hurtful work. He spoke the name Kitty Crozier under his breath, and shouted it once and heard what he recognised as joy in his voice.

Kitty Crozier had only ever received postcards from her father. At intervals of months, or years, he sent her the briefest of loving messages, assuring her that he was alive and well, and as happy as a king with his newest wife or latest partner. He had never been alone or anything but perfectly contented, the cards implied, untruthfully, in all his time abroad.

She looked incredulously at the backward-sloping writing on the envelope. He had written her a letter. He had picked up his expensive pen and written her a letter. 'How is my Baby Cordelia?' it began. 'How is my one loving daughter?'

(She had been his Pretty Kitty for all her childhood. She'd become his Baby Cordelia when she and Daisy were twenty, after he'd seen a performance of *King Lear* in New York. He hadn't cared for the play; had endured it, he told her later, merely to keep the third Mrs Crozier – the 'culture-crazy' Linda – sweetly disposed towards him. The rantings and ravings of that tiresome old cove had made him squirm in his seat, while the Fool's jokes, if such they were, had brought everything except a smile to his face. He was more amused, he admitted, by the antics of Regan and Goneril, because they reminded him, the girls, of his own malevolent four-hours' first-born: 'Slightly, Kitty, slightly.' Daisy had applied herself to the business of hating him with a stamina that inspired her father's envy, and as he watched Shakespeare's prize pair of bitches turning nastier and nastier a bell of recognition started ringing wickedly in his head. 'They might be Daisy' was the thought that came to him. He'd tried to banish the thought, but it wouldn't go away. Then, late in the endless evening, with the corpses piling up on-stage, including Cordelia's, he'd realised that Lear's youngest had been as loyal and as true to her terrible dad as Pretty Kitty was, he hoped, to hers. 'You're my Baby Cordelia now, my dearest darling. You're your terrible daddy's one loving daughter.')

I hope Life is treating you kindly. I long to hear what you have been up to. Any Love Interest, perchance? You must be over forty now, my dearest darling, but I will bet a million you have not lost your looks! I hate to think

of your Beauty going unappreciated. I hope you are not wasting your Sweetness on the Desert Air.

As you can see from the Address I have written above, your terrible absent Papa is back in his Mother Country. And what is more, Kitty, he intends to stay. FOR EVER, which probably will not be very long. I do not want to die in America and I most certainly do not want to be buried there either. Now you know what I do NOT want, I must tell you what I DO. I want you to pay me a Visit soon. The Person who is caring for me is an excellent Cook and suggests you come for Lunch, preferably on a Sunday, as Dinner is too much of a Strain on the Pair of us.

So my dearest darling Kitty, would the last Sunday in the Month be suitable? Please write and say Yea or Nay. We are only an Hour from London by Car. I can trust you (CAN'T I?) not to let your frightful Sister know where I am living. Of course I can. Unnecessary Request. If she found out I was back in England, she would bombard me all over again with her awful Accusations. She has not exhausted her Supply of Insults yet and never will.

I have Lots and Lots of Monkey's Bums to give you and I hope you have saved up a Few for me as well.

Your ever loving Daddy.

She had monkey's bums and to spare for him – she wrote back immediately – and when they had finished exchanging them, his Baby Cordelia would listen while her terrible daddy brought her up to date with his terrible news. Why, she wondered, was he being coy, since coyness wasn't in his nature, about the person caring for him? Who was this ministering angel? Was she a mature woman, or someone younger? A pretty nurse who had fallen for his charms?

And yes, perchance – why was he using that antiquated word? – there was some 'love interest' in her otherwise dull life. She had met a Romanian. She would say no more than that.

Would he and the caring person mind very much if she brought the Romanian with her that suitable Sunday?

Needless to add that she sent her love.

He was in a field on the other side, the earth lit only by the morning star, when he remembered that the stretch of the Danube he had just swum across had once been spanned by Trajan's bridge – the greatest, his history teacher had said, in the vast Roman Empire. The Emperor's cavalry had clattered over that mass of intricate woodwork on its way to besiege Decebalus.

'You are Roman Romanians,' their father had instructed him and his brother Aureliu when they were boys. 'You must always be conscious that you have Roman blood in your veins.'

For Constantin Florescu that precious blood might have belonged to Trajan himself – or if not Trajan, then a soldier near to him, an officer in the Imperial Legion. Their father had them imagine a noble warrior, a man of learning as well as strength, fighting for five arduous years against the superstitious, ignorant Dacians, who had the courage of beasts. They were to think of themselves as that warrior's descendants: proud, strong, fearless. It was more than probable that the Florescus' share of Barbarian blood had been refined down the centuries to the point of vanishing.

'How does blood vanish, Papa? Where does it go?'

'Ah, Virgil, when you and Aureliu are older, and know of men and women, and love and marriage, and blood joining blood, what I have said will not be a mystery.'

He heard a shot in the near distance and shouting, and then the squawking and shrieking of panicking birds. A red-legged falcon flew low above him, low enough to be captured in his upraised hands. But his hands were clasped about him, because he was wet and cold and naked,

23

impatient for the still unrisen sun to dry and warm his shivering flesh. He had used up all his strength and fearlessness, and craved only the light and heat of the coming day.

He rose, now, from the London grass, his short rest over, and picked up his spike and pretended for a ridiculous moment that it was a javelin and he was Don Quixote, and then he saw a keeper approaching and decided not to charge.

She lifted his head from her breasts and told him she had a twin sister. 'Her name is Daisy, Virgil.'

'She looks like you? She is – what is the word – identical?'

'Not exactly. It's easy to tell us apart.'

'I am relieved.'

'What do you mean? Why relieved?'

'I am not happy to see you in another. Please assure me that Daisy cannot be mistaken for Kitty.'

'I do assure you, sweetheart.'

(She would remember, when he was gone from her, calling him sweetheart for the first time and the strange pleasure she had felt on hearing him say: 'I am not happy to see you in another.')

'Daisy is older than me by four hours. She has always, and I do mean always, behaved as if those four hours were four years. From when we were very little she treated me as her junior. I was the helpless younger sister who needed protecting.'

'Four hours? How painful for your mother.'

'Yes, Virgil. Daisy rushed into the world. Even then she was anxious to set it to rights and as quickly as possible. I'm not unkind. That's her character. I was different. I was reluctant to leave the safety and security of Nelly's womb. I had to be coaxed out. Enforced.'

'You call your mother Nelly?'

'Yes.'

'Not Mother? Not Mama?'

'Oh, no. The three of us had to be friends, so it seemed natural to call ourselves Daisy and Kitty and Nelly.'

'*Had* to be? Why *had* to be?'

'Why? Because our daddy, Eleanor's husband, left us, abandoned us. Daisy and I were five years old and Nelly was still young. We had to be friends and we were.'

'Your father fell in love with someone else? Was that the reason he left you?'

'That's the reason he gave Nelly. That's the reason he gave Muriel, I should imagine, and Joan, and Linda, and Carol, and – well, all of them.'

'He is a Casanova, a Don Juan?'

'Not quite, Virgil. He usually marries the women he loves. Do you want to meet him?'

'Do you want me to meet him?'

'I think I do.'

Her father was back in England, she said, after spending most of his life in America, where he had worked – thanks to his excessive good looks – as a model. He had a new companion, who was caring for him, so he might be frail at last – though it was hard for her to associate him with frailty.

'We have talked enough, Kitty Crozier, and I have asked too many questions.'

'I am a wanderer, Mr Razelos. I do not care to remain long in one place.'

'It upsets me that you are going. What is your next destination? Port of call?'

'I am staying in London.'

'Well, well, well, then – you do not have to leave the Aphrodite. There is no necessity. There is no problem. Why move from here if you don't need to?'

'I am a peculiar man, Mr Razelos –'

'None more peculiar than myself and don't I know it. You cannot excuse yourself on grounds of peculiarness.

You are the least peculiar of all the peculiar persons who have come to the Aphrodite. That is the solemn truth.'

'Thank you. You are kind. Mr Razelos, I wish to move because –'

'You have found somewhere better? More luxurious?'

'No, I have not.'

'I am confused, Mr Florescu. If there is nowhere better, then why are you trying to tell me you wish to move?'

Virgil Florescu, unable to answer, began to laugh. Nicos Razelos patted him on the shoulder and laughed too.

'I am trying to tell you –'

(That I cannot, will not, tell you of sadness and anguish and melancholy; that I cannot mention a carpet from Oltenia and an icon of St Peter and a mother reading the story of Harap Alb to her two alternately incredulous and frightened sons; that I cannot talk of not wanting to be attached, however tenuously, to any room in any building in any country – and that all these things are mine not to reveal, dear Mr Razelos.)

'I am prepared to lower the rent a fraction, Mr Florescu. I hate to see the back of a clean-as-a-whistle tenant who makes no noise and brings no drugs on to the premises. I have not met too many of your kind, believe me. Think again. Reconsider. I shall have an unhappy Miss Eunice on my hands otherwise.'

'Miss Eunice? Unhappy?'

'Certainly. She hasn't stopped speaking about you – in glowing terms – since you had your conversation.'

(Miss Eunice had opened her door one evening to introduce herself to the Romanian gentleman her friend Mr Razelos had told her about. She was elegantly dressed in dark-blue silk and wore a pearl choker like the one Virgil Florescu's mother had kept in her 'box of treasures'. 'I am pleased to meet you, Madame,' he said, to which she responded with 'Are you wondering why Nicky calls me

Miss Eunice rather than plain Eunice?' and before he could say 'Yes', she was providing him with the answer.

'When Nicky was first courting me – and it *was* courting, despite his being married, as he still is, bless him, to a lovely woman, Irene, who understands – when he was first courting me – Mr Florescu, isn't it?' He nodded. 'When he was first courting me, Mr Florescu, he used to take me wining and dining, no expense spared, restaurants and night-clubs, smart places filled with the famous people of the day, and once a week, a Wednesday, we caught the latest big film at a very clean cinema where one of Nicky's friends – a Greek, of course – was manager. This particular Wednesday I'm concerned with, they were showing a picture – I can't remember the title, always have been hopeless with titles – set right down in the Deep South, in America, in a huge house with verandas and whirring fans overhead in every room, and there was this lady of the house played by that tall actress with blonde hair and greeny eyes whose name escapes me, and she was having this affair – "torrid" was the word they put on the posters – with a man who'd come to do some work for her, manual work, which meant he never had his shirt on, and naturally she looked at his rippling muscles from behind her shutters and that's when the idea of being torrid came into her head. What I do recall is the name they gave her in the film. She was Miss Geraldine. Not Geraldine, as with Geraldine here in England, but *Miss* Geraldine. Everyone addressed her as "Miss Geraldine" – her servants, the sheriff and even the man with the muscles who broke her heart, but he said it with a sneer. Anyway, Mr Florescu, when we were coming out of the cinema, Nicky said to me "You're going to be Miss Eunice from now on" and I said "Come off it, Nicky, don't be a fool" and he said he was serious, I deserved the respect of Miss and he wouldn't listen to me telling him it was daft – I wasn't a Southern belle – and he was that insistent, the Miss Eunice stuck, he calls me nothing else, except for very

27

personal endearments, and I have to tell you, Mr Florescu, it does embarrass me a bit. Does that answer your question?'

'Yes, yes, it does,' he replied, adding his thanks for the explanation.

'I can't leave this house any more, Mr Florescu,' she continued in a quieter voice. 'I'm frightened of the outside world. I can't even stand on the front steps. The traffic terrifies me. A man came at me once with a knife and I've had no courage since. Still, Nicky's nice to me, bringing me that delicious baklava, which ought to make me fat but doesn't, due to my phobia. Nicky's promised me that if Irene dies first, which I shouldn't hope for, he'll sell all his London properties and buy a country mansion in the middle of fields, way away from cars and strangers. One fine day, perhaps.'

'Yes,' he said, pitying her. 'Yes.'

'You must excuse me for not inviting you over my threshold, but if Nicky turned up earlier than usual he'd go mad if he found you sitting in my flat, especially with me dressed the way I am, in his favourite wining-and-dining outfit. He's very possessive of me and I'm grateful; it's wonderful to be loved, but I wouldn't want to encourage his jealousy, because it's not worth the awful trouble. I mustn't keep you, you look tired, it's been a real pleasure talking with you.'

'Yes, it has. Good evening.'

'Good evening to you, Mr Florescu.')

'Ah yes, our conversation in the hall.'

'There aren't many people she gets to talk to, apart from yours truly.'

'I do understand.'

'She's given the other residents the cold shoulder. Their faces aren't sympathetic to her, like yours is.'

'Mr Razelos, I *will* leave eventually, but not as soon as I intended.'

'Weeks are you considering? Months?'

Days, Virgil Florescu thought. It has to be days. 'Weeks or months, months or weeks, whichever, whichever.'

She was in his arms when she learnt her first Romanian word.

'*Suflet* means "soul", beautiful Kitty Crozier.'

(How apt, how appropriate, she would think afterwards, that it was *suflet*.)

'I am going to speak a poem for you.'

'Is it one of yours?'

'No. It is not. It is by Lucian Blaga.'

'I'm disappointed, Virgil,' she teased him. 'I was beginning to enjoy the fact that I might become your Muse. It isn't every middle-aged wreck who gets to be a poet's source of inspiration.'

'Muse, inspiration – oh, Kitty, if you can be my Muse, if you can be my inspiration, you will be, I promise. I shall hire you for the job. What salary does a Muse command? Is there an agent for Muses, who will barter and barter until a price is fixed? "Mr Florescu, I am prepared to sell you the services of our Crozier Muse, but I have to warn you that she is not cheap. Her speciality is the wistful lyric – a song of love that opens joyfully but soon invokes the shadows. She is adept with irony, too, though if it's satire you are after I would recommend our lesser Muses – they are guaranteed to bring a snarl to your verses in double-quick time. Clever girls! You are not a satirist, Mr Florescu? That's very useful information. That really narrows the field. Our Crozier Muse would seem to match you perfectly, but again I must warn you that she does have ambitions. She wants to broaden her scope. She is seeking epic status. Before you know it, she will be commanding you to write a latter-day *Odyssey*, a modern *Aeneid*. She will lure you into waters too deep to fathom, if you aren't watchful and wary. Now, Mr Florescu, are you absolutely certain you wish to sign the contract? You are? Then expect the Crozier

Muse to be at your disposal *tout de suite*, or just as soon as all the formalities have been agreed to our mutual satisfaction. I guarantee that you will not be disappointed, Mr Florescu. You have chosen wisely."'

'Fool, Virgil. Heavenly fool that you are. What *am* I supposed to be worth? My agent didn't come clean.'

'That's my business and his. You are worth what you are worth. Listen now, Kitty. Listen to Blaga's little poem.'

He spoke the poem quietly, as it should be spoken, in his own language, and then he translated the untranslatable for her.

'The opening line is easy enough – *Spune-o-ncet, n-o-spune tare* is "Say it softly, do not say it loudly". The poet is saying to his lover, softly, that when we are not together, our souls are separated from us, isolated. But when we are next to each other, when we are two, our souls are there in our bodies. That is it, more or less. I thought you might like the sweet Romanian sound of it.'

'I do.'

'I am sleepy, Kitty Crozier, my Muse-to-be.'

'You won't be here in the morning, will you?'

'For the present, no. For a while longer. Have patience with me. For the present, Kitty, I have no home to go to and I must see if it's still there.'

Perhaps she should begin by saying: Daisy, your irresponsible, flighty younger sister is excelling herself. It was necessary to make Daisy aware from the outset that no one appreciated the absurdity of the situation better than she, Kitty, the twin with the brains who never stopped to think.

Yes, Daisy would delight in the flattery; the reminder that she was neither flighty nor irresponsible. She welcomed such reminders.

The facts, the facts: Daisy would want the facts, the nitty-gritty, the details. These were the details. Her affair, her romance, could be said to have started ten whole months ago, when she was in hospital. She had been under heavy sedation following her hysterectomy, but when the drugs wore off and she awoke in an ordinary ward the first person she saw was a man with dark eyes smiling down on her. She would not describe his smile, with the glint of silver that wasn't silver. She would omit that detail.

The most important detail, the single fact that would cause Daisy concerned discomfort, was that she, Kitty, had met the stranger again by accident in Green Park. It was the ideal afternoon for leisurely walking and she was on her way to have tea with the latest biographer of Warren Hastings when the man from the hospital called out to her. They had exchanged names almost instantly, and she had written her address and phone number on a piece of chocolate wrapping he removed from his spike.

His spike?

Yes, Daisy, his spike.

'The rehearsal's abandoned,' she said and laughed, and poured herself a second cup of strong black coffee.

This was the sixth of the London rooms he had passed hours in and the only one not to have contained even the traces of an icon: a torn and faded poster of Marilyn Monroe in a billowing skirt; a yellowing photograph of James Dean, seated on the edge of a bed, playing a flute; Jim Morrison, posed Christ-like, a lipsticked kiss still vividly red on his throat, and Che Guevara, bedecked with flowers, prepared for burial – in Clapham and Fulham, in Hackney and in Chelsea, these were the sacred images their worshippers had left behind.

He opened the small leather suitcase his friend Dinu Psatta had given him and started to pack his few possessions. The next room awaited him: the next wardrobe, the next bed, the next table, the next chair, and – decorative addition in Clapham and at the Aphrodite – the next Chianti bottle with a nearly spent candle stuck in it.

It was the idea of an icon that had brought him trouble – serious trouble, Radu Sava warned him; deadly trouble. He wished, now, that he hadn't written the poem – not because of the danger it had meant for him, but because it was banal. He had composed it with suspicious ease, the words running ahead of his pen. He had not revised it, honed it, put it aside for later and closer inspection, as was his custom.

'Icon' had come to him at the very time portraits of the Conducător began to appear everywhere. It became impossible not to notice the benign leader. There was no escaping his kindly gaze – unless you walked with your eyes closed, or spent your working day in the lavatory, or stayed at home and starved. The nation's benefactor was most often depicted in uniform, with medals honouring feats achieved in unfought battles pinned to his chest. Then there was that other picture, the one that still adorns hotel lobbies, the foyers of theatres, shops, schools, railway and bus stations, airports, universities and the Hall of the Palace of the Socialist Republic; the picture that heretics, long accustomed to disbelief, can hardly believe: the picture that shows the Conducător, his consort at his side, wearing the ancient Order of the Garter, the gift of Elizabeth, Her Britannic Majesty.

He was alone in the tiny apartment he shared with Radu Sava on the morning the young intellectual paid him an unexpected visit.

'Virgil Florescu?'

'Yes.'

'The poet Virgil Florescu?'

'I write poetry.'

'It is poetry I wish to discuss with you. In a friendly fashion.'

'I have to leave in a few minutes. I have a class at nine.'

'Your first class has been cancelled. Your pupils have been instructed to do revision exercises. We have a good hour, at least, in which to chat. You will be inviting me inside?'

32

'Come in.'

'Compact,' the young man observed.

'Small,' Virgil Florescu responded. 'Confined.'

'What is confinement to a talented man? Many great works have been conceived in – shall we say? – spaces no bigger than cells. I have written a paper on Emily Dickinson.'

'Have you?' he said, keeping curiosity and interest out of his voice. 'I thought she lived in a family mansion at Amherst.'

'She did, indeed. I have been there, to savour the atmosphere. It did not tax my imagination to see how much, with what severity, she confined herself. You have not visited the States, Virgil?'

'No, I have not visited the States, or anywhere else. I have not travelled outside Romania.'

'That is a tragedy, considering the many languages in which you are fluent. You ought to be free to practise them with the natives. That kettle in the corner reminds me I am thirsty. Shall we drink some herbal tea?'

'Let us.'

The young man removed his expensive overcoat, which he folded neatly and placed on the floor beside the chair he now occupied.

'This is a remarkable carpet, Virgil.'

'It is from Oltenia.'

'Then it is historic. It is an antique.'

'Probably.'

'I am ignorant, I confess, on the subject of antiques. Poetry is my domain. Please enlighten me, Virgil – was there a period when the manufacture of Oltenian carpets flourished? A period when anybody who was anybody had to own one?'

'Poetry is my domain as well. There was, I think, a period when they flourished, at the end of the eighteenth century. That is as precise as I can be.'

'I am Corneliu, Virgil. We need not bother with my family

name. This exquisite carpet – that wonderful red; that wonderful blue; those flowers that seem to have been thrown into the pattern rather than formally designed –'

'It belonged to my mother. It is my inheritance.'

'A valuable inheritance. A useful inheritance, Virgil, should you find yourself in real hardship.'

'Here is your tea.'

'I shall leave it to cool for a second. I do not have an asbestos tongue.'

Virgil Florescu was determined not to break the ensuing silence.

'Robert Frost is another American poet I have studied. "I have walked out in rain – and back in rain/I have outwalked the furthest city light" – these are appealing lines.'

'You spoke them with an American accent.'

'It came with my studies, Virgil. I find Frost a problematical case. Wouldn't you agree?'

'You will have to explain what you mean by problematical.'

'With pleasure. In many of his poems, Frost is anxious to be recognised as a good citizen, a responsible member of the community. Civic decency is a major concern of his. And yet – and this is where the subject of Frost takes on the nature of the problematical – and yet the biographical evidence indicates that he was anything but decent. He was cruel to his wife – or was it wives? – and children, and he drank to excess. Speaking for myself, it is a problem that the poetic Frost is so markedly different from the Frost of lax morals and perverted habits. I recall the white-haired old gentleman, full of the wisdom of years, whom John F. Kennedy invited to the White House and I shudder.'

'Do you?'

'Yes, I do. Are you a drinker, Virgil?'

'Of alcohol?'

'Of course of alcohol. I am not alluding to the drinkers

of tea, coffee and water. The human race, in short. Are you a drinker of alcohol, Virgil?'

'Yes. When it is available. I sometimes drink a beer or a glass of wine.'

'Not *țuică*? You would not be a true Romanian if you did not like the taste of *țuică*.'

'Yes, *țuică*, too.'

'I have a sudden urge to smoke. May I offer you an American cigarette? A Kent, no less.'

'No, thank you. It is perhaps un-Romanian of me, but I do not smoke. I will fetch you an ashtray.'

'A moderate drinker, a non-smoker – you do not appear to fit the picture most of us have of the prototypal poet, Virgil. Are you immoderate in other ways?'

'No.'

'Are you, then, the model citizen Robert Frost aspired to be?'

'I doubt it.'

'You are not so perfect, I hope, that you will not welcome a little praise. I am a sincere admirer of your poetry. I find it resonant and subtle. The smell of my cigarette is not displeasing to you?'

'No.'

'In America I made a joke. I neglected to eat their cereal, their fried eggs and ham and their hash browns – such a *mélange* of food was all too heavy on my stomach at the start of the day. Instead, I drank coffee – the real thing, Virgil, not our acorn substitute – and smoked my first ciga-rette of the morning. I called the combination my cooked breakfast. My American friends were most amused.'

'Yes?'

'Yes. As I say, Virgil, your poetry impresses me. There is, however, one poem, and one alone I must emphasise, that I do not care for. Can you guess which one I am referring to?'

'I cannot.'

'I'm sure you can. If I were asked to write about it I should describe it as a squib. You are not an indulgent artist, but this poem is an indulgence. In this exceptional poem you give full rein to your crudest feelings. You eschew subtlety. You employ an obvious conceit to obvious purposes.'

'I do?'

'Oh yes, Virgil, oh yes. You are your own harshest critic normally, which is why I respect you. But with this poem, this solitary poem, you were not harshly critical. That is the reason I enquired about your drinking. Were you drunk when you wrote it?'

'Was I drunk when I wrote *what*?'

'"Icon".'

'You have read it?'

'Closely. Scrupulously. Did you think that by allowing a callow youth to publish "Icon" in a student magazine in Tirgu Mureş your host of admirers would somehow overlook it? We Florescu fans are eager for our hero's every word. Do not underestimate us. "Icon" was brought to my immediate, and disappointed, attention. How many copies did the poor child publish?'

'I don't know.'

'No more than two hundred, I have been reliably informed. He is not planning a second edition of that issue. Your discerning readers, who have been denied access to "Icon", may consider themselves fortunate. Or "blessed", Virgil, if I may borrow the word you put to such feeble and repetitive effect in the poem. And those of us, myself included, who are not "blessed", what must we do? I will supply the answer, Virgil. We must overlook your aberration. We will cast "Icon" from our minds, in the course of time. The poet himself may, or possibly will, do likewise. You are aware, aren't you, that there is no official censorship in our country?'

'I am aware.'

'Were you a Hungarian, say, or a Czech, you would not

36

have the same freedom to censor your own writings, to be self-critical, to show restraint. A freedom, I suggest, you have temporarily abused. Honour that freedom, Virgil. While I was in America, researching Emily, I was saddened by the fact that no one outside the university seemed to read the great American poets. Here it is different. Here the poet is respected. Here he has a public role to play and, should he be so inclined, a public duty to fulfil.'

The young man rose, picked out a wrinkled apple from a bowl on the table, and remarked '"Ye shall know them by their fruits". This one was not picked from the forbidden tree.' He bit into it. 'No, Eve would not have been tempted. You will eat the remainder?'

'Leave it in the ashtray, with the stub of your Kent cigarette.'

'You have a class at ten thirty, I believe. Your pupils are expecting you. I will accompany you down to the street. Ah, my overcoat. I nearly forgot it. I bought it, along with the Fair Isle pullover you have been staring at throughout our discussion, at Orly airport, in the duty-free shop. The *perks*, as I heard them say in America, of travelling in style.'

Dear Nicos Razelos: I fear I am having to make a get-away. The reason for my departure cannot be expressed in ordinary terms, in the language we speak to one another. I have not been unhappy at the Aphrodite. I have to move on. It really is as simple as that.

Please say goodbye to Miss Eunice on my behalf and wish her happiness from me. I hope she will be cured of her phobia some day.

An extra week's rent is enclosed.

With thanks to you and kind thoughts. Virgil Florescu.

There was no one else on the premises – except for Miss Eunice, who was in her bathroom, singing – when Virgil Florescu closed the front door of the Hotel Aphrodite behind him for the final time.

2

Cerberus

'I have jowls, Kitty,' was the greeting Felix Crozier accorded the daughter he had not seen in eight years. 'You'd be blind not to notice them. I am *jowly*, my darling.'

'"Vanity, vanity, all is vanity."' The man who spoke – Kitty Crozier could not resist observing – had eyes that shone with a fierce brilliance. His large bald head would have fitted more comfortably on to a taller, broader body. 'Shut up about your jowls, Crozier, and give the poor woman a kiss.'

Felix Crozier did as he was commanded.

'You promised me a monkey's bum, Daddy. Lots of them, in fact. Let me have a monkey's bum.'

'A monkey's bum, Crozier? What on earth is she demanding of you?'

'It's from when I was a child, Mr – I'm sorry, but I don't know your name.'

'That's because I haven't told you and Crozier here isn't exactly quick off the mark when introductions are necessary. I am Derek Harville, your jowly father's companion, adviser, nurse, gardener, cook, bottle-washer, general factotum, and if there's any other post of a menial nature I haven't mentioned rest assured I fill it. I am pleased to make your acquaintance at last.'

'And this is my friend Virgil Florescu. Virgil, meet my father – and Mr Harville.'

'So you are the mysterious Romanian?'

'I am Romanian, yes, Mr Crozier.'

'He doesn't look remotely mysterious. He looks perfectly normal and ordinary from where I'm standing. What is mysterious, Crozier, is this monkey's bum business. I shan't serve drinks until I've had a satisfactory explanation.'

'It's from when I was a child, Mr Harville. Daddy took my twin sister, Daisy –'

'I've heard masses on *that* subject. Masses and masses. Do continue.'

'Daddy took us to the zoo, and we watched the monkeys scampering up and down in their cages, and I started to laugh at the sight of their pink bums. Then Daddy said "I can shape my lips into a monkey's bum" and he put his lips together and stuck them out, and I laughed even more. Then Daddy said "Do a monkey's bum for me, Kitty" and I did, and then he said "Let's share a monkey's bum kiss" – and that's the explanation.'

'Shall we demonstrate for them, dearest darling?'

'Yes.'

They kissed in the manner Kitty had described and Derek Harville said, 'Well, now that you've solved the monkey's bum mystery, we're all suddenly very much wiser. Was Daisy amused, Crozier? Did she join in the fun?'

'I honestly can't remember, Derek.'

'Neither can I, Mr Harville, but she probably didn't.'

'Daisy's my secret weapon, Kitty. I assume the use of the familiar Kitty is in order?'

'It is.'

'Yes, Kitty, your sister is my trump card, the trick I intend removing from my sleeve, as it were, when Crozier here

39

becomes especially difficult and cantankerous. I shall threaten the old roué with one of Daisy's alarming telephone calls and watch those jowls wobble with fright.'

'She doesn't know I'm living in England.'

'From what you have told me, *ad* almost *nauseam*, Crozier, nothing deters the resourceful Daisy when she is in patricidal mood. She'd find you anywhere, under any stone. Did she not track you down in Aspen, Colorado, once?'

'That wasn't so clever of her. That was in my Carol days. Carol's face was never out of the magazines and papers. Daisy read somewhere that Carol was taking a much needed vacation with the dashing new man in her life and, hey presto, there she was on the line shouting obscenities at me.'

'With every good reason, I have no doubt, Crozier. Now, why don't the three of you disport yourselves on the lawn while I nip inside and fetch us all something refreshing to drink?'

'Champagne, Derek. The vintage Krug. Today's a very special occasion. It isn't often that dearest darling Kitty and her terrible father are reunited.'

Derek Harville made a snorting noise and disappeared.

'Follow me,' said Felix Crozier leading Kitty and Virgil along the side of the cottage into the back garden. The huge lawn had been recently trimmed, and on its borders Kitty saw roses, marigolds, delphiniums, pinks, sweet-peas and an isolated patch of love-in-a-mist. 'Serene, isn't it? It's Derek's handiwork. He's the chap nature's favoured with green fingers. Let's sit in the shade, under the willow by the pond.'

'When you wrote in your letter – and what a surprise it was, Daddy, receiving a letter from you – when you wrote that there's a person caring for you, I didn't expect –'

'Derek?'

'Well, a man.'

'I bet you didn't. And I hope you're not thinking what I think you may be thinking.'

'What's that?'

'That I've started playing funny buggers in my dotage. Because I haven't. I can say this while the coast is clear for a minute, but Derek's not what he seems. I know he gives the impression that he's as queer as a chorus boy's backside, but he isn't. He's no oil painting either, but that hasn't stopped the women chasing after him and fighting over him. Can your Romanian understand what I'm saying?'

'I can, Mr Crozier. I understand, too, that you are confiding in Kitty. I am Virgil,' he added, pronouncing his name the English way.

'Ah, right. Virgil. I didn't quite catch it when Kitty said it. Virgil, eh? Unusual.'

'It's pretty common in Romania.'

'Is it? How fascinating. There aren't many Felixes in Britain and America, not in my experience. In all my seventy-plus years I've never bumped into another Felix. Makes me feel a wee bit unique. Yes, well, that's Felix for you. Call me Felix.'

'Daddy, have you been very indiscreet about Daisy? How much have you told your companion?'

'I'll be honest with you, Kitty darling. I've been silence itself on the little matter of her – of her – disorder. It's just her terrorist tactics I've remarked on. And the fact that she hates me.'

'Hasn't Derek asked why she hates you?'

'I suppose he has.'

'And you've replied?'

'That I haven't an idea. Disliking me would make sense, Kitty. What's the phrase? Healthy dislike. Why doesn't the wretched creature simply dislike me? I don't deserve her hatred. I'm not worth hating.'

(Some months earlier, when she was only days out of the hospital, she awoke from an afternoon nap and switched

41

on the radio. She was alert within seconds, because the man who was giving the talk on Kurt Weill's music was praising a song she had not anticipated ever hearing again. 'That's Him', the expert revealed, was written for the character of Venus in the show *One Touch of Venus* and Mary Martin had sung it seated on a wooden chair she had drawn down to the footlights, the better to entrust the audience with her happy news. As Kitty Crozier listened to the same record she and Daisy had heard several times over during the course of that momentous Easter holiday, she hoped that her sister was tuned to a different station, or walking the dogs, or preparing in the quiet of her kitchen one of her plain and wholesome meals for Cecil and the children:

> You can shuffle him with millions,
> Soldiers and civilians,
> I'd pick him out.
> In the darkest caves and hallways,
> I would know him always
> Beyond a doubt.

Venus was singing, and Kitty and Daisy were once more in the doorway, watching their handsome father as he clipped his moustache.)

'And as for Baby Cordelia, that's still *entre nous*. It's too silly, too private.'

'My ears are throb, throb, throbbing,' said Derek Harville as he approached them, bearing a tray which he placed on an iron table. 'Does that mean, perchance, that I am the topic of conversation?'

'Yes and no, Derek. Perchance it does; perchance it doesn't.'

'May I assist you, Mr Harville?'

'That's extremely courteous of you. It's Derek, please. Remind me of your name.'

'Virgil will suffice.'

'Thank you, sufficient Virgil. I hereby appoint you passer-

42

round of the nuts and olives.' He opened the champagne –
'Not a drop spilt. Aren't I the dexterous one?' – and filled
the glasses.

'To Daddy, and to Derek.'

'To my dearest darling Kitty.'

'To sufficient Virgil.'

'*Noroc.*'

'Which means?'

'Happiness. *Noroc* is the word we use when we toast
each other. *Noroc* is good luck, or happiness.'

'Then loads of *noroc*, heaps and heaps of it, for all of
us.'

They drank.

'Nectar. Sheer nectar. I should have treated myself to
much, much more of this when I was younger.'

'Then you would not have been svelte and you wouldn't
have sustained a career as a model, and the rich ladies
wouldn't have lusted for you if you'd had a paunch and a
boozer's flushed complexion. What nonsense you evacuate,
Crozier. Tell me, sufficient Virgil, is Romania one of those
plum brandy countries?'

'We have such a drink: *ţuică*, it is called. I prefer it
flavoured with apricot.'

'If it's anything like slivovitz it's not for me. Firewater,
absolutely diabolical firewater. Thirty years on, the ghastly
memory of losing my memory persists. Two days went missing from my life, thanks to a mere half-bottle of slivovitz.
It still rankles with me – the idea of having lost control.'

'Derek's a controlling sort of person. Aren't you, Derek?'

'Someone has to be. Think of a world consisting only of
Crozier here multiplied by billions, with nary a factotum
in sight, and you'll soon have a picture of total chaos blur-
ring your vision. No, let's not think of it, it's too upsetting.
I run a trim ship.'

'With a helpless second-in-command, eh, Derek?'

'You said it, Crozier.'

The old men chuckled at this rejoinder, and the gentle noise they made struck Kitty and her lover as not unaffectionate.

'My glass is empty, Derek.'

'Is it, by Jove? And what of your daughter's? And sufficient Virgil's? In polite households, Crozier, the needs of guests usually take priority.'

'I have enough, Derek. I must be careful.'

'I'll fill you up with gallons of coffee, so don't be worrying this early in the proceedings about driving home. There you are, Kitty. There you are, Virgil.'

'What has happened to my "sufficient"?'

'Missing it already? It'll be back in time for lunch. Oh, Crozier, there's just a smidgen, the merest smidgen, of bubbly at the bottom. It's for you.'

'Open some more.'

'No, no, no. You have Sauvignon to come and a heavenly Margaux, and a Monbazillac with dessert, and if you're coherent after those I might allow you an Armagnac to settle your stomach. But for now, Crozier, be strong-willed and be patient. Meanwhile, the stove beckons me. Bring Kitty and her sufficient Virgil into the house at your leisure – that is to say, this month, this week, this afternoon, *today*.'

'How did you meet Derek, Daddy? And where?'

'Wait for him to vanish. He'll come back and correct every damned thing I tell you otherwise. There, he's gone. Yes, well, dearest darling, I met him first when I was with the frightful Joan. Was it Joan, now I think of it, or was it Linda? No, it *was* Joan. It has to be Joan. Yes, it was in the Joan days. Joan had this thing about the English aristocracy, thought the sun shone out of their arses. Her idea of ecstasy was to stand outside a stately home and wonder what Milord and Milady were doing behind those great windows. I got to dread coming to England with her. Do you remember Joan, Kitty darling?'

'Yes, Daddy, I do. I liked her more than Muriel.'

44

'Anyone would. She's dead, the bitch. Muriel, that is. Well, yes – Joan. It's Joan we're dealing with. Joan found out there was this viscount or duke or what the hell he was who was begging for money to restore his south wing or north wing, whichever wing it was, where his collection of paintings by that chap who specialised in barges – no, they're not barges, what are they, the tiny boats the men dressed as barbers' poles steer along in Venice –'

'Gondolas, Felix. The paintings must be by Canaletto.'

'Gondolas, yes, thank you. Yes, by Canaletto. Yes, thank you, Virgil. Yes, well, Joan sent this viscount or duke one of her nice big healthy cheques, with the result that she and her husband, me, were invited to dine at the family pile. And that's where I came across Derek, who was the duke's or viscount's butler. My God, did Derek turn that into a memorable evening for me. The nerve of the man. The gall.'

'Why, Daddy? What did he do?'

'What didn't he, the rogue. He caught my eye at the reception in the picture gallery – oh, Joan was in her element being presented to Lord This, Lady That, and a couple of doddery near-royals – and he winked at me. He actually winked at me. The next thing was that he walked over to me and asked if the wine was to my taste, and I was on the verge of the expected "Yes" when he came out with "Because if it is, your palate is beyond salvation. You would have been safer with spirits, sir, but His Grace keeps those under lock and key." And then he was off, nodding here, bowing there, to all appearances the perfect servant.'

'Did he speak to you again?'

'Yes, yes. Out of the corner of his mouth, like a clever ventriloquist. I was stuck between an ancient crone in a tiara and some inbred young oaf at dinner – Joan, of course, was up at the top with His Grace – and every time Derek passed he'd mutter something to me. Of the crone, for instance, he said "She had a booking on the *Titanic*, but cancelled at the eleventh hour. Very inconsiderate of her" and – this one I'll never forget – "There's an excellent fish-and-chip shop in the adjoining town. Warmly recommended" and "Be frugal, sir, it is Cook's worst night in living memory." The laughs, the laughs. I can't recall everything he muttered in whichever ear was convenient for him, except for what he said as we were leaving: "I trust this has been an instructive experience, sir. You have seen how the turds live." He winked at me again while he was helping madam, Joan, into her cape. "Oh, it's been totally, totally wonderful, Harville," she was gushing, and Harville – Derek – bowed and scraped and assured madam that he and his devoted staff were only content when they were certain that His Grace's distinguished guests were contented also.'

'Crozier!' Derek Harville bellowed from the conservatory. 'Today!'

'Trouble, trouble. Let's go in, Kitty darling. And your friend.'

Kitty and Virgil followed Felix Crozier into the cottage.

'I bought it for the beams,' said Derek Harville. 'A few of them are the genuine originals. Before we seat ourselves at table, does anyone want to wash those euphemistic hands?'

Virgil did, and was told that the bathroom was to the right at the top of the not-genuine and not-original stairs.

'He's quite gloomy, your friend.'

'He's serious.'

'His clothes, Kitty darling. His awful clothes. Forgive me for saying so, but he is drabness personified.'

'I'm not bothered by what he wears.'

'What's his job?'

'At the moment he's working in one of the London parks. Virgil's a poet.'

'Airy-fairy type, eh? Can't you do better for yourself, Kitty?'

'What's better?'

'Someone with an income. Someone with a bit of dress

sense. Someone, Kitty darling, with some flesh on him.'

'You must excuse an intervention from the factotum. He *is* skinny, Kitty. What do they eat in Romania?'

'Not very much, Derek. Unless they're politicians, or privileged.'

'I'll feed him up for you. There's plenty of everything. We've scallops, and roast lamb and –'

'Lamb? I forgot to say. I'm sorry, but Virgil can't eat lamb. He has an aversion to it.'

'He's vegetarian?'

'Not completely. It seems to be red meat he's averse to. I'm very sorry, Derek. He'll have the scallops, I'm sure.'

'I assume it goes with being a poet, Kitty – not touching red meat.'

'Quiet, Crozier. Ration your inanities, if you would be so kind. What lies was your loose tongue imparting to Kitty and her poet out there?'

'No lies, Derek. No lies. Honestly, Derek, no lies.'

Derek Harville mimicked her father – ' "Honestly, Derek, no lies" ' – with an accuracy that would have caused Kitty to laugh in recognition had she not found herself slightly shocked by it.

'He does me perfectly, doesn't he? Uncanny, isn't it? Gets my voice to a T. I wish I had his knack. I'd have earned myself a fortune as an entertainer.'

'You are not exactly impoverished, Crozier, and in certain respects you were employed in the entertainment industry. Night after gruelling night.'

The old men's second outbreak of chuckling was interrupted by the return of Virgil. 'I smell meat cooking,' he said.

'Yes, and it is not for you. Kitty has forewarned me regarding your – your aversion, isn't it?'

'Aversion, yes.'

'I shall ply you, sufficient Virgil, with a sufficiency of beans and baby, baby carrots. There's masses of hearty

47

lettuce, too, delicately enhanced with my own vinaigrette. You will not starve.'

'No, I won't. You are a kind man.'

'Did you hear, Crozier? Did you catch Virgil's compliment? Please don't pay me any more, I beg of you, or my already sizeable head will swell. One will suffice, sufficient Virgil.' He clapped his hands. 'To your places, to your places.'

(In later years, in the years of utter desolation, Kitty Crozier would be seated at the exquisitely set table with the vase of sweet-peas from the garden at its centre; would be seated in that low-ceilinged, oak-beamed room, marvelling that the constant banter of her father and his Mephistophelean companion had progressed to a state beyond words, had become a kind of fearsome music, high and shrill; would be seated there, again, looking across at the soulful man in a stranger's cast-offs, willing his eyes to meet hers in fond conspiracy – willing them and willing them for ever.)

'You're obviously not averse to coquilles Saint-Jacques.'

'No. I am not. Thank you.'

'Crozier's partial to them, aren't you? The first time I prepared coquilles for him I had to stop him trying to consume the shell.'

'That's a lie, Derek. I'm not a gastronomic cretin, whatever else I am. And I wasn't telling lies to darling Kitty and her Romanian out on the lawn. I was regaling them with stories about the evening I had the misfortune to meet you, you scoundrel.'

'Ah, yes. A truly nightmarish occasion, even by the nightmarish standards maintained by the Duke. He was meanness incarnate. Fund-raising to restore the west wing gallery, indeed! He could have restored it a hundred times over and still have had tons of shekels left in the family's – beg pardon – kitty. The only thing he was generous with – to the point of being lavish – was his ignorance. He *was* a gastronomic

cretin, to purloin your phrase, Crozier, and by far the worst
of many I worked for. All in all, however, I was happiest
in his employment.'

'Why was that, Derek?'

'Because, Kitty, he afforded me the greatest scope for
insolence. I was cautious to start with, testing the waters
of sarcasm, as it were, but little by little I ventured out of
the shallows and into the depths, the sublime depths, of
rudeness. I despised him. I despised him – I can say it now,
calmly – with a ferocity that was uncontainable. I considered quitting his service when my feelings became – yes,
murderous. I wanted to, needed to, murder him. But then,
one morning, he and I were both saved – he from a possible
violent death; I, as a possible consequence, from the hang-
man's rope – by his response to a comment I was convinced
would render him puce with fury. There was a moment,
and what a moment, of silence between us – he stared
at me, gasping; I stared back, astonished at my daring.
"Goodness, goodness, goodness," he spluttered, eventually.
"Goodness, Harville, what a bold man you are. Goodness
me, is it your intention to be always so frank with your
master?" I nodded and thus began a working relationship
that survived until the monster died of bowel cancer in his
ninth decade.'

'What was the comment?'

'It was of a personal, a very personal, nature. I was privy,
it dismays me to recollect, to a knowledge of the ducal
anatomy otherwise only in the possession of himself, his
wife and his doctor. I made use of my knowledge on that
historic morning by suggesting – none too subtly – that his
notorious parsimony was not unconnected psychologically
to the scanty object on his person that the Duchess needed
a magnifying glass to discover. That was my comment,
Kitty, of September the twenty-third nineteen forty-seven –
a rare day; a joyous day; the day I exhibited true courage.'

49

'Derek's being untypically modest. He was decorated in the war. He –'

'Silence, Crozier. Pour the red wine, if you please. Are you aware, Virgil, that John Keats enjoyed a glass or two of Margaux? Hence the "purple-stained mouth", I presume.'

'No. I was not aware.'

'You are now. Is there, perchance, a Romanian Keats? Someone similar?'

'Yes, there is. Eminescu. Mihai Eminescu.'

'And is he as melancholic?'

(The moon appearing above the tree tops melancholic? A sad heart stirring at the faint sound of a distant horn melancholic? The poet's sweet wish for an early death melancholic?)

'Yes, Derek, he is as melancholic as Keats. More so, in my opinion.'

'Dear, dear. Poor man. He must have had a rotten time of it. Died young?'

'Yes.'

'No doubt a happy release, as they say. I shall carve the joint in the kitchen, sufficient Virgil, to lighten your burden somewhat. Crozier and I favour our lamb on the bloody side.'

'Excellent cook, isn't he, Kitty darling.'

'He is.'

'Derek's making sure I go to seed in the grand manner. It's marvellous not having to watch my figure any more. Not watch it so closely, rather. I was never quite as skinny as your Romanian friend, God forbid, but I had to be jolly careful with my diet. Derek chose the right word when he said I was "svelte". You remember me as being svelte, don't you, dearest darling?'

'How could I forget, Daddy?'

'That's my daughter.'

Derek Harville advised his guest with the aversion to concentrate on the vegetables while the carnivores disposed of the lamb. 'Your agony will be short-lived, I guarantee, since Crozier here is already showing the remnants of his fangs. This decanter is yours to empty.'

'Thank you.'

('Why didn't the shepherd listen to what the faithful lamb of Birsa told him? Why didn't he kill the traitors with his fierce dogs and German knife?' Matilda Florescu patted the head of her son Aureliu and smiled. 'You don't wonder how it is that the lamb, Mioriţa, can speak human speech?' Aureliu answered that if Harap Alb could have a clever talking horse, why couldn't the shepherd have the clever talking Mioriţa? 'Yes, Aureliu, why not? And you, Virgil, what are you thinking?' He was thinking, he said, of the star falling to earth, of the mountain suddenly becoming a priest, of the singing birds with bright features and of the old woman with tired feet wandering everywhere in search of her son, the shepherd with hair like the wings of a raven.

'You have a lot to think about,' his mother whispered, 'but sleep first.'

Aureliu, his voice thick with drowsiness, murmured, 'That shepherd was a fool, Mama. That shepherd was stupid.')

'Each Monday morning, at nine o'clock, I was summoned into His Grace's presence to be given a cheque made out to cash for the coming week's household expenses. "Same as usual, Harville?" was his rhetorical question prior to the autumn of nineteen forty-seven. "Not exactly the same, Your Grace," I replied on the second Monday in October and elaborated: prices were rising; certain items of linen had to be replaced, et cetera, et cetera. The amount on the cheque grew marginally bigger. "You are worse than those damned Socialists in Westminster where my money's concerned, Harville," he complained once as his writing hand set off on its reluctant journey towards his fountain pen. It was that half-humorous remark of his that inspired what I consider my *pièce de résistance*, my wiliest ruse. I asked myself what was really worse, in his blinkered eyes, than the Labour Party (which, unbeknown to him, I supported) – and the answer I came up with was of a radiant simplicity. Why, the Communists were worse. Their guiding star shone over Moscow. Oh, the excitement, the giddying excitement I felt when I wrote that inaugural letter – as it were from the Duke, on the Duke's embossed notepaper – to Mr Pollitt, the leader of the British Communists, expressing his, the Duke's, enthusiasm for Mr P's ideas and ideals. I forged the Duke's signature and enclosed five pounds and advised the worthy Mr P not to write in response to this no doubt surprising missive as the Duchess was a tartar who always opened his mail on the look-out for evidence of an adulterous kind. She was also – it saddened him to report – a dyed-in-the-wool Tory, who would emasculate him for his treachery. This one-sided correspondence continued on a regular monthly basis, a regular fiver attached to the Duke's wilder and wilder endorsements of the Communist faith, for a satisfying lengthy period. I think it was those zestfully composed letters that led the Communists to put up a candidate for election in the Duke's constituency. I voted for the pitiful wretch, as did fifty-six others.'

'That was your luxury, Derek.'

'Luxury? Yes, I suppose it was.'

'The luxury of choice, any choice, is one we do not have.'

'Ah, yes. Your countrymen are under Communist rule.'

'No, Derek. We have a ruler and the ruler has a wife, and the people who let them rule over us call themselves Communists or Socialists, but any name would do. If Communism is a doctrine of equality then we are not under Communist rule.'

'Aren't you?'

'We are not. It is my belief, if I may be serious, that Communism is an impossible concept – an impossibly good concept. Mere human beings cannot be trusted with it. It is too good for them.'

'I assume you have escaped from Romania. How did you get out?'

'Ways, means. There are ways and means, not all of them ingenious.'

'And yours were?'

'Mine were ordinary. Mine were simple-minded.'

'No details? Or is that going to be sufficient, sufficient Virgil?'

'No details. Sufficient, yes.'

'Take some nourishing salad.'

The appearance, minutes afterwards, of an apple pie, warm from the oven, caused Felix Crozier to exclaim, 'Your masterpiece, Derek. This is your quintessentially English masterpiece. This is what I've denied myself for most of my life. And with lashings and lashings of cream as well. How could I have lived without this?'

'The time for the evacuation of sheer nonsense has come round again, alas. You lived without apple pie with lashings of cream because you very sensibly understood that your willowy shape was your fortune, along with your profile and the various enchanting attributes that were yours, Crozier, and yours alone.'

'I have a scrapbook upstairs, Kitty darling, that Derek's helped me put together. It's very bulky. It contains the best pictures of your terrible daddy from way back when. There I am, the epitome of the English gentleman, in naught but the smartest magazines and more often than not on the cover. And all my women are in it, except Eleanor.'

'Why isn't Nelly included?'

'Two reasons, Kitty dearest. One is that I don't seem to have a photograph of her, and the other is – and I'm serious, I'm serious – I respect her too much to place her in their company.'

'That's considerate of you. She's in Egypt at present.'

'Is she? Rather her than me. No, Eleanor isn't in. It kicks off with my Muriel days, then there's my Linda days – dear

God, the ballets and operas and art shows and plays and concerts I had to endure for Linda – then it goes on to my Joan days and into my Carol days. Susan and Peggy are in there somewhere, but they were briefer –'

'Their days were numbered, Crozier?'

'In a manner of speaking, Derek. The fortnight with Barbara merits a few beach snaps and it ends, the scrapbook, with a picture Derek says gives him the shivers. It's one of the last woman, and she is the last, I involved myself with – the dreaded ST, who killed off the old Adam in Felix Crozier after a single night of love.'

'S and T are not the lady's initials, Kitty. They represent an abbreviation of Silicone Tits, the sobriquet Crozier gave her when he had recovered from the shock of encountering them.'

'They were cold to the touch, I swear to you, Kitty. I thought I was fondling light bulbs, gigantic light bulbs. They bruise a person, too.'

'ST is responsible, in a circuitous fashion, for the Crozier and Harville partnership. I had agreed to spend a year in California factoting for a Mr Landau, the least parsimonious of men, at his opulent mansion in Bel Air. ST and her ageing beau were among those invited to Mr L's summer ball – their first and last public appearance together. We soon identified ourselves, Crozier and I, he by observing "You're the so-and-so who winked at me", I by responding "The very same". Over lunch the following Sunday I told him that I had purchased a quasi-Tudor cottage in the rolling English countryside. He expressed envy. I was persuaded, the longer we chatted, that he would make passable company for me – and that is why the recently bejowled Crozier is sitting where he is, waiting to be offered another portion of apple pie.'

'I tell you what I'm looking forward to, dear darling Kitty – well, no, not exactly looking forward to, "looking forward to" sounds too gloomy in the circumstances; "looking forward to" isn't quite right, and yet I am looking forward, in one sense, to it, and that's dying in England. There's a part of me that's looking forward to being boxed up in solid English wood and lowered into English earth. I shan't be able to hear them, of course, but the thought of good old hymns like "Abide With Me, Fast Falls the Evening Whatsit" and "Onward Christian Soldiers" being sung by the choir and congregation is very reassuring and heart-warming. Yes, and heart-warming. There's a lovely country church across the fields yonder with a peaceful churchyard full of family graves, some of which have been standing for centuries, and that's where I've decided I want to take my eternal rest. I shan't be able to hear him, of course, but the vicar, who has a pleasant – not to say melodious – voice, will send me off with the ashes to ashes, dust to dust speech, and I'm sure he'll deliver it, from what I've heard of him, quite, quite beautifully. I visit the churchyard when the weather's fine, and I sit on the wall and I think to myself how I'll be lying there, in my own precious plot, with the four English seasons coming and going, going and coming.'

'And friendly Master Robin Redbreast will call on you every winter, and the cheery cuckoo will serenade you with a special rendering of his song each spring, and nary a pigeon will shit on your stone. What a mawkish outpouring, Crozier. Heart-warming? In your case there isn't one to warm. Why is it that the most egocentric of our benighted species are so often the most – the most repellently – sentimental?'

'Yes, why is it?' Felix Crozier chuckled as he spoke. 'Why oh why oh why?'

Soon Derek Harville was chuckling too, and then the companions were joined in hooting, honking laughter.

They are like a pair of satyrs, Kitty Crozier thought, and had a vision of them both with horns and furry legs and cloven hooves. It was scarcely more fanciful than the reality her startled ears and eyes were hearing and seeing, and telling her she must believe.

He journeyed at night, when sleep was elusive, spurred on by the prospect of reaching Italy; by the possibility of talking easily to strangers in a language as familiar to him as his own. He craved those familiar words, the words of streets and squares and public gardens, the words of the quotidian life he tried to celebrate and honour in his poetry. He often rushed towards them.

He had few words in this country.

On the third morning of his seeming freedom he was almost lured into a village by the smell of newly baked bread. His stomach announced its state of emptiness to him with a noise that signalled happy anticipation of being quickly filled and silenced. He watched the red-faced woman arranging the loaves on a rickety table outside her modest one-windowed house. His hunger, the hunger he had not assuaged by feeding on tufts of wild herbs or bitter red and black berries, advised him to approach her. He would have no difficulty making her understand that he needed to buy a loaf, but what money could he use for the purpose? It was too risky, this early in his travels, to offer her one of the notes Radu Sava had amassed for his escape. She might look askance at an American dollar, and grow suspicious and alert her customers to his presence.

He went back into the woods, away from the still tempting, still powerful aroma, away from the loaves gleaming golden in the sunlight. Although he was hungrier now he walked on with a willed determination.

He heard the stream before he saw it. He stopped and drank. Then he squatted nearby, and noticed that the stool the berries and sage had formed was coming out of him in tiny pellets similar to those left everywhere by the forest's nocturnal animals. If there were trackers on his path they would not be led to him by his droppings, which constituted

– he smiled at the notion – his sole means of disguise. He was indistinguishable, for the time being, from the rat, the weasel, the mouse, the stoat.

He drank again, and took off the shirt, the trousers, the underpants and the runner's shoes he had borne with him across the Danube. He doused his tired body in the cool, trickling water. He washed his blistered, blackened feet. He found a spot the sun was warming and, using his bag as a pillow, lay down and attempted to rest.

When he awoke his flesh was burning. He assumed he had slept for two or maybe three hours, since it was now the middle of the day. He put on his clothes, slaked the thirst that sleeping had induced and set off in the direction suggested by the crude map his troubled but envious friends had prepared for his benefit.

He knew there was a town ahead, which he would be foolhardy to enter. He was not yet far enough from the border, from the men – and women – who were eager to do business with the guards whose lights had failed to pick him out as he swam to Yugoslavia. Perhaps the shot that surprised the catchable falcon had met its target: another swimmer, perhaps, whose successful capture, half-alive or dead, might ensure the present safety of the renegade poet. Perhaps, perhaps: perhaps allowed of no certainties; perhaps was not to be trusted.

He came to a clearing and realised he would soon be at the very edge of the forest. He slowed his pace and moved cautiously. Then, as he left the protective trees behind him and took several wary steps into the field, there occurred the second of those events that Dinu Psatta, in Rome, would deem his miracles. A man was sitting on a stone, calmly looking at him.

The man greeted him in words Virgil Florescu could barely understand. I shall have to run, he thought, I shall have to turn round and dart off like a hare. But he didn't run, even as his brain was insisting that he should. He

57

remained transfixed instead, because the man was inviting him to eat.

'Branko,' said the man, pointing at himself. '*Nom*. Name.'

'Virgil. *Nom*. Name.'

They shook hands.

His fear suddenly gone, his feeling of panic replaced by one of strange secureness, he sat down on the grass in front of the man called Branko.

Branko had salami, a piece of orange-coloured cheese and bread.

He indicated, with what he hoped was a clownish expression of distaste, that his belly would not be pleased with the slice of salami Branko had cut off for him.

Branko snatched at a clump of grass, pressed it into his mouth, chewed it, spat it out and said '*Vous*? You?'

'*Oui*. Yes.'

Branko removed the slice of salami from the tip of his knife and ate it appreciatively. '*Moi*. Me,' he said, pointing at himself again, at his own strong, sturdy body – by this means implying that his strength and sturdiness were the result of his liking for meat. He was proud of his chest and stomach, and glanced sadly, but not unkindly, at Virgil's skinny, bony frame.

He acknowledged the regretful glance, with its implication that he, Virgil, ought to be stronger, healthier, by pulling a clown's face. It's my lot in life, Branko – this puny chest, this flaccid stomach; it's what I have to bear, with humour, with patient acceptance, but mostly with humour.

Branko nodded and shrugged, catching the clown's drift. 'Virgil,' he said, hacking at the loaf and passing him a chunk of it.

The bread was grey and stale, very much like that he had waited in line to buy each morning in Bucharest. It was bread, even so, and because it was hard he could not wolf

58

it down. He broke the chunk into pieces, savouring them one at a time, softening them with saliva.

'*Vous.* You,' said Branko, handing him the cheese.

'*Non.* No,' he replied, and had to resort to the limited language of signs and pulled faces and pointed fingers they had forged between them. His mime conveyed to Branko the message that they must share the cheese and Branko in turn was adamant that it was for him, Virgil, alone.

'*Vous.* You. *Oui.* Yes.'

'*Merci.* Thank you.'

The cheese was bland and lacking in flavour, a processed Communist cheese of the kind the Conducător and his consort would not have at their table – the table that was blessed with Brie, Gorgonzola, Camembert. No, this cheese was for *them*, the cake-eating mob beyond the gates. He ate it, though, with a delight he did not have to feign. It tasted good because of the generosity of the smiling man who had given it to him; it tasted of selflessness, of kindness.

'Beer,' said Branko, producing two bottles from his sack. '*Bon* beer. Good beer.' There was a bottle opener attached to his versatile knife. '*Vous.* You. Virgil.'

It *was* good beer and he had to stop himself gulping it, from drinking it as he had drunk the water in the stream. He swallowed it as slowly as he could and chastised himself for wishing, fleetingly, that Branko had supplied him with a glass. He wanted to sip this beer, not have to swig it. Want, want: why should he want more from his benefactor? Had he slept longer in the forest, had he chosen a different path, he might not – no, might never – have chanced upon Branko, or, indeed, anyone like him.

Yet Branko, to Virgil's astonishment, did have more to offer. There was a third bottle – the last, a sigh informed him. '*Vous et moi.* You. Me,' Branko explained. They would drink it together; they would share now the '*bon* beer'. Branko drank first, then wiped the top of the bottle with his sleeve before passing it to '*bon* Virgil', who copied '*très bon*, Branko'. The ritual once established, they continued until the beer was finished.

Branko stood up and mimed the act of digging, to tell '*bon* Virgil' it was time to return to work. He put the bottles and the remainder of the salami in his sack, which he tied with string. He put out his arms and so did Virgil and the two embraced, Virgil's stubble grazing Branko's cheek.

'Goodbye, Branko. *Merci.* Thank you.'

'*Vous et moi.* You. Me.' He pretended to eat, to drink. '*Bon.* Good. Beer. *Bon* beer.'

'Goodbye. *Au revoir.*'

He watched Branko walk down the field towards a building in the distance he supposed must be a farm. Branko turned and waved, and he waved back. He waited for the gracious man to disappear from sight, and then he picked up his bag and resumed his journey.

'Your father is not so terrible,' he said, ending the silence that followed their love-making.

'He's terrible enough. That's always been his word – "terrible". He thinks that by using it, by making it plain that he knows how terrible he is, he is somehow apologising to me.'

'He is not so bad.'

'It's as if I don't need to see him again,' she said brightly. 'Now that he's happy at last. Now that he has the devilish Derek to care for him.'

'That man who is Derek is his own creation, Kitty. He speaks an English I do not hear on the lips of the people I work with or the people I listen to in London. He is presenting Derek to the world, which is his stage. He is not so bad either, whoever he is. He is diverting.'

'I suppose he is.'

She lay there, with Virgil curled about her, and spoke no more of the father she felt she did not have to pity any longer. The vain daddy of the past – the elegant, handsome

60

victim of demanding wives; the improbable husband and impossible parent who, on his rare meetings with his one fond daughter would send her flickering signals of the discomfort he was undergoing with the inevitable new woman – was hardly to be detected in the present Felix Crozier. He was vain still and would die vain, with a convenient mirror by his deathbed to reflect his last moments. But the slightly desperate man of the signals was gone and with his departure – this was the revelation that came to her there, in the dark – yes, with his departure went a measure of the pitying love he had inspired. It was only a measure, because the past of her daddy, his Pretty Kitty and Baby Cordelia, remained the past, not to be obliterated.

'I might not even attend my father's English funeral,' she told her sleeping lover. 'With the hymns and the sermon and the beautifully spoken words. I might even give it a miss.'

The afternoon heat and Branko's beer were making him drowsy, but for the moment there was nowhere he could safely stop. He hadn't completely skirted the town – the ruin of an ancient church was visible and he could hear, faintly, the excited noise of children at play. He walked on.

He walked till dusk, over fields and along country roads and lanes, with the curious energy an anxious mind bestows on a tired body. He was conscious of being stared at by the few people he passed and kept his gaze averted whenever he saw someone approaching. But it was the concerted stare of a group of men, who had ended their conversation abruptly as he came in view, that caused him to feel terror. His hot sweat became instantly cold and a rank smell filled his nostrils. His feet were suddenly heavy beneath him and each step he took to get beyond the stare, beyond the sheer intensity of it, had to be calculated, planned. He knew he had achieved his immediate purpose when he heard their mocking laughter behind him. He guessed that they were calling him a lunatic.

(Dinu Psatta would be amused by this episode when his friend recounted it to him on one of the many steps leading up to Santa Maria d'Aracoeli. 'Not one of your miraculous escapes, Virgil. You should have returned their stare. They were simple country folk, probably. They were harmless. They hadn't seen your strange like before. That is my interpretation.')

The light was already beginning to fade when he saw the dilapidated cattle shed by a bend in the road. He found himself being unwary, so acute was his desire for rest, and went inside. The door was gone, but most of the roof was intact and from the part that was least decayed there was coming a steady, gentle sound of snoring – barn owls, he realised, enjoying the last of their day's sleep. He ought to have been afraid, for, as he prepared to lie down in a corner, he had to clear away innumerable cigarette stubs, a couple of cigarette packets and a used contraceptive. He was in a meeting place for lovers, and it was a warm evening and they might appear at any moment.

He awoke in darkness. The owls had left for work. He stood up and stretched his limbs. He was aware that he was filthy and dusted himself down as best he could with the backs of his dirty hands. He pissed on the grass behind the shed and renewed his walk to beckoning Italy.

As he walked that night, he spoke – in a quiet voice, under his breath – those poems, in a jumble of languages, he had memorised. He began with the white trees, the black trees of George Bacovia – a poet not admired by Constantin Florescu, nor by the young intellectual – and then the souls invoked by Blaga were briefly mingled, and here was Lorca sorrowing that his brain was stained with ink, and Ruth was standing in tears amid the alien corn, and the Arab without a country was dying in Paris, and suffering was taking place while someone else was eating, and Rimbaud's

Ophelia was beautiful like the snow, and Ovid's Corinna was dressed only in a long, loose gown ... The ghosts were gathering at Pascoli's hearth in the morning light in a narrow village street and a man was addressing him.

'Dollars?'

He stopped and turned round. A small, fat, white-haired man was standing in a doorway, grinning at him.

He asked the man, who was dabbing at his freshly shaven face with a cloth, 'Do you buy? Do you sell?' in English.

'Dollars? Yankee doodles? Dollars?'

The grinning man put Virgil Florescu in mind of the wicked character known as Smooth-Face in the story of Harap Alb their mother had read to them as children, and with the reminder came the thought that this man might be as devious and cunning.

The man came over to him and touched his bag. 'Dollars?' He raised a hand, fingers separated. 'Dollars?' He raised both hands. 'Dollars?' The man produced notes from one trouser pocket, coins from the other. 'Dollars?'

Virgil moved away from the man and opened his bag. He fumbled inside it and brought out a ten-dollar bill.

'Yippee!' shouted the man, thrusting all his notes, all his coins, at him, and ran into the house. A grinning woman emerged a moment later, and thanked the stranger with a gesture of prayer and a curtsey.

'I hope you're being sensible.'

'Sensible, Daisy? How sensible should I be?'

'With your health, silly. I hope you're looking after yourself.'

'Yes, I think I am.'

'You can't be too careful –'

Before Daisy could continue, Kitty finished the next part of the litany for her. 'Not at my age.'

'Exactly.'

In the ensuing silence Kitty wondered if her sister would now say, 'We're neither of us any younger.'

'We're neither of us any younger. Middle age is well and truly upon us. You at least won't have to endure the menopause, which must be some consolation for you.'

'Yes, I suppose it is.'

'Are you still having those tired spells?'

'No, not so much. Not at all, in fact, lately.'

'Dare I ask if that's the result of your taking my advice for once in your life? You've been eating plenty of fresh fruit, as I advised?'

'Yes, Daisy,' she said, adding Daisy's expected: 'All that natural sugar.'

'Precisely.'

'As distinct from unnatural,' she muttered to herself as she went into the kitchen. 'Follow me, sister dear.'

'I hope you haven't prepared anything fancy, Kitty. None of your complicated sauces.'

Kitty's complicated sauces were Daisy's invention and the phrase 'None of your complicated sauces' was invariably delivered, as it was now, with an expression suggestive of Daisy's uncomplicated, and by inference superior, culinary skills.

'No, Daisy, I haven't prepared one of my sauces. I haven't prepared a sauce of any kind.'

'I'm pleased to hear it. You, of all people, ought to know that my tastes are plain and simple.'

'I, of all people, Daisy, think I do.'

Kitty served the plain and simple meal of baked cod and boiled new potatoes, and Daisy, at Kitty's invitation, talked about her husband, Cecil, and their children, Andrew and Janet.

'Oh, Cesspit's his usual solid old self, expanding gradually round the middle and thinning a bit on top, but not too drastically, thank the Lord. You know how it is with Cesspit – how he's caught up in his share prices and his

64

stocks and bonds. No, Kitty, I've no surprises to offer you on the Cesspit front. And no complaints, I'm afraid, either.'

And there were no complaints, no surprises, where Andrew and Janet were concerned. As usual – with Daisy, everything was as usual – her son and daughter, always referred to in the order of their births, were not doing exceptionally well at school, but they were not, thank the Lord, doing badly. Then Daisy used a Daisy phrase that touched her sister whenever she heard it: 'They're really quite splendidly average.'

It was that 'splendidly', spoken with such warmth, such glowing pride, that moved her. Daisy could not have been more fulsome were Andrew a musical prodigy or Janet a mathematical genius.

'I think they're splendid, anyway, and that's what matters.'

'Yes, Daisy.'

'All things considered.'

'I'm in love, Daisy.'

'You are what?'

'I am telling you that I am in love.'

'No, Kitty, you can't be. No, Kitty. No, Kitty, you're not.'

'I am.'

'Is this another of your infatuations?'

'I do not have infatuations.'

'Yes, you do, silly. There was the kaftanned creature.'

'Freddy belongs to my vanished youth, Daisy. I was young then. There has been no one since Freddy who has captivated me. Until Virgil.'

'Who?'

'Virgil.'

'Whoever is he?'

'He's a Romanian.'

'What sort of Romanian?'

'The human sort, Daisy.'

65

'No, silly, don't be clever with me. What does he do? Is he important? Is he a diplomat?'

'I find him important. No, he isn't a diplomat. He isn't smooth enough for diplomacy. He doesn't possess the required charm.'

'Then what does he have? What is his appeal, Kitty?'

'I love him. I simply love him.'

'That's no answer. That tells me nothing. Where did you meet him? Give me some details.'

'Where did I meet him?' She stared across at her frowning twin and said, 'I didn't meet him properly to start with. I saw him. I saw him looking at me.'

'Where did you see him?'

'In hospital, Daisy. After the operation.'

'When you were drugged. When the drugs hadn't quite worn off. Is that when this meeting of the eyes took place?'

'Yes.'

'Your drugged eyes met his, and it was love – was it – at first sight?'

'I do believe it was.'

'You stagger me, Kitty, you stagger me. You've been out of hospital for almost a year and you haven't once mentioned this great Romanian lover of yours. Not to me, anyway.'

She hadn't mentioned him because she had been alone for ten months, not even thinking of the man she had seen in the ward. Then, a mere matter of weeks ago, he had called out to her in Green Park and she had recognised him, and the next thing was that she had written her address on a scrap of paper and he had visited her the following evening, and now they were lovers. Those were the bare, the very bare, details.

'Make of them what you will, Daisy.'

'I wish I could make sense of them, that's for certain, you silly. I take it this Virgil is as handsome as sin?'

66

'No, he isn't. I can say, in truth, that he isn't. My Virgil Florescu is not at all handsome.'

'What age is he?'

'Mine. Ours.'

'I'll bide my time,' Daisy promised, 'before I predict disaster.'

In a copse not far from the village he sat down and counted the money the smooth-faced man had thrust at him.

('The miracle of the dinars,' Dinu Psatta would remark on learning of his friend's morning encounter and its outcome. 'A very minor miracle,' he would add with a grin as they entered the church that had once been the Temple of Jupiter and an imperial palace. 'Not a gigantic miracle, like the one that happened here.' They would stand where it was said the Emperor Augustus had stood when the heavens opened and the Virgin appeared to him, robed in light, holding the unborn Saviour of the world in her arms. 'Your modest miracles are small fry in comparison.')

The extent of the man's generosity or improvidence became clear to him later the same day when, with two of the twenty notes, he bought a shirt, some socks, a razor, a bar of soap, a tube of toothpaste and a bottle of mineral water. The woman at the cash desk glared at the insanely smiling customer who refused the change she was offering him.

There was a railway station in the town and he headed towards it. The sudden furious barking of a Dobermann pinscher chained to a post outside an official building with boxes of red geraniums in each of its windows startled him out of his reverie.

The dog growled on seeing him and began to move backwards, easing the tension on the chain it had extended to the limit. 'Good boy, good boy,' he said softly, and the Dobermann cocked its ears. 'Come, boy, come,' he whispered, bending low and putting out his right hand, palm upwards. 'Come to me.'

The Dobermann flopped to the ground. 'Good boy,' he repeated, stroking the shiny black-and-tan coat slowly and gently. The animal rolled over and he now rubbed its belly, and as he did so he thought of the three-headed beast that guards the entrance to the underworld. 'You are just like Cerberus,' he told the delighted, wriggling Dobermann. 'It only needs a few honeyed words and you change character.'

The dog bared its teeth and resumed its furious barking as soon as he rose to go.

He spoke the poem he called 'Cerberus' to her while she sponged his back. The idea of the versatile three-headed dog with a single brain had come to him early in his travels, he explained when he finished, but the words were new and the last words were the newest, having arrived only the day before in Green Park.

'My father, Constantin Florescu, is its inspiration, Kitty. He is the cunning dog with three heads.'

He invited his beautiful Muse-to-be, the Muse of sweetness and contentment, to join him in the water.

3

The Fisher of Perch

Daisy and Kitty Crozier, wearing the gingham dresses their mother had specially made for them, were driven to London by a uniformed chauffeur in the biggest car they had ever seen. They were gawped at throughout the journey – by pedestrians in the streets or waiting at traffic lights and by the occupants of other, much smaller, vehicles. They were whistled at and waved to, and frequently saluted.

'You are very privileged young ladies. It's not many little girls who get the treatment you're getting today – riding along in luxury as if you were a couple of princesses.'

'We aren't little any more, Mr Jackson,' Daisy corrected him. 'We are ten now. *Under* ten is little.'

'I sincerely beg your pardon. Which one are you?'

'I wouldn't like to have your money. Nelly's already told you who I am. I am Daisy. I'm older than Kitty, even though we're twins. I act older than she does.'

'Is that so?'

'Yes, it is. I've always acted older.'

'Then you'll be a mature woman, Daisy, before you know it. Has the cat run off with Kitty's tongue?'

'She lets me do the talking when we're out together. She's shy in company.'

'You mustn't be shy with me, Kitty. I love listening to children babble.'

'Babble? What's babble?'

'Babble's how boys and girls speak when they're not on their best Sunday behaviour.'

'Is babble babyish?'

'It can be.'

'We don't babble, Mr Jackson.'

'That's a pity, Daisy. I'm really disappointed. I was hoping you would keep me amused. You are enjoying the ride, aren't you?'

'Yes, thank you, Mr Jackson,' said Kitty. 'I'm enjoying it.'

'Are you both looking forward to your holiday with Mr and Mrs Crozier? Are you both excited?'

There was a silence.

'Which of you is going to answer? Kitty? Daisy?'

'We think he should have come for us this morning, not you.'

'Your father's a busy man, Daisy.'

'Does this big silly car belong to him?'

'Big it certainly is, but you'll have to tell me why it's silly.'

(The Daisy phrase 'big silly car' was coined that day in March 1956. The 'big silly car' would signify for Daisy Crozier and Daisy Hopkins something vulgar, ostentatious. The 'big silly car' was one of the more obvious trappings of vanity. It was in the 'big silly car' that her lasting hatred of Felix Crozier was first made manifest.)

'I don't have to, if I don't want to.'

'Of course you don't, Daisy. Perhaps Kitty will tell me why instead.'

'She can't, because she's not me. I'm the only person who can tell you and I don't want to.'

'I shall have to carry on in ignorance in that case. There was I, convinced that I was driving a smart motor car and now I learn from you it's really a silly one. I must admit I'm baffled.'

'It's silly because it's not necessary, Mr Jackson,' Daisy pronounced, adding – so that Kitty alone could hear – 'Like him.'

'You're a strong-minded young lady and no mistake.'

The admirer of Emily Dickinson called on Virgil Florescu a second time. 'Good morning, Virgil.'

'Good morning.'

'Your pupils have been instructed to do further revision. We have another hour in which to talk.'

'Very well.'

'I have brought my thirst with me again.'

'I will make tea.'

'It is excessively cold in here.'

'That is how it is for us,' said Virgil Florescu without rancour. 'The radiator seldom serves its purpose. Radu Sava and I regard it as a Dadaistic object. We should be stupefied if it were to run warm. And as for *hot* –'

'You are almost voluble today, Virgil. You were more restrained in your speech during our previous meeting.'

'You gave me no opportunity to extol the pointless qualities of the radiator then. You appeared to be preoccupied with poetry.'

'I still am, Virgil. The condition of your radiator is of no interest or significance to me. I have come to chew the poetic cud with you. There are many, many topics I wish to raise for discussion.'

'Are there?'

'The affair of "Icon" not being one of them, you will be relieved to discover. Whatever there is to say has already been said, in the clearest possible terms. "Icon" is Virgil

71

Florescu's folly and that is that. I can offer no embellishments.'

'I understand.'

'Let us turn our attention to George Bacovia.'

'Why? He is out of harm's way.'

'You are not coming to harm, Virgil. I am aware that Bacovia is dead. It is his influence on the young poets of our country I am considering.'

('You are learning the words of a pathetic drunkard,' Constantin Florescu chastised his thirteen-year-old son. 'The man was a weakling. A man who was kept alive by his wife is no man for you to look up to.'

'I am not looking up to him, Father. I am memorising one of his poems.'

'Yes, and what a poem it is. A boy of your age should be seeking excitement and adventure, not reading this graveyard stuff. Where is your spirit, Virgil?'

His spirit, he could not disclose, was with the pathetic drunkard's words and rhymes, with the beguiling music they made. That was where his quiet spirit was and where he knew it was going to stay, somehow or other.

'He was mad. He was sick. He was a hopeless case.')

'I am thinking in particular of his self-absorption and his morbidity.'

'Are you?'

'Yes, Virgil, I am. They are not attractive attributes. Certainly not attractive or healthy enough to be emulated.'

'His despair was his own and so was his irony. They cannot be assumed by anyone else. Here is your tea.'

'Thank you. This will warm me up. Perhaps I am inferring, Virgil, that Bacovia's work belongs to the darker times he lived through. He died a quarter of a century ago. Things are different with us now. We shall soon have a palace here in Bucharest that will be bigger and grander than Versailles. There is new hope burgeoning in our country.'

Virgil Florescu stared pointedly at the radiator. As he

was doing so, the young intellectual just as pointedly poured the hot tea on to the Oltenian carpet. 'That was clumsy of me, Virgil. My hand slipped.'

'I will fetch a cloth.'

'You seem extraordinarily calm. I realise how precious this carpet is and what memories it provokes.'

'Yes.'

'Yes?'

'Yes.'

'Is "yes" to be your only response?'

'Yes.'

'If I were you I would curse me for my clumsiness.'

'But I am not you.'

The intellectual, whom Virgil Florescu refused to address or recognise with the name Corneliu, watched as the poet dabbed at the sodden carpet with a dry cloth. 'I fear you are doing more harm than good. I shall take it with me and have it cleaned by a professional.'

'There is no need.'

'There is every need, my dear Virgil. An antique must be treated with care and reverence. The expert I have in mind will treat it with both.'

'It needs no expert.'

'I insist that it does. I shall curtail our interesting discussion and bear your treasure to the expert restorer without delay. You are trying not to look distressed, Virgil, and you are not succeeding. Shall I carry it rolled or folded?'

'My darlings.' Felix Crozier was standing at the top of the stairs, his arms outstretched in welcome. 'Come and be cuddled by your long-lost daddy.' He bent down and embraced his daughters, kissing each of them in turn. 'You're both so pretty, my little darlings.'

'We aren't little any more,' said Daisy. 'Your darlings.'

'You look little to a tall chap like me. But, yes, you have grown since I last saw you. By leaps and bounds, Daisy.

73

You are less little than you were. That is the long and short of it, you might say.'

'We're ten now. We were five when you left us.'

'It isn't healthy, Daisy, to dwell on the past. It's best to live in the present. Muriel and I have made all sorts of plans to keep you happily occupied. You are going to have a simply wonderful holiday, I promise you.'

'Is she here?'

'If you mean Muriel, the answer's yes. She's in bed at the moment. You'll meet her as soon as she's recovered from her migraine.'

'What's a migraine, Daddy?'

'I was beginning to worry that you'd lost the power of speech, Kitty. A migraine, my dearest darling, is the worst headache you can imagine. Worse than worst. You feel sick and you can't see straight, and the pain, Muriel tells me, is shocking. Poor Muriel. She's lying in the dark, in peace and quiet, and praying for the migraine to stop, because she is longing to meet her stepdaughters. She has heard so much about the famous twins from their proud father that she feels she knows them already.'

'Are we really her stepdaughters?'

'Yes, Daisy. Muriel is my wife, my second wife, and since you are my children it follows that she must be your step-mother. And if your mother marries again you'll have a stepfather.'

'Nelly won't marry again.'

'You sound very certain, my darling. How do you know?'

'Because she's told us. She keeps her word. Nelly means what she says.'

('Nelly has been lying to us all these years,' Daisy Hopkins would complain to her sister when she returned from India. 'She could have told us the truth.'

'Which truth is that?'

'The truth that Grandfather McGregor shot himself. The

74

coward blew his brains out. He absolutely did not die of malaria.')

'I'll keep my word with you, Daisy. I'll mean what I say.'

'I decided not to write in code and that was my undoing, Kitty. I wrote in anger instead. And if I hadn't written "Icon" I might never have had to find ways and means of leaving the country. It's almost as simple as that.'

'Why almost, Virgil?'

'Because, because – as the man with the ring on his lip says. I must not confuse you. Let me tell you the simple story of the one truly bad poem I allowed to be published.'

She mashed the pulp of some aubergines she had baked earlier that day while he described the genesis of 'Icon'.

It was on a spring morning that the idea first came to him. The long winter was just over and the streets of Bucharest were filled with people delighting in the unexpected warm weather. He and his close friend Radu Sava – one of those rare doctors who is actually concerned with the well-being of his patients – were walking along the Boulevard Magheru when Radu remarked that the kindly gaze of the nation's benefactor seemed to be more prevalent suddenly, as if the photograph had both propagated and multiplied itself during the night. Then, a week later, another friend revealed that she had visited a kindergarten in Constanţa where the dormitory beds were so arranged that the children slept with the eyes of the benefactor looking down on them, as it were from heaven. 'They are meant to feel protected, especially when they wake in the dark and see that his watchful eyes are still open,' she had said. And as she was speaking, he thought of the icons of St Peter and the Virgin and Child his mother had treasured and prayed in front of year after difficult year, and the benign face of Romania's saviour, coloured and shaped in the Byzantine mould was there before him – an icon, no less; a graven image, inviting prayer.

75

'Have you ever heard angry laughter, Kitty? It's short-lived. It dies quickly in the throat. I was laughing the moment I started writing "Icon", but only for a line or two. The joke wasn't fantastic enough, absurd enough, to be funny. It was hardly a joke at all.'

He had been pleased with the poem; pleased with its blasphemous allusions to the consummate blasphemer: the man who had neither doubts nor qualms about assuming the role of God. The editor of a student magazine in Tirgu Mureş, a friend of the friend from Constanţa, had shared the deluded poet's pleasure in 'Icon' and the complacent Virgil Florescu had granted him permission to publish it. The poem appeared in *Magpie* ('That's *Coţofană*, Kitty. Do you like the word?') in the issue of May 1985, above the initials F. V.

'I saw it in print and was horrified by its obviousness. It was no longer the poem I had believed I had written.'

(In Paris, after Virgil was gone from her, she would hear Dinu Psatta praise the poem that went underground in the dark times, passed from hand to hand on scraps of paper. 'Virgil hated it because he hated having to write it. Even a poem that mocked Ceauşescu was one poem too many on the subject. That was his opinion. But he was wrong, Kitty. The true subject of "Icon" is *anyone* who thinks he is God.')

'They were horrified, too – the authorities. But for a different reason.'

'Blasphemy?'

'Yes, of course, Kitty. Sacrilege. Heresy. I became known as the renegade poet. I became news. They, the authorities, sent a young man with intellectual pretensions to talk to me. They did not send an obvious brute. Oh no, not them. He claimed to have studied the poetry of Emily Dickinson and Robert Frost. He considered Frost lacking in moral fibre. I might have found him diverting had I met him any-where else in the world.'

Virgil Florescu said nothing, that Sunday afternoon, of

the young man's appropriation of his mother's Oltenian carpet. He watched Kitty, the undoubted love of his life, add a finely chopped onion, the juice of a lemon, salt, pepper, a sprinkling of paprika and a dribble of olive oil to the mashed aubergines. She whisked the mixture into a smooth paste with a fork and put the bowl into the refrigerator.

'My very first stab at poor man's caviare, Virgil. I hope it tastes as it ought to.'

'It will.'

'We'll eat it this evening, sweetheart. I know how I wish to be occupied till then.'

Felix Crozier opened the door of the sitting-room, where a maid was waiting to serve them tea. 'Allow me to introduce my lovely daughters, Beryl. My twin blessings. This is Daisy and this is Kitty.'

'I'm pleased to meet you, Miss Daisy, Miss Kitty.'

'Hullo,' said Daisy.

'Good afternoon,' said Kitty.

'Is that cake what I think it is, Beryl?'

'If it's a simnel you have in mind, it is, Mr Crozier, sir. It's shop-bought, to be honest, but none the worse for that.'

'Shall we sit down, my darlings, and tuck in?'

Daisy mouthed 'My darlings' to her sister, who whispered 'Stop it' in response.

'I remember how you both like marzipan.'

'I don't like marzipan. I don't like it at all.'

'But, Daisy –'

'I don't like marzipan any more, Kitty.'

'Daddy will eat it for you, in that case. Please be so kind, Beryl, as to give my daughter a slice without marzipan. What about you, Kitty? Do you still have a sweet tooth?'

'Yes, Daddy. Thank you.'

'That's a relief. That's my Kitty.'

'Perhaps Miss Daisy would prefer orange or lemon squash rather than tea, Mr Crozier, sir.'

'Why is she calling me Miss Daisy?'

'Beryl is showing you respect, and Kitty too.'

'Then why don't you call her Miss Beryl? Don't you respect her?'

'No one respects Beryl more than I. It's the Beryls of this world who keep the wheels going round. Beryl and her kind are the salt of the earth.'

'Thank you, Mr Crozier, sir.'

'You haven't answered my question.'

'Beryl calls you Miss Daisy for the same reason she calls me sir. Because she knows her place. We are fortunate in our family to be higher up the ladder than Beryl is.'

'Which ladder? I can't see any ladder.'

'Squash or tea, Miss Daisy?'

'Tea, please, Miss Beryl.'

'And yourself, Miss Kitty?'

'Tea, please, thank you.'

(Kitty would remember how Daisy picked at her slice of simnel cake; how she carefully dismantled it, crumb by crumb by crumb; how she popped each tiny morsel into her mouth and said 'Munch, munch'; how she stared at their father during this performance and how he maintained a tolerant smile, despite her provocation. The memory would surface in dreams, mostly, with Daisy and Kitty, in their red-and-white gingham dresses, poised on the edge of the chesterfield, under the huge, glittering chandelier, in the sitting-room of the house in Mayfair, in the 'smartest stretch of London'.)

'Muriel, my darling, there you are. Has the pain gone away?'

'Only just, Felix. Only just. So these are your daughters. Why are they wearing table-cloths?'

*　　*　　*

His new no-home to go to was in a part of London with a beguiling name. 'Gospel Oak, Kitty.'

'But that's miles away.'

'There are trains and buses. It is not so far.'

'Come and live here with me. Yes, Virgil?'

He smiled at her and took her hands in his across the kitchen table. 'Not yet. Not quite yet. Put up with my temporary madness. It will pass. I promise you will see the sane Virgil Florescu one day.'

(In Scotland, the following summer, she would wake beside him in small hotels and boarding-houses. Mr and Mrs Florescu, as they styled themselves when propriety seemed particularly in order, would take breakfast together, morning after happy morning.)

He was in an attic now, he said; an eyrie. He could look out at the city, with the dome of St Paul's always visible on the horizon. The servants of the house's original owner had slept there, he'd learned from its present owner, an exuberant old woman who had once sung opera.

'You must phone me, Kitty. It will be an experience for you. You will hear her sing "Mis-ter Flo-res-cu, tel-e-phone" up the stairs. Yes, yes, she sings. I shan't respond instantly, so that you can hear her summon me twice – her second "Mis-ter Flo-res-cu, tel-e-phone" will be even more resonant than her first.' He kissed the palms of her hands. 'Your poor man's caviare is the best – the very, very best – I have ever eaten, my beautiful Kitty Crozier.'

Because it was Good Friday, and all the shops were closed, they went to church dressed in what their stepmother kept on calling table-cloths. These were blue-and-white, and no more to her taste than the red-and-white ones they had worn the previous day.

After the service Daisy and Kitty sat between their father and Muriel Crozier in the back of the Rolls-Royce. The journey from Knightsbridge to Mayfair lasted five minutes.

'We should have walked,' Daisy grumbled. 'We should have walked through the park. We didn't need to go in the big silly car.'

'I tested the weather earlier, Daisy, and decided it was too chilly for walking.'

'We have jumpers. Nelly packed extra jumpers for us.'

'If it's fine on Sunday we'll take a stroll in the park, I promise.'

'Why not tomorrow?'

'Tomorrow? Muriel has plans for you tomorrow.'

'I surely have. We're going on a shopping spree – just you, and me, and Kitty.'

'Aren't you excited, my darlings?'

'Yes, Daddy,' Kitty lied, and spoke the words again to compensate for Daisy's studied silence.

The door of the house was opened by Beryl, who curtseyed as they entered.

'Hullo, Miss Beryl,' said Daisy. 'We've been to church. The vicar had a runny nose.'

'Who's going to race me to the top of the stairs? You, Daisy? You, Kitty?'

Daisy shook her head vigorously.

'I will, Daddy.'

He let Kitty win, as she guessed he would. 'Well done, Kitty. You've pipped me to the post again, as you always used to.'

'Is this house yours, Daddy?'

'No, my darling. It belongs to Muriel's first husband. We hire it from him when we come to England. Jackson belongs to him, in a manner of speaking, and so does Beryl and so does the cook. The car's his, too. He disappears to Switzerland with his valet – that's his personal servant, Kitty – while we're in London.'

'Are you and Muriel happy, Daddy?'

'Over the moon, my darling. Believe me. Over the moon.'

She did not believe him, because of the forced brightness in his voice.

'Slowcoaches, that's what you are,' Felix Crozier joked when Muriel and Daisy joined them. 'Absolute slouches.'

There was an hour to kill before lunch – or luncheon, as Beryl called it – and Daisy and Kitty occupied the time by playing I-spy in those parts of the house they felt it was safe to enter. They descended the stairs and commenced their game in the hallway.

'I spy with my little eye something beginning with "n".'

'"N", Daisy?'

'Yes, "n".'

'I can't see anything beginning with "n".'

'Yes, you can. Look, look. Actually, there's two of them.'

'Do you mean the statues? The black boys holding the candlesticks?'

'Yes, silly. Say the word.'

'Niggers.'

'Your turn.'

'I spy with my little eye something beginning with "u".

'Where?'

'If I told you where that would be telling.'

'Down here?'

'Of course, Daisy.'

'The only word I know beginning with "u" is umbrella and there's no umbrellas.'

'You're warm. You're very warm. What's that thing against the wall as you come in?'

'It's an umbrella stand, Kitty. An umbrella stand with no umbrellas in it. Umbrella stand is two words and you only gave me one letter. That's cheating. You should have said "I spy with my little eye something beginning with 'u' and 's'" – then I'd have got it straight away.'

'I'm sorry, Daisy. Let's go upstairs again. There's more bibs and bobs to choose in the sitting-room.'

They had already spied the chandelier, the sofa, the chest

81

of drawers ('I spy with my little eye something beginning with "c" and "o" and "d",' Kitty had been careful to emphasise), when their father entered and put a record on the radiogram. 'Muriel and I adore this song, my darlings.'

(Thirty years later, in her modest, sparsely furnished, book-cluttered house, Kitty Crozier would hear

> He is as simple as a swim in summer,
> Not arty, not actory.
> He's like a plumber
> When you need a plumber . . .
> He's satisfactory!

and remember the opulent mansion off Park Lane in which she and Daisy spent what Nelly was to refer to for ever as the 'Easter of Easters'. She would picture the dapper Felix inviting his darlings to listen to the clever lyrics and ask herself if it was then that she felt her first slight stirrings of pity for him.)

'We never tire of it. Shall I play it again before we eat?'

'Yes, Daddy.'

'Muriel knows it off by heart.'

'Does she think it's you the woman's singing about?'

'Me? No, Daisy. Certainly not. Me? Heaven forbid. Me, Daisy? Why should Muriel think it's me?'

'Because of the silly look on your face.'

'I don't understand, my darling.'

'I do.'

'I'm no plumber, Daisy. Definitely not. I'm hopeless at anything practical. When Muriel needs a plumber she very sensibly phones for one.'

There were extra-special Easter presents waiting for his darlings on the dining-room table, he told them when the song was over.

'What's extra-special?'

'You'll soon see. After you've closed your eyes, that is.'

82

'I don't want to close my eyes. It's babyish.'

'I still close my eyes, Daisy, whenever I'm lucky enough to be given a present.'

'Who gives you presents?'

'Lots of people. Friends. I have lots of friends.'

'Friends like her?'

'Please call my wife by her name, Daisy. Please be polite and call her Muriel.'

Attached to the boxes that contained what Felix Crozier described as 'ostrich-sized Easter eggs' – 'It will take you at least a year to eat them' – were cards which read 'With love and kisses from Step Mummy and Daddy'.

In bed that night, Daisy ate and ate and ate all the broken pieces of her Easter egg until she was sick.

He wrote to Pamela Florescu in Bristol, informing her of his seventh London address. He hoped his kind token wife was well and happy, and he thanked her, as was his grateful custom, for making it possible for him to remain in England. He had completed two poems and was still wielding the fearsome spike with determination. He could say truthfully that, as a result of his efforts, the park was cleaner and tidier that it was usually. He sent his greetings to Tom. He had nothing else of any consequence to report.

He stared at the words 'nothing else of any consequence' and wondered at his reticence, his timidity, even. Kitty was of consequence, of deep and lasting consequence, so why was he loath to mention her? He smiled at the idea of Pamela, to whom he was married in name alone, becoming jealous. Pamela had lived with her doting Tom for many years. She would be overjoyed to learn that the husband she had never slept with ('One chaste kiss to fool the registrar, and that's your limit, Mr Virgil Florescu') was in love with, and loved by, an exceptional woman. Although he was confident Pamela would welcome such news, his reluctance to disclose it persisted. He shivered, then, and the sudden blast of icy January air that seized him on that balmy September night persuaded him, when he was warm once more, to leave 'nothing else of any consequence' intact.

After posting the letter he went into a pub and ordered a beer. He sat down in a corner, next to three old men who were talking drunkenly of courage and guts. One of them, he learned, had been a conscientious objector and his companions were mocking him for his cowardice. 'Cowardice? I was shoved in prison. I was forced to do the most terrible donkey-work for six long years.'

The other men cackled. 'You didn't risk life and limb, the way we did.'

The pacifist banged on the table, causing a metal ashtray to rise in the air and spill its contents into his lap. 'You only ever bring up my pacifism when you're thoroughly pissed. You can call me gutless as much as you want, but I know different. I'm not afraid of death. I wasn't then and I'm not now, so keep your bloody tongues civil.'

The man's outburst provoked further derisive laughter. 'Temper, temper. You'll be trying to fight us in a minute.'

Virgil Florescu thought of the unsteady trio later as he rested on his bed in the slowly gathering darkness. He'd wanted to speak to the enraged pacifist, to ask him why he had elected not to serve in the army (or navy, or air force), but the man had shouted 'You bloody sneering bloody bastards' at his friends and stomped out.

He lay there, in the London attic, willing his mind away from Constantin Florescu's proud revelations – 'We were young and impetuous, and obeying the will of our Christian God' – and his mother's descent into numbness. It was better not to think, either, of his own brief and ignominious military training or of Aureliu's progress through the ranks of the army. 'I have just one spirited son, Virgil, and he is not you.'

He began to mutter familiar lines from Book Twelve of the *Aeneid* –

84

'... et iuuenum exosum nequiquam bella Menoeten,
Arcada, piscosae cui circum flumina Lernae ...'

– and was momentarily perplexed that he was doing so. Then
he heard a voice from the past telling him that he, young
Florescu, was an unusual student and it was suddenly clear
why the frustrated Menoetës of Arcadia was in his thoughts.
The unusual young Florescu had written an essay for his
classics tutor, Teodor Costea, in which he'd reflected on 'the
names in the dark' – *'multi praeterea, quos fama recondit'* –
in the great epic poem he and his classmates had been reading, and translating, and pondering over for several months.
Costea – whose beard was stained by, and smelt of, tobacco
– had praised him for his obtuse originality in concentrating
on those anonymous hordes the mightier Virgil assigns to
the periphery of the story and seldom describes. 'Your fellow students have chosen less original, but more pertinent,
subjects, young Florescu: the torment of Dido, for instance,
and the rescue of Anchises from the flaming ruins of Troy,
and Aeneas's journey down to the nether world – but you,
you have devoted page upon intriguing page to nonentities.
To "the unremembered dead", as you rather elegantly put
it. The only character you discuss in detail is the poor
Arcadian fisherman, Menoetës; one of the hundreds of soldiers slain by King Turnus. You have contrived, clever
young Florescu, to make a hero of him. He appears to be
as heroic, in your eyes, as the heroes themselves.'
    And still is, the middle-aged Florescu would have said to
the yellow-bearded Costea twenty years on. He remembered
writing of the unremembered – the sailors, soldiers, slaves;
the maidens, mothers, wives, widows – and how he had
singled out Menoetës, the hater of war whom circumstances
deprived of a quiet life, for his considered attention. As,
indeed, the poet had done, in five lines that preserve the
fisherman's humble, thwarted ambition – to leave the scenes
of battle and return to the brooks at Lerna – for ever.

85

Menoetës was no warrior and held no public office, and might have been nothing but a minor impediment in Turnus's path – except that his name is recorded, his very ordinariness honoured. 'Oh yes, Professor Costea, I have not forgotten him.'

The phone rang at the bottom of the house and soon Freda Whiteside was singing up the stairs: 'Mis-ter Flo-res-cu, tel-e-phone.' He waited, in ordered to ensure a repeat performance. 'Dom-nul Flo-res-cu,' she sang the second time. 'Tel-e-phone. A Miss Cro-zi-er for you.' He called out that he was coming and went down to the hall, where his beaming landlady passed him the receiver.

'Kitty –'

'I think I recognised the tune, Virgil. The words didn't quite fit, though. It was "Casta Diva", wasn't it? From Bellini's *Norma*?'

'If you say so. I am ignorant about opera, as Mrs Whiteside has discovered.'

'I've almost finished my work on the book, sweetheart. Will you come to supper on Tuesday?'

'Yes. Yes. Yes.'

'I'm missing you.'

'It's been four days, a mere four days. That's all.'

'That's all, I know. It seems longer. Virgil, my sister has invited us to lunch next Sunday. She needs to inspect you. Could you suffer another family gathering?'

'The first one was diverting.'

'I can't promise that Daisy and Cecil and the children will entertain you as much as my terrible father and Mephistopheles did. There certainly won't be any badinage.'

'I don't expect badinage, Kitty. The badinage between Derek and Felix was a rare surprise. A bonus.'

Back in his room, he wondered which fish Menoetës might have caught in the brooks at Lerna. Then he recalled that one of the translators of the *Aeneid* – was he French? was he English? was he American? – had suggested perch.

'The brooks of Lerna, crowded with perch' was his phrase. He would steal that convincing suggestion. His own Menoetës would be a fisher of perch.

'What a treasure trove this store is,' Muriel Crozier exclaimed as she led her stepdaughters through the toy department at Harrods. 'Is there anything here that takes your fancy?'

'We're too old for toys. I keep telling you we're ten. There's nothing here for us.'

'I'm sure that's not true, Daisy. My grandpa just adores jigsaw puzzles and he's older than most folks alive. You can never be *too* old for toys.'

'Well, we are.'

'Is that so, Kitty?'

'Yes, that *is* so.'

'I asked Kitty the question, not you, Daisy. I should like to hear Kitty's answer. For once.'

'Kitty hasn't been listening. She's got her miles-away face on.'

'Would you like a jigsaw puzzle, Kitty?'

'Yes, please. Thank you.'

'Choose the one you want then, dear. The really complicated, difficult ones are the best, I find. They take longer to fit together.'

Kitty chose a puzzle with a windmill, which Muriel said was a famous painting by a Dutch master.

'Delft is in Holland, Kitty. These water pieces will drive you crazy, I can guarantee. Happily crazy, of course. That's the joy of jigsaws.'

'Thank you.'

'And you, Daisy? Which puzzle for you?'

'None of them.'

'Oh, come on. Don't be such a curmudgeon. I shall pick one for you. How about this? Look, Daisy, it's a grand lady in period clothes. Why, she's Madame de Pompadour, no

87

less. Those jewels alone will occupy you for hours.' She smiled down on the glowering Daisy. 'And hours. You will have hours and hours of quiet amusement.'

Muriel Crozier handed the boxes to a shop assistant with the instruction to wrap them and charge them.

'What's "charge"? What do you mean by "charge"?'

'Are you talking to me, Daisy?'

'Yes.'

'I do have a name. I told the polite young man to charge them because I have an account. The store sends me a bill and that's when I pay it. Does that satisfy you, Daisy?'

'Doesn't he pay? Our father?'

'Sometimes. When he has to. Oftentimes.'

Daisy must understand, Muriel Crozier said, that it was rude, it was the height of vulgarity, to talk about money, other people's money, in a public place. Enough was enough. Now they had dresses to look at. Finding pretty dresses for Daisy and Kitty was the real purpose of their little trip.

'We've got dresses.'

'I know you have, Daisy. But these will be different. These will be beautiful.'

'We don't need them.'

'We'll see what Magda has to say about that.'

'Who's Magda?'

'Come and meet her.'

'Why?'

'Magda is an expert – *the* expert – on clothes for girls. She rules over her department like an absolute queen.'

(For Daisy and Kitty Crozier, Magda more resembled a witch than a queen, such was the trepidation they felt in her presence. Her charm had them cringing; reaching for the security of each other's hands. Her mouth seemed to contain as many empty spaces as it did teeth, and in those spaces tiny bubbles of spittle formed and burst as she talked enthusiastically of the latest heavenly designs she had bought for the daughters of her clients. 'Or stepdaughters, should I say,' she remarked to the Mrs Crozier she had once had the privilege of dressing as an enchanting teenager. 'Nine years ago, wasn't it? How time does fly.'

The classroom at Alder Court would be decorated with Daisy's paintings and drawings of gap-toothed witches stirring nasty stews in cauldrons and riding aloft on broomsticks. These near likenesses of Magda would one day join the garden refuse for burning when Nelly decided that Daisy, at the age of fourteen, ought to be painting and drawing from life rather than fantasy. 'Open your eyes, Daisy. You can turn out those awful midnight hags in your sleep. Draw a plant or a flower for me. Why not start with the datura?')

'Who is who?'

'Tell Magda – is it all right for them to call you Magda?'

'I don't think their tongues will take easily to Mrs Esterhazy-Williams.'

'Tell Magda your names, girls.'

Daisy and Kitty stood in silence.

'They're very shy, aren't they, Mrs Crozier.'

'Kitty is,' Muriel Crozier responded, patting Kitty's head. 'But not Daisy.'

'They have quite ruddy complexions. Do they live in the country?'

'Yes.'

'Rosy cheeks do not go well with rosy shades. I have a motto, Mrs Crozier: the ruddier the skin, the colder the colour to offset it. I look at Kitty and Daisy, and pale green speaks to me. Or a really icy blue.'

'Anything would be better than the table-cloths they're wearing.'

Magda snorted and said, 'Yes, yes – so very bistro, aren't they, those dresses. And obviously run up.'

'Obviously.'

(They thought and felt as one that Easter Saturday, Kitty Crozier was to remember. It was as if they were possessed of the same distaste for Magda, the same loathing of their

89

father's new wife, the same protectiveness towards Nelly, whose 'run-up' dresses were being mocked. They disliked the 'lovely, lovely', 'professionally finished' dresses Magda made them get into and then out of, but they hated most of all the pale-green and Arctic-blue 'creations' that Magda Esterhazy-Williams and Muriel Crozier finally chose for them. They heard themselves described as 'sweet little pieces of Dresden' and were sickened by 'sweet little' and confused by 'pieces of Dresden'. They watched as Magda's nervy assistant folded the four dresses and wrapped them in fine paper, and still they said nothing. Theirs was a united silence. 'They must be overawed, dear Mrs Crozier. Or overcome. It's their country upbringing, I assume. They need their rough edges softening. What a pity they can't spend more time in your care. But you are a woman of the world and your husband is such a busy man.'

They mouthed a joint 'Thank you' at Muriel Crozier's insistence, and Magda Esterhazy-Williams kissed them both and told them they were now the two most elegant girls – '*Très, très chic*' – in London.

Once they were out of the store, Daisy released her hand from Kitty's and ended their state of unity. She spoke as only she dared to. 'Do we *have* to go back in the big silly car?' she asked Muriel Crozier, as Jackson opened the door of the waiting Rolls-Royce.)

The following day Felix Crozier took his daughters to the zoo in Regent's Park. Since the zoo was 'nowhere special' and 'open to everybody', and Muriel was 'laid low' with a migraine, Daisy and Kitty were allowed to wear the 'table-cloths'.

Whenever Kitty glanced at her sister that afternoon Daisy seemed distracted, deep in thought. 'What's the matter, Daisy?'

'You'll see. You'll find out. You'll see, Kitty.'

Of all the animals and birds they gawped at in wonder or terror – it was the stillness of the coiled cobra that had Daisy flinching – only the monkeys, leaping from branch to branch and scampering up and down the trees in the large monkey house, looked glad to be in London. Kitty began to laugh at the sheer happy sight of them. 'Their bums, Daddy,' she cried out and her father said, 'What about their bums, dearest darling? Is it the pinkness of them?'

'Yes, Daddy. And some of them are red as well.'

'I can shape my lips into a monkey's bum, if you'd like me to, Kitty.'

'Yes, please.'

Felix Crozier put his lips together and stuck them out, and Kitty laughed until she was in stitches.

'Now you do a monkey's bum for me, Kitty darling. When you've recovered.'

So Kitty put her lips together and made them stick out, and her father said she'd done a perfect monkey's bum at her first try. Then he lifted her up and rubbed noses with her. 'Let's share a monkey's bum kiss, my dearest darling,' he whispered. They kissed and laughed again.

When he lowered her to the ground, Kitty noticed that Daisy had disappeared. 'Where's Daisy, Daddy?'

'Up to her tricks, I don't doubt. She can't have gone far.'

She had gone as far, they discovered, as an ice-cream kiosk, where she was buying a vanilla cornet with one of the two half-crowns Nelly had given each of them as pocket money.

'Shall I buy you an ice-cream, Daddy? I have enough in my purse.'

'That's very thoughtful of you, dearest. I have to consider the size of my tummy, but I'll be greedy just this once. I'll have strawberry, if the man has it.'

Kitty bought her father a strawberry-flavoured lolly and chose a raspberry ripple for herself because it sounded funny.

That evening was to be the last Daisy and Kitty spent in the Mayfair mansion.

It was Muriel Crozier's wish that the twins dress for

dinner. 'But not identically. Let me see Daisy in the pale green and Kitty in the Arctic blue.'

To everyone's surprise, Daisy did not protest. 'All right, if that's what you want. I'll put on the green frock, if that's what you want.'

'Don't say "frock", Daisy. "Frock" is common. "Frock" is a word people like us try not to use.'

(In the summer of 1978, when she was working on the index for a scholarly book on English etymology, Kitty Crozier – locating the entry for the word 'frock' on page 105 – would recollect Muriel Crozier's advice to Daisy. She would smile on learning that 'frock' had been in use since the fourteenth century. Who had been using it, preserving it, in all that time? A few 'people like us', surely. A few million dead people like us.)

'Go and bathe, girls. Beryl will wash and brush your hair.'

Daisy made no complaints while her hair was being washed and brushed, and she did not scream when some drops of shampoo ran down into her eyes, causing them to smart.

'What have you done with the devil inside of you, Miss Daisy? Giving it a day off, are you? You're almost as good as gold tonight.'

'Am I, Miss Beryl?'

'Yes, you are. I say almost because you're still calling me Miss Beryl, which you shouldn't be.'

'I like calling you Miss Beryl, Miss Beryl,' said Daisy, giggling.

'Are you planning to be sick again this evening?'

'No, I'm not. It was that horrible chocolate's fault.'

'That chocolate, young lady, is the best money can buy. It didn't make Miss Kitty sick.'

'Kitty only nibbled hers. She's still got plenty left.'

'I'm puzzled, Miss Daisy.'

'Why's that, Miss Beryl?'

'I'm puzzled why, if the chocolate Easter egg was so horrible, you gobbled the whole thing up.'

92

'It was a present, Miss Beryl. From them. That's why I ate it up. I was being polite.'

Beryl sniggered. 'You were, were you? "Polite" wasn't the word Madam used when she caught sight of the state of your bed this morning.'

'I couldn't help myself. Honestly, Miss Beryl.'

'I'll try to believe you, you scamp.'

'What's a scamp, Miss Beryl?'

'It's what you are and it's what Miss Kitty isn't, and that's my way of telling you what a scamp is.'

When they were dressed – Daisy with a matching green ribbon in her hair; Kitty with a matching blue – Beryl told them they looked like miniature mannequins from Paris. 'Let me show you off to Mr and Mrs Crozier.'

But Mrs Crozier was suffering with her head again and would be lying in the dark for at least another hour. They would have to be content with their father's approval.

'Let's give him a lovely surprise, shall we? Come along, mannequins.'

'What's mannequins, Miss Beryl?'

'Mannequins are models. Models who model clothes.'

They found Felix Crozier peering at his reflection in a mirror. He was trimming his moustache with a small pair of scissors. The woman on the record was singing the song Muriel Crozier knew by heart.

'He loves himself, Kitty. He loves himself more than anyone else in the world.'

'Mr Crozier, sir. Miss Daisy and Miss Kitty are here to see you.'

'So they are, Beryl, so they are. What beautiful, beautiful daughters I've been blessed with.'

'Madam has such refined taste, Mr Crozier, sir.'

'She certainly has, Beryl.'

'I hate him,' Daisy muttered. 'Listen to the stuff he speaks. I hate him.'

'No, Daisy.'

93

'Yes, Kitty.'

They were beautiful, beautiful; they were his dearest, most precious darlings and the dresses simply enhanced Nature's perfect achievement.

'Listen to him.'

'Tomorrow evening,' Muriel Crozier announced when dinner was over, 'Daisy will be in blue and Kitty in green. What do you think, Felix?'

'Felix thinks that's a wonderful idea.'

'You may leave the table, girls.'

'Felix also thinks that his darlings ought to give us both a grateful good-night kiss.'

Kitty waited for her sister to object, but Daisy was the first to rise, the first to peck Muriel's cheek, the first to say an unexpected 'Sweet dreams, Daddy' to an astonished Felix.

'You kissed them, Daisy,' Kitty remarked after Beryl had tucked them into their beds. 'Why did you?'

'I was being polite.'

'Why?'

'Y is the last but one letter of the alphabet, Kitty. That's why.'

'I don't believe you.'

'You know it is. It comes between X and Z.'

'I don't believe you were just being polite.'

'Well, I was.'

Towards dawn, Kitty was awakened by her twin's laughter. Daisy was seated on the floor, the new dresses scattered about her. 'Snip, snip, snip,' she was saying to herself. 'Snip, snip, snip.'

'Daisy, what are you doing?'

'Having fun with his scissors. Snip, snip, snip.'

'Daisy, you mustn't. You can't, Daisy.'

'Oh yes I must. Snip, snip, snip. Look at them, Kitty. Look what I've done to them.'

Kitty switched on a bedside lamp and looked. She gasped at what she saw. 'You've cut them in pieces. You've ruined them, Daisy. We shan't ever be able to wear them now.'

(She had cut the dresses in pieces, it was true, but her snipping had been inventive. Daisy had scored and scarred the expensive material – shantung silk – of which the four 'creations' were composed. Because she had only a pair of nail scissors at her disposal she had laboured throughout the night at her enjoyable task. She was especially pleased with the way she had altered the hem of the Arctic-blue dress Magda the witch and the horrible Muriel had chosen for her. 'I've scalloped the edge, Kitty,' she crowed, using an expression she had learned from Nelly. 'I've scalloped it good and proper.')

'I don't want to wear them, Kitty. Ever again.'

'Nor do I. But you shouldn't have cut them. We could have taken them home and let them go mouldy.'

'Snip, snip, snippety-snip.' Daisy giggled. 'She's going to be so angry with me. She's going to be so cross.'

'Aren't you frightened?'

'No. Not me. Not of her.' Daisy yawned. 'I'm tired. I'm sleepy. Turn out the light.'

'There's no need to ask which of you two did this,' said Beryl, gathering up the ruined dresses at eight that Monday morning. 'She may be sleeping the sleep of the innocent, but I'd bet on my life this is little Miss Daisy's handiwork.'

Kitty was silent.

'I shall have to show these to Madam, Miss Kitty. Did you try to stop your sister? Did you tell her she was doing wrong?'

'Yes,' Kitty answered, then corrected herself. 'No. I was too late to stop her.'

'I haven't seen Madam in a temper. I expect a few sparks will fly today, though, thanks to the sleeping beauty.'

Beryl left the room and Kitty waited for flying sparks. She waited for raised voices, for shrieks and shouts. Minutes passed. She heard nothing upsetting. Daisy slept on, her unworried features indicating to her anxious twin that she was in the middle of a happy dream.

95

Then Beryl returned with the news that Sir, Mr Crozier, was expecting Miss Kitty and Miss Daisy to join him for breakfast.

'Let's have you both washed and dressed.' She yanked the sheet that was covering Daisy. 'Come along, little devil. Rise and shine, naughty Lazybones.'

Daisy opened her eyes and smiled. 'Hullo, Miss Beryl.'

'Don't you "Hullo, Miss Beryl" me. I know what you've done and so does Madam.'

'Snip, snip, snip.'

'You should be ashamed of yourself. Where's your gratitude? Where's your respect? How many other girls of your age, do you imagine, get to wear such beautiful clothes?'

'Snippety-snip,' said Daisy, miming the act of cutting with two fingers.

'Snippety-snip, is it? I'll give you clippety-clip with my hand if you don't behave.'

'Is she very angry with me?'

'I presume it's Madam you're asking about and not the cat's mother. What do you expect her to be, you minx? Tickled pink?'

'Your holiday is over,' Felix Crozier told his daughters once they were seated at the dining-table. 'Muriel has no wish to see you again. She has no wish even to say goodbye to you. You have hurt her, Daisy, which means that you have hurt me as well. Jackson will drive you back just as soon as you've finished eating.'

'I'm sorry, Daddy.'

'You have no reason to be sorry, Kitty. I should like to hear the words on Daisy's lips.'

Daisy shook her head.

'I'm sorry you're not sorry. I am very sorry indeed.'

In the hall, soon afterwards, Kitty and her father exchanged monkey's bum kisses. When she began to cry softly he took the handkerchief from his breast pocket and wiped away her tears. 'There, there, my dearest. One more monkey's bum, if you please.'

'I love you, Daddy,' she whispered in his ear.

'Bless you, my darling.'

He carried her out to the Rolls-Royce and kissed her hair, before lowering her to the ground. He stared at Daisy, who returned his stare.

'I want to say goodbye to Miss Beryl.'

'Beryl's busy. Beryl's working.'

'She could come outside for a minute.'

'She could, but she won't. Goodbye, Daisy. Perhaps you will be a nicer young woman the next time we meet.'

'Snip, snip,' said Daisy. 'Snip, snip.'

'Be off with you.'

Daisy sulked during the journey home. Kitty sensed her sister's frustration and disappointment at being denied the sight and sound of their stepmother's anger, but knew that she must not be comforted. What Daisy had done with the scissors was wicked. What Daisy had done with the scissors, Kitty had begun to realise, was mad.

And yet, when the 'big silly car' – which seemed bigger and sillier than ever to both of them as Mr Jackson attempted to steer it up, down and along narrow hedge-lined country lanes – yes, when it approached Alder Court, Kitty was suddenly pleased that Daisy's snipping had brought their Easter holiday to an early end. Although she loved her father, she was relieved not to be in his company any longer. She thought she would prefer to pity him – for hers was now a pitying love – from a distance.

Nelly welcomed Mr Jackson into the kitchen, where she sat him down at the refectory table to drink Darjeeling tea and eat the bread she had recently finished baking. She offered him marmalade, too. 'Kitty had a hand in making it. She has the patience a good cook needs.'

'She is a credit to you, Mrs Crozier.'

The chauffeur brought out an envelope from his jacket

and handed it to Nelly, who made a groaning noise.

'This, I suppose, is the record of Daisy's misdemeanours. It feels bulky enough.'

'Mrs Crozier wrote it at white heat, Mrs Crozier.'

Daisy smirked at this remark and at Jackson's evident embarrassment. Nelly, looking directly at her, said, 'I'm sure she did. I shall read it with interest.'

She read Muriel Crozier's letter, quickly, in front of her daughters as soon as the chauffeur had gone. Then she scrunched the three lavender-coloured sheets of notepaper into a ball and tossed it on to the fire. She waited until it had burnt before she said, 'You will send her a few words of apology, Daisy.'

'I can't.'

'You can and you will.'

'I can't, Nelly. I honestly can't.'

'Nonsense. You are going to be dishonestly apologetic for the first and, I hope, last time in your life. You will write your father's wife a very short note, Daisy. With very few words.'

'I can't.'

'You can, you can, you can. Fetch a piece of paper and a pen, Kitty.'

Nelly stood over Daisy and watched as she wrote: 'Dear Stepmother, I am very sorry indeed that I ruined the dresses you kindly bought for us. I am ashamed of myself. Please try and forgive me. Yours sincerely, Daisy.'

'That's it. That's done. Now, perhaps, you will stop wailing.'

'Shall I write to Daddy, Nelly? Saying thank you?'

'Yes, Kitty. Put your message underneath Daisy's. We don't want to waste paper and it will save the cost of an extra stamp.'

'Virgil Florescu?'

'Yes.'

'This is Corneliu Ursachi speaking.'

'Who?'

'You surely have not forgotten me already. I am the clumsy individual who spilt tea – accidentally, or course – on your exquisite antique carpet.'

'Oh, yes.'

'I have very good news for you, Virgil. The carpet cleaners have excelled themselves. Your treasure is as new. I wish to return it to its bereft owner without more delay. Would tomorrow morning be convenient?'

'It isn't, but no doubt it will have to do. You do not usually go to the trouble of fixing an appointment.'

'But our relationship is different now. No more surprise visits. I shall arrive at nine precisely.'

'My class, I assume, has been informed of my absence?'

'Naturally. Revision, revision, Virgil. Your students will be gainfully occupied, have no fear. Until tomorrow.'

The young intellectual was accompanied by an unsmiling older man when he appeared, several minutes later than he had indicated, the next day.

'Good morning to you, Virgil. Allow me to present my colleague Adrian. He will take no part in our conversation. Adrian is not a lover of poetry. Adrian prefers football.'

'Is he here, then, to drink tea?'

'He is indeed. We have been visiting certain people since dawn and we have both developed a thirst.'

'Be seated.'

'There are only two chairs, Virgil, neither of them sturdy. You see how solid Adrian is. Adrian will remain standing.'

'As he chooses.'

'Before you prepare the refreshing herbal tea, Virgil, let me suggest that you open this parcel. It contains your Oltenian carpet, restored to its former glory.'

He took the parcel, untied the string that secured it and pulled out a carpet he knew immediately was not his mother's. The design was identical and so was the size, but this carpet was a modern copy, a synthetic reproduction of the original. Even though he was convinced he was holding a fake, he looked on the back for his mother's maiden name, the letters sewn into the fabric in blue and gold thread by the skilled hand of her beloved nurse Gabriela. But 'Matilda Popescu' wasn't there and Matilda Florescu wasn't there either – no, not in any sense at all.

'It is as new, yes, Virgil?'

'Yes, it is as new. It definitely is as new.'

'You seem dazzled by it. Aren't you going to place it on the floor, where it belongs?'

'Not yet.'

'I promise you I shan't spill tea on it. I have my clumsy days, Virgil, but this is not one of them.'

'I am thinking that I may have other plans for this carpet.'

'On one of the walls, perhaps?'

'Who knows? I must prepare the tea. You say that you and your colleague are thirsty.'

'That is true.'

'Be patient with me.'

(He thought, as the water boiled, that his mother's carpet – wherever it was; whatever fate had been decided for it – had become a precious memory now. The object itself was gone, yet everything it represented for him endured.)

'Your expert cleaners,' he said, 'have put a sheen on my poor fading carpet. It almost glows.'

'That is why they are experts, Virgil. They are dedicated workers. They do what they are required to do supremely well.'

'Such dedication is wonderful. And rare.'

'In other countries, perhaps, Virgil. But not here in Romania.'

'How thoughtless of me. How very rash. There are – there must be – many dedicated workers here.'

'You are beginning to sound excited, Virgil. Relax. Relax and call me Corneliu.'

'The tea is ready. I am sorry for keeping you and your colleague waiting.'

'We have not waited long. Do not apologise. Adrian will require sugar. Adrian needs plenty of sugar to sustain his energy.'

'Would your colleague care to add the necessary sugar himself?'

'Four cubes will suffice, Virgil.'

He plopped the cubes into the glass and passed it to the man who might or might not be Adrian.

'The last time we had the pleasure of one another's company we discussed, I recollect, the poetry of George Bacovia.'

'You spoke of him. I listened. I did not – I do not – share your view of his art.'

'But I have altered my view, Virgil. I have altered it radically, drastically, in the light of your impassioned contribution to our discussion. You have made me think again.'

'Have I?' Virgil Florescu responded incuriously.

'You are really too modest. Yes, you have. What an insensitive reader I was, failing as I did to discern the irony – the irony you drew my attention to, Virgil – in Bacovia's verses. He is very ironical, even tongue-in-cheek. He lived through black periods in our history, when it was incumbent on our artists to be ironical. That I have come to understand. Were he alive today, he might perhaps be more attuned to the spirit of the age. Yes? What is your opinion?'

'My opinion is that were he alive today he would be the same Bacovia.'

'But the circumstances have changed, Virgil. And for the better.'

'Circumstances do not change for poets like him. Their circumstances are unchanging. From the birth of their poetry to the death of their bodies, their circumstances remain constant.'

'This is a Romantic speaking, Virgil.'

'Possibly.'

'Undeniably. You seem to be favouring the idea of the doomed and fated poet – the man whose gift is also his burden. Your multitude of admirers, Virgil, who include Corneliu Ursachi, are thankful that your own resonant and subtle poetry does not read like the work of such an unfortunate person.'

'A thankful multitude? Virgil Florescu is not the sort to inspire multitudes. My admirers, gathered together, would be able to mingle comfortably in a small room. A room no bigger than this.'

'You do yourself an injustice, Virgil. You are almost as famous – in our country – as –'

'As?'

'As the one talented poet incapable of writing anything so uncivil as "Icon". There, I have broken my promise to you by mentioning it. Forgive me. When we meet again I shall not allude to your aberration. Now Adrian and I must say our farewell. Actually, Virgil, I shall say farewell on Adrian's behalf. He is proficient in silence.' The man who claimed to be Corneliu Ursachi laughed, and said – in an assumed voice that was meant to be Adrian's – 'Farewell, Virgil.' He then reverted to his own way of speaking. 'In my case, Virgil, it is *au revoir*. We shall see each other soon. In the meantime, Adrian and I have more visits to make. Surprise visits. Good day to you.'

He closed the door of the apartment behind the intellectual and his silent assistant. He leaned against it, his heart suddenly thumping, and listened to their footsteps on the stairs. He heard Corneliu curse the lift for being out of order – 'The cunt of a weary old whore is in better condition' – and did not move until he was sure they had left the block.

He walked across to the window and looked down to the street. The men were standing on either side of a dented and battered Dacia, arguing vociferously. Adrian was the more animated. He was gesticulating with both hands and at one alarming moment he inflicted further damage on the car by banging his fist repeatedly on its roof. Adrian's taciturnity, Virgil Florescu was not astonished to discover, had been a temporary affectation. Adrian and Corneliu were, of necessity, actors, since their peculiar profession demanded that they play the roles expected of them – the brooding, silent henchman; the loquacious academic, employing a script mapped out for him by some invisible official.

Virgil Florescu watched impatiently as the men continued their argument. Then, to his relief, Adrian got into the tiny car and hunched himself over the steering wheel. A petulant Corneliu joined him and the Dacia juddered down the street, leaving a trail of pitch-black exhaust in its wake.

There was a curfew that evening and by seven o'clock the city was in darkness. In the urinal behind the morgue of the hospital where Radu Sava was on duty, Virgil Florescu and his cherished friend pissed on the glowing, hated carpet.

'We are naughty schoolboys again, Virgil.'

Arms linked, they walked back to their apartment. The lights were on in the Hotel Athénée, and as they were passing it Radu Sava stopped and said, 'Our not-so-secret secret police are everywhere, even in *pissoirs*. The Securitate will find the sodden carpet. It is time you fled Romania.'

He arrived at her house, after their four-day separation, and they went instantly to bed.

They talked later, in the kitchen – she of the Easter of Easters; he of the glowing carpet that precipitated his exile.

He had written another poem to speak to her. It was about a man whose highest ambition was to live quietly and humbly, fishing for perch in the river where his father had fished. 'I have stolen him, Kitty. I have stolen him from my mighty namesake and made him my own.'

4

Breaking the Glass

_____

'You are our first ever Romanian, Mr Florescu. He is, isn't he, Cecil?'

'Not quite. I had a Canadian Jewish Romanian financier pass through my office once. He told me a little bit of his family history after we concluded business. Pretty sad stuff, as I recall.'

'Then Mr Florescu is our first complete Romanian. You're not Canadian as well, are you? Or Jewish?'

'No, Mrs Hopkins. I am neither. And as for being complete, I suspect I have Hungarian blood. My father, who is now an old man, insists that I am a Roman Romanian, rather than one of Dacian origin.'

'Does he? Well, Roman or whatever it was you said, do sit down and make yourself comfortable.'

'You are kind. Thank you.'

'Kitty tells me you can't eat meat.'

'That is correct, yes. I cannot.'

'She says you're allowed fish.'

'Yes, I am.'

'I hope fried sole with a plain parsley sauce will be acceptable, Mr Florescu.'

'Thank you, yes.'

'He is Virgil, Daisy,' said Kitty, putting an arm about her twin. 'He is Virgil to us.'

'It occurs to me, Virgil – if I may –' Cecil began, and stopped.

'What occurs to you, Cecil? You obviously find it amusing.'

'Yes, I do. Rather. Yes, it is amusing. Or rather, to be accurate, it's more droll than amusing. On balance, I would say it was droll.'

'What is droll, Cecil?'

'The fact that here I am addressing Virgil, Daisy. What is droll is that two years ago, in Chicago, I found myself sitting next to a banker named Homer Bradley at dinner. All through the meal it was Homer this and Homer that. So, you see, I've made the acquaintance of Homer and now I've met Virgil. It's almost as if I've started to move in classical circles.'

'I don't know how many Homers there are in America, Cecil, but I am one of thousands of Romanian Virgils.'

'I shall pretend I didn't hear that. I wonder what the chances are of shaking hands with a Socrates or an Agamemnon. Pretty remote, I should think.'

'You might come across them in Greece.'

'That's an idea, Kitty.'

'Please don't give my husband ideas, there's a good baby sister. I'm happy with him as he is.'

Cecil laughed and said what a disgraceful host he was, forgetting to do the honours. There was something in the cabinet to satisfy every tippler's taste, though Daisy and he were in the habit of drinking a sherry before Sunday lunch. But to each his own, to each his own.

'Do you approve of our house, Virgil?'

'Approve? Why, yes, Daisy.'

'We have put a lot of love and work into it.'

'I can see.'

'Do you have nice houses in Romania? Does your family own one?'

No, he answered. No, his family, his present family, owned no property. They lived in apartments, none of them spacious. Politicians and those in favour with the authorities – they had large apartments, houses in the countryside. No one else. 'My mother kept photographs of the house she was born in. It was built in the old Romanian style, with the dining-room stretching the length of the ground floor. There was a gallery, or balcony above, and once a year, on his feast day, my grandfather would invite gypsy musicians to play and sing in the courtyard below the gallery. He was a farmer. He was a good man, kind to the people who worked for him. So my mother impressed on me. The house was taken from him, along with his land.'

'He's dead, is he?'

'He died when I was seven. My mother is dead also.'

'But your father is alive?'

'Yes, he is alive. He still has all his wits. Constantin Florescu is imperishable.'

'Imperishable? What's his secret?'

'His secret, Cecil, is a secret.'

'Very mysterious.'

'Before we get lost in secrets and mysteries, why don't we drink a toast to our complete Romanian's health?' Daisy suggested. 'Here's to Virgil.'

'To Virgil.'

'To Virgil.'

'Thank you. You are kind. The sherry is exquisite. I am touched. *Noroc*.'

'*Noroc* means happiness,' Kitty explained. 'It's one of the few words I have learned.'

'You'll learn more, sister dear, if I know you. That's one

106

of the many differences between Kitty and me, Virgil. She has brains, whereas I have common sense.'

'Really?'

'Really and truly. Look at this room. See how tidy it is. No dust, no mess. Now think of the chaos Kitty lives in. Books everywhere you turn, newspapers scattered over the carpet, clothes left on the backs of chairs. I haven't peered behind her bedroom door lately, but I can imagine – from past experience – the sheer awfulness inside.'

'I find Kitty's bedroom very pleasant.'

'You do? Do you? Oh, well, yes, of course. You would. I understand what you're saying. You would, of course.'

'Very pleasant.'

'Are you planning to marry Kitty, Mr Florescu? I mean, Virgil.'

'Virgil's married, Daisy. To a woman who lives in Bristol with her lover.'

'It is a marriage of convenience. For political reasons. We shall divorce when times change. If times change.'

'Let's hope they do. If there is anything in this world that would make me happier than I am already it's the knowledge that my younger sister has finally settled down. She has had too many, far too many infatuations. Far too many infatuations for my liking.'

(There has been one infatuation, Kitty Crozier did not remind the sister she had reminded so often, and so ineffectually, before. She had only once been infatuated and that was with the 'kaftanned creature', the blond, beautiful, grey-and-green-eyed Freddy. She had tried to tell Daisy that her other involvements were of the uninvolved kind, with friends and acquaintances, for mutual gratification. But Daisy had chosen not to hear her, Daisy-fashion.)

'Kitty and Virgil must follow their own course, Daisy love.'

'As long as it ends in marriage, that's all I ask.'

'Perhaps they will keep your request in mind when the

opportunity arises. I can just imagine Kitty saying to Virgil, "Daisy wants us to marry, therefore we should." Or rather, I can't imagine it.'

'Cecil's being sarcastic now, which isn't the way he is usually.'

There was a sudden sound of buzzing. 'Cook's call to arms,' said Daisy, rising from the sofa. The timer on her good old faithful cooker was commanding her to get those vegetables on the boil and to baste the joint of beef – beef for Sunday lunch was a Hopkins family tradition – which she was sorry Virgil wasn't permitted to eat. And she must fry his fish. And would Cecil rustle up their offspring, wherever they were, and have everybody around the table in, well, ten minutes flat?

She left the room. The buzzing stopped and Cecil let out an exaggerated sigh. 'I've persuaded Daisy to go to India, Kitty.'

'You have what?'

'I'm not surprised you're astonished. It is surprising, isn't it? But yes, indeed, Daisy is about to take the proverbial plunge and spread her folded wings, as it were. Majorca is the furthest she has ever been away from home, so this will be quite an undertaking for her. Quite a trip.'

'Why India?'

'Well, when I tell you it's India, perhaps I should be more exact and say Nepal. Rather, she's going first to India and then on to Nepal. Daisy has this friend, a widow, a rather splendid woman, very enterprising, not the sedentary type, who loves the great outdoors. It's been her dream for years to walk in the Himalayas. She invited Daisy to join her and Daisy, not surprisingly, declined. Usual excuses – children at a difficult age; Cecil incapable of boiling an egg for himself; India on the other side of the world, so not easy to get back quickly in case of an emergency, et cetera, et cetera. Whereupon Harriet – that's the widow – asked me to come to the rescue. Which I did. I explained that walking in the Himalayas was not the same as climbing Everest and mentioned her grandfather, who died in Darjeeling. Why not dabble in some family history? I suggested. That did the trick. Oh, and the fact that I'm footing the bill. But I won't believe she's going until I've waved her goodbye at the airport. No, not until then.'

'When does she leave?'

'On Wednesday, at eleven in the evening, God and Daisy willing.'

Cecil remembered that he was supposed to be rustling up his young ones rather than imparting matters of state – when Daisy finally got round to telling them about her Indian trip, would they pretend to be ignorant of it? – and excused himself for a moment.

In the dining area adjoining the kitchen Kitty introduced Virgil to her niece and nephew.

'Hi,' said Janet.

'Hi,' said Andrew.

'Hi.'

'Mr Florescu, Virgil, is from Romania. You've probably done Romania in your geography class, haven't you, Andrew?'

'Probably, Ma.'

'My children are shy, Virgil, and given to few words in company. But we love our pair of Trappists, don't we, Cecil?'

'Do we? I think we do, sometimes.'

'That's only Cecil's joke. Of course we do. I hope you are hungry, Virgil. You'll pardon my saying so, but you look as if you could do with a square meal.'

'I am thin, yes.'

'I have to warn you that simple food, simply cooked, is the way we like it in the Hopkins household. Nothing too rich or fancy. That's another difference between Kitty and me. She adores making complicated sauces, with ingredients

109

the majority of people have never heard of, whereas I stay content with the traditional recipes.'

'You are kind to invite me.'

'I can't tempt you to some beef?'

'No, Daisy. Thank you. I have an aversion. The fish in your uncomplicated sauce will give me satisfaction enough. I shall eat it with pleasure.'

(Kitty Crozier would recall how quietly courteous her vanished lover was that day; how he spoke of his aversion, yet again, with no hint of its genesis; how he persuaded the timid Janet to exchange a little French with him, to Daisy's startled delight; how he sat across from her at lunch, in his approximately-fitting 'charity suit', looking almost at ease amid so much domesticity – family chatter, family phrases and rare family silences.)

'We thought we might take a walk later, after our stomachs have settled. That's our Sunday routine, unless it's raining heavily. It's the dogs' favourite time of the week.'

'You have a dog?'

'We have two, Virgil. Buster and Bruiser.'

'But where are they?'

'At the back of the house, in their own special extension that Cecil built for them. They come inside once a year, for Christmas dinner, but otherwise they're out of bounds.'

'They're not out of bounds when they're running, Daisy love. They bound like the very devil the moment they're let off the lead.'

'I've lived with Cecil's jokes for nineteen years,' said Daisy, 'and they don't get any better. Did you understand that one, Virgil? The play on words?'

'Yes, yes, I did.'

'I couldn't live without them now – his jokes, I mean. They have grown on me. That's the funniest thing about them, the way they grow on you.'

'You make them sound like fungus, dear. Some more pears and custard, Virgil?'

'Please. Thank you.'

'I'll have a second helping as well.'

'Sister Kitty, you do surprise me. Isn't custard a bit too common, a bit too ordinary for your sophisticated taste?'

'Not when it is as smooth and delicious as this, Daisy, no.'

'There was I thinking you were above my custard.'

'Oh, Ma,' sighed Andrew.

'We've been prattling on, Virgil, and no one's bothered to ask you the important question. How did you manage to leave Romania?'

'I had ways and means, Cecil.'

'Legal ways and means?'

'Yes. I would say legal, for me. Legitimate ways and means.'

'You escaped?'

'In a manner of speaking, Andrew. I have nothing adventurous to report, though. I crossed the border. I have been in Italy. That is all.'

'Do you speak Italian, Virgil?'

'Yes, Janet.'

'Anything else?'

'Spanish and Portuguese. The Latin languages. And a little Greek. And awkward English, as you can hear.'

'And French.'

'Yes, and French. Like you.'

'Please say something in Romanian.'

'What shall I say? Listen. *Asculţi. Asculţi* is "Listen":

'*Mai bine singuratec şi uitat . . .*
În ţara trista plina de humor . . .'

He paused. 'I will translate for you – roughly, I'm afraid, crudely. "It is well to be alone and forgotten, in a sad country full of humour." That is as close as I can get. Poetry has its own language in every language.'

'Virgil is a poet, Janet.'

'I write poems, Daisy.'

'I have to confess, Virgil, that I've never been much of a poetry person. Poetry's Kitty's province. Nelly, our mother, tried and tried to tune my ear to it, and she didn't succeed, more's the pity.'

Why, Cecil wanted Virgil to tell him, was a man with his gifts working in a park, picking up leaves and litter and stuff? Why was it that he, a writer, hadn't found, with Kitty's help, a job to do with books?

'I do not need such a job here. Believe me, it is not necessary. As it is, I meet diverting people. I have time to think. I have no wish to do with books.'

'You might earn more money.'

'I earn enough for my needs.'

'Yes, I suppose you do,' said Cecil, without malice or irony. 'Are you a famous poet, over there in Romania?'

'I am infamous. I have become infamous.' He smiled. 'I am more famous than famous by being infamous.'

'Now that's a riddle if ever I heard one. I'll hazard a guess you wrote a poem that caused offence, that the boys in power considered unwarranted. Have I hit the target?'

'"Boys in power" is very good, Cecil. I am taken with "boys in power".'

'You have my permission to quote it.'

'Thank you.'

Since the days were already beginning to shorten, wouldn't it be sensible, Daisy proposed, if they went for their stroll a trifle earlier than usual. Now, for instance. The Baskervilles, Buster and Bruiser, were probably champing at the bit, anyway, and Virgil was obviously curious to meet them. 'Baskerville' was Cecil's family name for the dogs, and another of his inimitable jokes. Had Virgil read *The Hound of the Baskervilles* by Conan Doyle? Nelly had read it aloud to her frightened daughters on winter evenings in Alder Court, with the trees howling in the wind outside. Kitty and she had huddled together as the horrible plot thickened and Nelly's voice grew steadily – no, unsteadily – more excited. A happy memory, though, despite the fear they had felt. Yes, a very happy memory of being absolutely terrified.

'No, I have not read it.'

'It's a Sherlock Holmes story. He unravels the mystery. You have heard of Sherlock Holmes?'

'Oh, yes. And the dependable Doctor Watson, too. They are well-known in my country.'

'Just as your Count Dracula, it suddenly occurs to me, is well-known here.'

'I must correct you, Cecil. He is *your* Count Dracula, not ours. The preposterous undead Count in his preposterous Transylvanian castle is the invention of an Irishman. He is one blood-sucking demon who does not belong to us. We have no claim on him.'

'Is Transylvania a real place?'

'Yes, Janet. It is as real as England. I have been there in spring and it is beautiful.'

Daisy rose from the table, clapped her hands and said it was time to put their skates on – an English expression, she remarked to Virgil, not to be taken literally – and set off. They had had some fascinating conversation, but some healthy exercise wouldn't come amiss either.

'Let's be going, everyone. On your pins. Marching orders.'

'Oh, Ma,' sighed Andrew.

Kitty and Virgil waited with Daisy on the steps leading up to the house while Cesspit – that was Daisy's private nickname for Cecil, not to be used in polite company – and the offspring fetched the Baskervilles.

'They are hard to tell apart,' said Daisy when the dogs appeared, panting, tongues lolling. 'That's Bruiser with Andrew and Janet is trying to control the uncontrollable Buster. They are Labradors, Virgil, in case you don't know. Thoroughbreds.'

'Yes, yes. I can see. Yes, yes.' He sniggered, then began to splutter and soon he was laughing loudly, helplessly.

'What is so funny about a pair of black Labradors?'

He was unable to answer Daisy's question immediately, because his laughter was rising higher and higher – just as it had risen, Kitty recollected, on their first evening together, when she had asked him if his gleaming tooth was made of silver.

'Our beloved leader –' he managed to say before being overcome again. 'Nicolas Unpronounceable?' Cecil ventured. 'The little chap with the little wife? Him?'

'Yes, yes. Forgive me. Be patient.' He breathed deeply, cleared his throat, patted his chest and said: 'Our beloved leader, our Conducător as we call him, was given a black Labrador by one of your politicians. He is called Comrade Corbul. That dog is treated like a god and we wretched creatures, we humble, patriotic Romanians, must pay him our respects. I am serious. One day, in Bucharest, our capital city, I was walking along Calea Victoriei, the Street of Victories, when I saw an enormous car, with an armed guard on a motor bike on either side, caught in the traffic. I looked, I blinked, I looked, I blinked – yes, it was not a dream; I was not hallucinating. What I was looking at was a dog – no, not *a* dog; *the* dog – seated in splendour behind the driver. He had a medal of some kind attached to his collar. I looked until the car started moving and the dog – *the* dog – returned my stare. I may have saluted him; I think I did, because of his medal. What are medals for but to be saluted?'

'Is this true?'

'On my honour, Cecil. Everything I am saying is true. Some say that dog is now an honorary general in the Romanian army and a member of the government. He is said to vote on important issues with his left front paw and mastermind military campaigns by wagging his tail. When Comrade Corbul barks – woof, woof – heads roll. When he goes on barking – woof, woof; woof, woof – it means there is a national emergency. But when he growls – grr, grr – a curfew is imposed, alarms are sounded, arrests are made. Now I am being fanciful, perhaps. Or perhaps not. It is possible that the sleek, shiny, well-fed dog is the real ruler of my country. A dog's obeyed in office, isn't he?' He paused and smiled. 'I must apologise for my outburst. Your dogs are handsome. Good afternoon, Buster. Good afternoon, Bruiser. I hope I have not frightened you with my laughter.'

'It would take more than that to frighten the Baskerville brothers,' Daisy assured him. 'Have you completely recovered?'

'Yes. I have.'

'Good.'

'You were concerned for me?'

'For a moment. For a moment I wondered if you were having hysterics.'

'I am calm again. Thank you. I was carried away. It does not happen often.'

'That's a relief.'

(Kitty Crozier would think of that privileged, pampered animal – the glossiness of his coat attesting to the refinement of his diet – when she visited Romania two years after her lover had gone. The strays she would see on city streets and country roads were mangy, warty, possibly rabid, with eyes either crazed or dulled by hunger. She would not be struck by the sight of a bemedalled canine general riding in sole splendour down Calea Victoriei, past the antique shops selling icons of the Virgin and Child, St Nicholas, St Peter and other, unfamiliar, saints: his time of glory was over. She would stare, instead, at a pregnant bitch with inflamed teats, her scrawny body covered in bleeding sores, stretched out on the cracked and dusty pavement. She would stare and then she would remember one of the poems-cum-proverbs Virgil had taught her:

De te latrã vre-un câine
Astupã-i guru cu pâine

which he translated as 'If a dog barks at you, stop his muzzle with bread'. But this sad beast was beyond barking, probably beyond feeding, too – lying there in the fierce midsummer heat, weighed down by all the unborn life inside her.)

In Richmond Park, that afternoon, Daisy warned Andrew and Janet, as she warned them every Sunday, not to let the Baskervilles disturb the deer.

'They're miles away, Ma.'

'You always say the same thing, Andrew. If Buster or Bruiser got it into his head to run off, there could be terrible consequences. The keepers have orders to shoot.'

'Yes, Ma.'

'The deer are the Queen's property, Virgil. They have what I suppose are grazing rights. It's one of my foibles, but I can't warm to deer as most people can. I don't deny they are pretty. It's their nerviness I have difficulty with. They start at the slightest noise, the sillies.'

'Yes,' Virgil responded, bewildered that Daisy should be in possession of such an odd foible. He was diverted by the word 'sillies' and by her use of it, but thought it impolite to say so.

'You're not actually living with Kitty, I believe.'

'That is correct. Not yet.'

'But you do intend to live with her, I hope.'

'One day, yes. When I am more settled. When I am feeling more at home here.'

'What about Kitty's feelings? Aren't you considering those?'

'Yes, he is, Daisy. I'll answer for him. I'm perfectly happy with our arrangement. We see a great deal of each other.'

'It's not an arrangement I'd care for, Kitty.'

'No, Daisy. But it suits me.'

'Until Virgil becomes acclimatised?'

'Yes.'

'Whenever that may be.'

(He wanted to say he was certain he would become acclimatised; that, even with the name Virgil Florescu, he might be accepted as a Londoner soon. He wanted to assure Kitty's sister, who was waiting for his assurance, that he would move into the untidy house with its surfeit of books and live in the present, beside the woman he loved. He wanted desperately to be free to make this promise with complete confidence in its being fulfilled. But he wasn't free. Not yet. He knew he had to stay silent.)

'Let me mention the unmentionable while Cesspit's occupied with kids and dogs. Have you heard from *him* lately?'

'Our father?' asked Kitty, knowing whom Daisy meant; knowing, too, how Daisy would respond.

'Who art not destined for Heaven.'

'He sent me one of his postcards,' Kitty lied.

'With news?'

'The usual. He has found a new companion. His ideal, it seems.'

'The poor deluded woman. What a lovely fate she has in store for her. She's rich, I presume.'

'He didn't indicate.'

'She must be. And he must be worse than ever, now that he's really old. Did he give you his address?'

'No, Daisy. He's somewhere in America.'

'I wonder what he looks like these days. If he has his hair, and his teeth, and his figure.'

'Forget him, Daisy. Please do. Cecil dropped a hint that you have a surprise for me.'

'Yes, sister dear, believe it or not, I'm going to India. I've been injected in the arms and the bum for every dreaded tropical disease you can think of. Cesspit will be ruling the roost in my absence.'

Then Bruiser dropped a large red plastic bone at Virgil's feet and Virgil threw it for the dog to retrieve.

'The moment my grandfather died, my Uncle Mircea went over to the window and broke a pane of glass. I asked my mother what he was doing and she said, "He is letting Tatā's soul escape" and I asked her, "What is a soul, Mamā?" and she told me, then and there, that the soul is the best part of a man or woman. "The soul is God's hidden gift to us and our gift back to Him. Tatā's soul is free now, in the free air." And then she began to weep.' He spoke as he spoke his poem to her, in a low voice, calmly, slowly.

She stirred in his arms.

He kissed her forehead and went on: 'I was seven years old, as you know. I watched my mother close my grandfather's eyes for the first and last time. She was his favourite child. It was the custom that the favourite should perform this one, loving task. I watched a lot that day, Kitty. There was a lot for a little boy to watch.'

'Tell me.'

'This was in the 1950s, when officially there was no God in my country. The decree from the Kremlin was that He had gone into history. But not for my grandmother and my Uncle Mircea and my Aunt Irina, and not for my mother. They were believers. So, when my *bunic* went to his Maker, my mother's family tried as well as they could to see him off in the traditional way. They moved his bed to face the window, and after his soul was released and his eyes shut on the world, Uncle Mircea lifted him up and carried him to the bath-tub. My uncle and aunt washed the corpse with hot water, and Uncle Mircea shaved him and Aunt Irina combed his few wisps of white hair. And all the time my mother wept.'

Virgil told her that they dressed his grandfather in a linen shirt – not a brand-new shirt, as it should have been, but the newest they could find among his small stock of clothes

– and decked him out in his smartest suit. They put a black cap made of lambskin on his head. They laid him on a table. While his Aunt Irina cut and trimmed the old man's nails, his Uncle Mircea filled a kettle with the cooling bath water and said to Virgil, 'Come with me.'

'I took my uncle's hand, and we left the apartment and went down to the street. We had to seek out the nearest tree and we walked for I can't remember how many minutes until we found it. In the old days, my uncle explained – in the days before the Germans and before the Russians – there were trees galore on Tatā's farm. But now the family were reduced to living like machines, we had no choice but to pour the precious water over the roots of a public tree in a public place. I was mystified, Kitty. Why did we need a tree and why did we have to pour the water over its roots? We stopped in front of a sycamore, I think it was, and Uncle Mircea bent low and emptied the kettle, drip by drip, on the earth around it. Then he put the kettle on the wet patch of grass. We moved back two steps and I saw that my uncle was looking at the kettle as if it were a sacred object. I understood, as children sometimes understand, that I dared not say a word. I watched and waited. Then my uncle said that Tatā's thirsty soul had had its fill, perhaps, God be praised, and now we should return to help Matilda and Irina. He gave me the kettle to carry.'

He kissed her again and, after a silence, he said: 'My intellect tells me the breaking of the pane of glass and the pouring of the water were acts of superstition, of centuries-old fear and ignorance. Mumbo-jumbo, to use your strange English expression. Yes, that is what my brain is telling me. Even so, Kitty, even so, I am fond of the memory. It still stirs my heart. I can see and hear the priest muttering from the Gospels over my grandfather, and the cousins and family friends who stayed awake all night to keep company with the body. Some of them cried and some of them laughed, recalling happier times. The priest was at the graveside, too, wearing ordinary clothes and it was he who whispered the final blessing *Fie-i ţârina uşoară* – "May the earth be light on him" – as the grave-diggers covered up the coffin. Tonight, beautiful Kitty Crozier, I am a reluctant atheist.'

(Whenever she opened his infirm copy of the *Meditations* of Marcus Aurelius she would remember that phrase 'reluctant atheist' and the hint of anguish in his voice as he spoke it. She would recollect how it had warmed her, his confession; how it had seemed, in that moment, to represent everything in him she loved.)

'Not just for tonight, sweetheart.'

'Tonight especially.'

'You haven't mentioned your father. Why is that?'

'He wasn't there. He was in the capital, with my brother. He was playing the devout Communist. No ancient rituals for Comrade Constantin Florescu. Not in nineteen fifty-three. Certainly not in nineteen fifty-three. Earlier, yes. He was swimming with the tide, Kitty, and the tide was of a different orthodoxy. He didn't want to be seen dead with the pious dead. He had his latest career to consider. He had to move stealthily. He tried to persuade his wife not to tend her dying Tată, but my mother, for once in her life, was unpersuadable. No, Kitty, he wasn't there. Perhaps that is why the memory is so dear to me.'

'I have a few surprises for you, Nelly. Three, in fact. The first is that Daisy is in India.'

'Was the subcontinent given warning of her arrival? Have the men joined their wives in purdah as a result?'

'She's walking in the Himalayas.'

'My sympathy is with the sherpas. Is this the truth you're telling me, Kitty?'

'Yes, it is. I never tell you anything else.'

'And is the sweetly boring Cecil scaling the heights alongside her?'

'No, he's not. She's gone with a friend.'

'A friend? I often wonder what kind of person befriends Daisy.'

'An adventurous widow, apparently.'

'This sounds very un-Daisy-ish. Do you think she'll encounter one of those Maharishis and come back filled with inner peace? I hope not. A serene Daisy would be quite insupportable.'

'And unimaginable, Nelly. My beloved twin revels in being irritated, as we both know well. Something is bound to exasperate her in the mountains. Rest assured.'

'What's your second surprise?'

'It concerns Daddy. He's living in England. He says for good.'

'Nothing Felix does is for good, Kitty. Have you seen the old beast?'

'Yes. And his new companion. With whom, he says, he intends to spend what is left of his life.'

'That strain again. None of this is surprising. I've always believed he'd return one day. And as for his new companion –' Nelly Crozier halted, put her hands to her mouth, lowered them and grinned at her daughter. 'Wait a minute. You said "new companion" rather than "new wife". It's a man, isn't it, Kitty? He's living with a man, isn't he?'

'Yes, he is.'

'I'm not totally surprised. Is the companion younger and attractive?'

'No, Nelly. Daddy would be horrified by your question. Derek Harville is in his seventies and strikingly *un*attractive. He resembles one of those gargoyles on Chartres Cathedral. He treats Daddy as if he were an imbecile and Daddy appears not to mind. The more Derek insults him – and Derek has a rare line in insults – the happier he seems.'

'Are you asking me to believe that Felix and his legendary libido have parted company?'

'I suppose I am.'

'You have failed me, Kitty. You have let me down with a wallop. I should have loved to hear that Felix has become a paederast. The vain, ageing lecher in search of his lost youth – what an irresistible picture you've denied me. You must pour me another hefty vodka to compensate for my disappointment.'

Kitty filled Nelly's glass.

'Are they in London, Felix and his friend?'

'They are in Sussex. In a restored Tudor cottage owned by Derek, who does the cooking and the housework and the gardening. Daddy is there to amuse him and to be his usual decorative self. Except that he isn't as decorative as he was. His first words to me in eight years were "I have jowls, Kitty" and he has. He also has – *quelle horreur* – a pot belly. Not a massive one, but conspicuous. He's a different Felix now.'

(And no longer pitiable, she might have added. Kitty Crozier saw the two satyrs with their furry legs and cloven hoofs, and felt saddened that something of her affection for the father she still called Daddy had evaporated.)

'Have you told Daisy that her father's within spitting distance?'

'Of course I haven't. I couldn't be so cruel. Not to him, or to her. You are full of terrible ideas today.'

'I only ever voice them to you, Kitty. It's only you I allow to see the nastier side of my nature. That's your special privilege and always has been. Have you forgotten the third surprise?'

'No, Nelly.'

'What is it, then? It obviously has to do with you because you're blushing.'

'Yes, it has got to do with me. And a man named Virgil Florescu.'

'And a man named Virgil Florescu? Is this love, Kitty? Are you in love, at last?'

'Yes, Nelly. Yes.'

'This is the nicest of your surprises by far. My remaining brain cells are signalling that a man named Virgil Florescu isn't English. Which language has names that end in "cu"? Let me guess. Is he Romanian?'

'He is.'

'My ears are alert, Kitty. And my tongue is prepared to stop wagging while you supply a few details.'

('You were right to love him,' Nelly Crozier would assure her daughter afterwards. 'You were radiant in his presence, Kitty. You glowed. How could you have begun to fathom the guilt he was living with? You'd have needed divine powers. You saved him for a time. You almost rescued him.'

Kitty Crozier became aware, in grief, of an aspect of her mother's character she had rarely considered before. The comforting Nelly had no use for terms of endearment. She said, simply, what she felt. Each 'Kitty' came without decoration, without the unnecessary adornment of a 'dear', or 'dearest', or 'darling'. Such had always been her affectionate way, Kitty acknowledged. 'Felix is the person for sweet nothings,' Nelly had once remarked. 'He gave me six years of them.')

'Do you intend introducing me to this swarthy paragon?' Nelly asked when Kitty finished talking.

'Of course I do.'

'Does Daisy approve of him?'

'I'm not sure. I think she would prefer him more domesticated.'

'Ah, yes. Safe and sensible.'

'Shall I bring him with me at Christmas, Nelly? If he's free, that is, and wants to come.'

'If Virgil Florescu is free and wants to come with you, then please bring him. I hope he finds me – what was the word? – diverting.'

'He will, Nelly. He can't fail to.'

*   *   *

Sometimes, waking beside him, she would marvel at the strangeness of his being there – at his glinting smile in the hospital, at their chance meeting in the park. Then she would scare herself with the prospect of his lasting absence – with the thought of his disappearing as inexplicably as he had come to her. 'Please don't go,' she often whispered when she was certain that he was sleeping. 'Please don't leave me, Virgil.'

He liked to tease her that she owned too many books. 'Far too many for a serious reader, Kitty. I despair at the sight of all those shiny covers.'

On this particular evening – the evening he first talked of Marcus Aurelius – she responded to his gentle mockery with the question, 'How many is enough?'

'Just as many as you really need.'

'What if I need hundreds, thousands?'

'Hundreds, thousands? No, no, such a need can never be satisfied.'

'But you must have read hundreds of books, Virgil. In each of your languages.'

'Yes, I have. But I haven't hoarded them since I was a youth. I stopped being a literary squirrel when I was eighteen. I can remember the actual day of my conversion. I went with two of my fellow students to the apartment of our professor, Teodor Costea, to drink tea and talk with him about the classical world. I was keen to see his private library, to look at the precious volumes I was certain he had collected. There *was* no library, Kitty. There weren't any shelves groaning under the weight of learning. I asked him why the walls of his study were bare. "My dear wife Liliana does not enjoy dusting," he joked. Then he gave me his serious answer. "I have twenty essential works by my desk," he said. "Twenty is a great number. These twenty are my friends. I read them again and again." His words opened my eyes. He made me see that most books are for

124

reading once and once only. A few become your friends. A very few remain your friends for life. I live with very few books.'

And one of those, he told her, was the *Meditations* of Marcus Aurelius. He had befriended the wisest of the wise Roman emperors on a winter's night in Sibiu, where he had gone to teach. He was beguiled by Marcus's personality within moments of opening the book, and soon he was oblivious of the drunken shouting and laughter coming from the room below. The next day he was snowed in and read the *Meditations* a second time, with increased pleasure. He marked, with a pencil, the passages, the sentiments that most appealed to him, that struck him as being incontestably true, and when he had finished there was scarcely an unmarked page. 'I had sprinkled the text with a thousand yeses.'

He was to lose that copy, which was in French, and replace it with the English edition he still carried everywhere. Professor Costea, hearing of his enthusiasm for Marcus, had chastised him for not tackling the *Meditations* in the original Greek. 'He was right to do so. I should have persevered.'

'In Greek, Virgil? Why did he write in Greek?'

'Because he found it difficult. It was a challenge for him. I think that's the reason. Or perhaps he wished to keep his journal a safe secret from his officers and servants. He was writing to, and for, himself and no one else. It is an accident – no, let's say it's a miracle – that his little book has survived.'

('Why don't you write your poems in English from now on?' she asked him that same evening. He stared at her across the kitchen table. He put down the fork with which he was eating spaghetti and said, 'I don't write my poems in English because English is not my *limbă maternă*, my mother tongue. Romanian is the language I heard at my mother's breast. I did not acquire it, as I acquired the other languages. It was given to me. Such a gift has to be respected, to be honoured.'

'Your poems would reach a wider public, Virgil.'

'Oh, Kitty. Oh, Kitty.' He shook his head slowly and smiled at her. 'What are you saying? A wider public? I am not concerned, believe me, with a wider public, a narrower public, or any public whatsoever. I am not interested in a public. If I wrote poems in English, they would be different poems. No, Kitty, I have need of the sounds I was born with.')

'It is a deep mystery to me why Marcus's son was so obscenely wicked. Of anyone in history, he had a father to look up to, a father to be proud of. And what did Commodus do when he was made Emperor? He betrayed his father's legacy. He chose to be bad. He was iniquitous, Kitty, more iniquitous – if it is possible to measure iniquity in quantities – than the present benign leader of my country.' He stopped and smiled, and continued: 'It occurs to me that the Conducător and Commodus have something in common. Commodus called himself the Roman Hercules because of his skill with bow and arrow. But Hercules fought with beasts in the wild and always at the risk of his own life, whereas Commodus killed them in the amphitheatre, from a safe distance. Hercules, indeed. No labours for him. He shot his arrows and down went the ostrich, the panther, the elephant and the rhinoceros. Easy prey, easy targets. Teams of trained hunters had captured them all for Commodus to slay in front of the admiring crowd. The glorious hunter took aim, the animals fell and the common people cheered.'

'I predict, Virgil, that you're about to have a laughing attack.'

'I am, I am.'

'I can see the Communist tooth.'

'It's ludicrous, ludicrous,' he said when he was able to speak again. 'Our great and merciful leader is a hunter, too.

Yes, yes. There is a story, Kitty, my friend Radu Sava heard from a patient he was treating. The man whispered it to Radu because he was afraid of being overheard, even though he was mortally ill. He spoke as a privileged witness.'

'To what, Virgil? Witness to what?'

'To the Conducător's prodigious brilliance as a hunter. He saw our leader shoot a big black bear.'

'Well? Why is that funny?'

'The bear was drugged, Kitty. The bear was so sleepy it couldn't stand up to be sacrificed. Two strong guards were needed to hold it aloft. They brought the dope-ridden bear to within a few yards of its mighty killer, who lifted his rifle and took aim. And missed. He missed, Kitty. The bullet grazed the arm of one of the guards, who stared at his master in total disbelief. The master had missed, at close range. He aimed once more and this time the bullet hit the bear. Everyone applauded the bear's conqueror and drinks were served to toast his triumph. The hero led his consort and their courtiers into the hunting lodge, and the guard whose arm hadn't been grazed dispatched the still living bear with a single accurate shot. The dying man who told this to Radu had been among the courtiers and begged Radu to be as indiscreet with the story as he reasonably could. It was his last request, he said, that everyone should know what only the Conducător's intimates knew – that the saviour of the nation fired at a drugged bear and missed.'

(The prematurely aged Radu Sava would confirm that he had examined the party official with advanced liver cancer and decided not to operate. The man, hearing that death was imminent, had confessed to the doctor who despised him and his kind that he regarded their leader as a figure of fun: 'He is a clown. No, no. Clown is too kind. He is a moron, a thickhead. I must tell you how the thickhead hunted a bear.'

Radu had listened to the story impassively. 'I did not

127

even smile, Kitty. Those were the days of wariness. I could not trust a man who had risen so high in the ranks of the party. He was a privileged witness, one of the chosen. He had shaken certain hands. I heard what he whispered to me and I did not respond. I was not going to be the fly to his spider. He urged me to be "carefully indiscreet' with his anecdote: "It's for safe ears, remember," he cautioned. But whose ears were safe? Virgil's, to be sure, and those of my dear ones, but otherwise . . . I said nothing more. I summoned a nurse to his bedside, wished him good day, and left.')

'Soon there will be no Romanian bears for him to shoot. What will he do when he has made them extinct? Will he have brown bears flown in from Russia, and polar bears from Greenland and Iceland, and other bears from wherever there are bears? When he has shot – after first missing; yes, Kitty, after first missing – all the bears in the world, will he be reduced to shooting the cuddly little koalas from Australia?'

'Open some wine for us, my mad sweetheart.'

'Oh, *India*,' said Daisy.

'Is that it?' Kitty asked, after a long silence. 'Is that all you have to tell me?'

'No, silly. No, of course it isn't. Oh, but India.' She went silent again. 'Thank God for Nepal and the fresh mountain air. But as for India, India itself, well, Kitty, I'm afraid I have to shudder just thinking about the place.'

(And shudder she did, Kitty noticed in amazement. This theatrical shudder, this not quite convulsive shiver, was to become Daisy's automatic reaction to every mention of India. 'Oh, *India*,' she would sigh, and shudder. Sometimes in later years, Kitty – in devilish vein – would goad her sister into shuddering with a seemingly impromptu reference to the one distant country Daisy had visited. 'Oh, *India*,' would result, accompanied by a shudder that varied in exaggeration, depending on Daisy's mood.)

'Was it the poverty that upset you? You were expecting to be shocked, weren't you?'

'Was it the poverty? Yes, yes, it was. But it wasn't only that, not in Calcutta anyway. And not just the constant noise, though that was irritating enough. It was all sorts of things put together, to be precise.'

'Which things?'

'The cows. The cows come to mind. Kitty, those sacred cows – and I have to say they don't look sacred; they look like what they are, which is cows – those cows are everywhere. They bring the traffic to a complete standstill. They do their doings right there in the middle of the road, with the cars and trucks and I suppose you'd call them rickshaws trying their best to avoid them. Avoid the cows, I mean. Not a sacred sight, if you want my opinion.'

'Come and eat, Daisy. I toyed with the idea of making you a celebratory curry, but I decided on grilled halibut instead.'

'I'm very relieved you did. You know me and spices.'

'Do I?'

'Yes, silly. I had to be very careful with food in Calcutta. Even so – I will spare you the grim details – I had an accident with what I took to be a simple bowl of spinach. Runs and runs for hours and hours. Some creepy-crawly hadn't been washed out of it, I suspect, and ended up wreaking havoc in my stomach. That's India for you.'

'Is it really, Daisy?'

'In my recent experience, it is.'

'But you managed somehow to enjoy Nepal?'

'No crowds, no dirt, no noise, no heat – yes, I was in my element up in Nepal. Which was just as well, given what I discovered in Darjeeling.'

'Not a skeleton in the family's Indian cupboard, by any chance?'

'You can remove that mocking tone from your voice, Kitty. There *is* a skeleton as a matter of fact. Is, was – I can't decide which. Our McGregor grandfather was a coward.'

'Was he?'

'He did not die of malaria. As we've been led to believe.'

'That doesn't make him a coward.'

'Yes, it does. He killed himself. He blew his brains out. That makes him a coward in my book. People who commit suicide are always cowards. They choose the easy way.'

'I rather think I'd find it difficult to blow my brains out. Have some horseradish.'

'Horseradish with halibut sounds complicated to me. No, thank you, Kitty. You do realise, don't you, that Nelly has been lying to us all these years? She could have told us the truth.'

'Which truth is that?'

'The truth that Grandfather McGregor shot himself. The coward blew his brains out. He absolutely did not die of malaria.'

'Perhaps Nelly was protecting us, Daisy.'

'We weren't even born when he did it. Why should she want to protect us from history?'

('Why, Kitty? I'll tell you why. When the two of you were very young and Felix started behaving like the Felix we know, it didn't seem appropriate to burden you with the sad truth about my father's death. I wanted my little girls to be happy. Foolish me. I'd planned to sit you both down one day and go through the whole sorry business, but then Daisy had her breakdown and I considered it wiser to wait. And then, as the years passed and you grew up, the fact that my father didn't die of a tropical disease wasn't of such consequence any more. *Mea culpa*, I fear, Kitty.')

'How did you learn the news? The historic news?'

From an old missionary, Daisy said. The vicar at the

130

Presbyterian church had advised her to call on him, because he would remember her grandfather if anyone would. He did, indeed, but he certainly took his time remembering.

'He meandered, Kitty. He actually apologised for meandering. I was itching to say to him "Get to the point" but stopped myself out of sheer politeness. He really tried my patience with his tittle-tattle. I couldn't believe my ears when he told me Grandfather had eaten porridge for breakfast on the last morning of his life. As if it mattered. Thanks to him, I know what Grandfather ate for lunch as well – a soup or broth with pieces of haddock floating in it. He drank whisky, too, that Christmas Day. Lots of it, I shouldn't wonder, to judge by what happened. Dutch courage for the coward. The missionary said he must have felt depressed.'

'People usually are when they put guns to their heads. I'm sure there are a few cheerful suicides – but not too many, I imagine.'

'He wasn't alone, apparently, our grandfather. According to the old missionary, there was a spot the locals called Suicide Hill. That's where he went, with his gun in his pocket.'

Kitty must realise that it hadn't been easy getting up to Darjeeling. She and her friend Harriet had to have their passports stamped at Bagdogra, and what an early afternoon nightmare that turned out to be. They'd had to queue in front of a hut – a hut, not a proper office – inside which three typical Indians were pretending to be efficient. The hut was dusty and cobwebby, with a filthy filing cabinet against the wall and on the top of it was a heap of mouldy ledgers which Harriet said were still offering nutrition to famished insects. Two of the men were writing in pen and ink in only slightly fresher ledgers while the third man, who did all the speaking, looked on.

'Scratch, scratch, scratch – I'll never forget the scratching sound of those silly pens. Scratch, scratch – I thought my nerves would give way, I honestly did. Harriet smiled, she has a smile for every emergency, she's that type of person, but I felt like screaming.'

'What were the two men writing?'

'Our names, our dates of birth, our passport numbers. That was all. The work of a minute you might suppose, but they stretched it out to eternity. In silence, Kitty, in total silence. Scratch, scratch. What a country.'

Then it was bump, bump, bump on the winding roads up to Darjeeling in a Land Rover driven by a man in a turban who certainly couldn't be accused of slowness. Although she'd feared for her life, especially when he was negotiating the bends, she had to admit that, after all the annoyances of India, she was excited. The pure air kept hitting her through the open window – pure, pure air, with no smells of sacred cow dung, or human dung either – and her spirits lifted.

'And dropped again when the old missionary told me how Grandfather died. I'm beginning to wonder if Nelly has fibbed to us about anything else.'

'Stop wondering, Daisy. Please stop. What we owe Nelly in gratitude can't be measured. Please stop wondering.'

They continued eating in strained silence.

'How is the Romanian lover?'

'Loving.'

'I should hope so. But not loving enough to want to marry you. You are strange, Kitty.'

'Am I?'

'Of course you are. I have to tell you that Andrew and Janet were quite impressed with him. Your Mr Florescu. They were actually moved to words, for once. Andrew thinks he's "real" and Janet finds him "doomy". "He's wonderfully doomy" was what she said to Cesspit.'

'Doomy? I guess he is.'

'She had a smitten look in her eyes, apparently.'

'You're making me jealous, Daisy. I can't cope with a

rival. Not at my age. You just warn her to steer her thoughts away from my wonderfully doomy Virgil. She hasn't seen her aunt on the rampage, but she will if she isn't wary.'

'You silly object.'

Her voice came to him as he waited to be served in the expensive confectioner's. It was the soft and gentle voice of the time before her numbness, when she still spoke of the past wistfully.

('Oh, Virgil, that *cofetărie* in Sinaia. I used to think it was a fairy-tale place. There is nothing here to compare with it. The pastries were so delicate, so fragile, and there were so many of them it was an agony which one to choose.'

'*Mămică*,' he whispered.

'Yes, Virgil, your *Mămică* loved her summer holidays in Sinaia because they meant a daily visit to Kalinzachis', where her eyes were treated to a bigger feast than her belly. I swear I have never tasted anything to equal those sweets and chocolates. Not here, not now. You have not been spoilt as I was spoilt, I regret to say.'

She had wanted to spoil him more – and his brother, too – during the precious years of his childhood. The Lord God had surely intended that those should be the carefree years, since the sad and difficult ones came along soon enough.

'*Mămică*,' he said again, tasting salt on his lips.)

The assistant behind the glass counter asked the quietly weeping customer if she could be of any assistance.

'Chocolates, please. I require a selection. I have twenty pounds to spend.'

'Are they for someone special, sir?'

'Yes.'

'Would you like me to gift-wrap the box?'

'Yes. Please.'

'With some pretty ribbon?'

'Yes.'

133

She handed him a couple of tissues and he told her she was kind.

'We all have such days, sir.'

'Tonight I am an expert on the life and mysterious ways of Teresa of Avila. At least I think I am, now that I've supplied the index to a book about her. That's the beauty of my little job, Virgil – the copious knowledge I acquire.'

This year alone she had become a specialist on the English in Sicily in the nineteenth century; on the first governor-general of Bengal, Warren Hastings – whose grateful biographer had taken her to tea at the Ritz the very day she had met the man with the Communist tooth; on the chanteuse Edith Piaf, awash in drink and misery; on – she couldn't keep up with all the subjects on which she was currently an authority – oh yes, the Albigenses, whom she'd had to distinguish between in the four hectic days she and Virgil Florescu were separated; on Louis Quinze and Madame du Barry; on the Iron Chancellor, Otto von Bismarck; on the Danish composer Carl Nielsen; on Diaghilev, the impresario, and, and – and on other things and other people, already too numerous to remember.

She was an expert, too – though she had no wish to be – on 'The Times and Crimes', to give the book's sub-title, of a man who modestly styled himself the King of London's Underworld. His unedifying life story had been a torment to index, or rather cross-index, because every one of the King's shady acquaintances possessed two names – the name that was chosen for him at birth and a nickname descriptive of his talent or character. There was 'Big' Jimmy Saynor, for instance, who was always referred to as 'Slasher' in the text. 'Slasher' Saynor's feats with a cut-throat razor on the faces of an assortment of anonymous enemies were recorded in manic detail by the admiring King, who also paid tribute to 'Growler' Gaisford, Morry 'Icepick' Maddox, and 'Flyweight' Walsh, alias the 'Kilkenny Killer'. They were lovable rogues at heart, the King or his ghost insisted, with doting wives and girlfriends and adoring children, whose victims had only got what was coming to them – a scar here, a chopped-off finger there; an eye gouged out, a nose squashed flat and worse, much worse. At this particular moment she knew almost everything anyone needed to know about the King of London's Underworld and his circle – but the moment would pass and she would soon lose some of her unwanted knowledge, she hoped.

'What is this ghost? Who is this King's ghost?'

'His ghost is the man who wrote the book for him. The King had to employ a ghost-writer. The King gave him the facts and his ghost set them down. The autobiographies of film stars and criminals are usually ghost-written.'

'Ghost-writer, ghost-written. I like the thought of such a ghost.'

She saw that he was smiling to himself, as he often did when he heard an expression that pleased him.

Then he looked up at her and said: 'He has ghosts galore, the saviour of my country. An army of them, a regiment. You, Kitty, have made me understand that the men – and women – who write the Conducător's sermons are ghosts. They are shadows of their true selves. Their typewriters are not registered and numbered for purposes of identification as the typewriters of the flesh-and-blood people of Romania are. They have no fear of being identified, these non-beings, these ghosts. Why should they be afraid? They have his words at their command, which is his command, and his words ensure their ghostly survival. They press the keys of their machines to the same rhythm, with the same ideas ready to be typed on to the page, and on they go with their joyless task, Kitty, until the factory alarm sounds and the rhythm is brought to a halt for another day. I imagine that is how they work for him, his regiment of ghosts.'

His voice was low, his speech measured, his body contained. There was none of the near-hysterical excitement

135

that took possession of him whenever he spoke of the Conducător.

'You see I am earth-bound, Kitty. I am not carried away.
Perhaps it is because I do not find his ghosts as amusing as
his dog or his hunting of the bears. Yes, that is it. Our
leader's ghosts – I thank you for the conceit – do not divert
me. I worry for them. The prose they produce for him has
no energy, no colour, and it has no grammatical errors. I
have listened to it. I have read it. It is perfectly lifeless. They
have fashioned it for him to drone. But sometimes, Kitty,
he loses his place in the sermon and his droning ceases, and
then – panic-stricken – he speaks his own words. He falters,
he fumbles with his glasses, he takes a sip of water and he
says whatever comes into his head, and it's only we who
are watching his performance on television who are free to
indulge in the luxury of a smile at his expense. He has dared
to improvise and his daring has revealed him for what he
is – a man ill at ease with language. The party officials in
front of him in the Hall of the Palace of the Socialist Republic do not have our freedom. They must hide their smiles
behind solemn looks of agreement. But we can laugh if we
want to, we writers and artists and intellectuals who use
the subjunctive when we ought to, and make our nouns
and verbs agree. We can laugh at this peasant who slaugh-
ters our cherished syntax the minute he strays from the
sermon his ghosts have prepared for him. He is suddenly
vulnerable, standing up there alone on the podium. He
reaches the end of his tortuous, unghosted sentence and
stops. It is a cue, a desperate cue, for applause. The clapping
begins and increases in volume. He finds his place. He is
secure. The massed ranks of officials sense his security.
Their applause has come to his rescue and is no longer
necessary. The droning resumes and our laughter is
silenced.'

She sat on the floor by his chair and rested her head on
his knee.

'I am crazy, Kitty. I am not there to join in the laughter. It is your fault for mentioning the ghost-writer.'

'I apologise.'

'I hate myself for bothering with him, for letting him into my mind.'

If it weren't for him, she refrained from saying, you wouldn't be here; if it weren't for him, my life would be merely jogtrotting along, as it used to jogtrot along, day after forgotten day, in all that time before I met you.

He had arrived that evening, in his faded and much washed overalls, bearing what was by far the most lavish of his gifts – a box of handmade chocolates from the shop in Bond Street to which her father had once taken her while he was briefly in London with the artistic Linda. Felix had requested a special monkey's bum kiss in exchange for mountains of her favourite mints and she had duly obliged. She remembered, now, that Felix and his third wife were dressed for the opera – 'Pity me, my darling, I'm in for an evening of Druids' – and that they looked ridiculously elegant to her young eyes, 'like a pair of chic fossils' she told Nelly. Virgil, in his working clothes, had stood in that same shop a few hours earlier, hardly the picture of elegance or wealth.

'That's Edward the Confessor over there in the corner, in those two bulky parcels. He's my latest assignment. It's going to take me a month, I suspect, to tackle him.'

(Kitty Crozier would recall that she was with the Confessor and his eleventh-century court and kingdom for ten arduous weeks. The memory of that happily occupied time would come to her after Virgil was gone, when she began to play a game in her head that made her heart ache at the loss of him. In this game she would think back to the Lives she had read – and indexed and edited – while he was with her, from Warren Hastings to Aubrey Beardsley. Bismarck and Piaf and Nielsen and Wally, the King of London's Underworld, and the saintly Edward, and Sergei Diaghilev, drenched in a perfume called Mitsouko, and Robert Louis Stevenson, and Michael Faraday and Frank Lloyd Wright, as well as a swarm of Albigenses, had all featured in the life she shared with her doomy lover. In some peculiar way their very names became associated with contentment, ful-filment; and in later years someone's remarking that Niel-sen's songs were finer than his symphonies or that Bismarck was the best kind of bad German would set her pulse racing at the thought of him. They belonged, for ever now, in her Virgil period.

The Lives she worked on, when she was capable of work, in the immediate weeks post-Virgil, soon formed into a blur. She would wonder if she had been in a trance or perhaps hallucinating, so indistinct had those celebrated figures become for her, their cares and concerns inextricably jumbled together by her numb intelligence. Their sufferings meant nothing to her and she viewed their triumphs from the limbo she was in, which was a place where human success seemed risible.

Then, one overcast day, a day designed for accidie, she opened a manuscript and started to read. Another Life, another task to distract her. At the end of the first chapter she felt curiously elated, and by the end of the book itself she was moved to tears of pity and deep commiseration. She went out to her small garden and let the rain fall on her. And as she stood there, she saw Virgil coming across the lawn, his Communist tooth gleaming in the dimness.

The Life that was to release her was scarcely more than a monograph – a short character study, simply written, running to a hundred and twenty pages. Its subject was Wilhelm Friedemann Bach, the eldest son of the great Johann Sebastian, a man desperate to escape from under his father's shadow. She learned that he was an accomplished composer at an early age, the pleasant harmonies coming easily and naturally to him, in the fecund manner the music-lovers of Leipzig expected of a Bach. Yet Wilhelm Friedemann grew disenchanted with the facility with which he was able to write for the orchestra, the keyboard and the cathedral choir, and took to experimenting. His ambition was to create a new sound, a sound distinguishable from Johann Sebastian's, a sound that would be recognised as his and his alone. But his father's shadow lengthened and darkened with each fresh composition, and Wilhelm Friedemann sought relief from his frustrations in drink. Alcohol mellowed him, dulled his demons, and in his final years he was one of the familiar sights of unrespectable Berlin – an amiable drunkard, shuffling from tavern to tavern in old and shabby clothes, his once tormented nature apparently at rest.

The shadow that Constantin Florescu had bestowed upon his eldest son was of a greater length, she understood, and of a denser darkness.)

'A month, God help me, with a saint in my house. Do you feel like being unsaintly?'

'Yes, Kitty, I do.'

He was shovelling leaves into a cart when a rasping voice behind him said, 'So this is the London park the poet honours with his presence.'

He turned abruptly, scattering leaves into the air, and saw that the speaker was Derek Harville, who doffed his bowler hat in greeting.

'I didn't startle you, did I, sufficient Virgil?'

'You surprised me, yes.'

'Not unpleasantly, I hope.'

'No.'

'Are you at liberty to take a short rest? I have a few minutes to spare. Will you incur your employers' wrath if you sit and chat with me on the bench over yonder?'

'I am allowed a break for tea. I shall be happy to sit with you.'

'Very good. I am in pressing need of intelligent discourse.

I spend most of my waking hours listening to the idiot ramblings of the admirable Kitty's preposterous father and I have just endured lunch with my witless, literally wit less, son.'

'You have a son, Mr Harville?'

'I have a son. The fruit of my irresponsible loins. I permit him to treat me to an expensive meal on the last Wednesday in the month, and today's meal was very expensive and very satisfying. And because serious drinking is against his new-found religion I had an entire bottle of Crozes-Hermitage all to myself. He glowered each time the *sommelier* topped up my glass. I am, I confess, ever so slightly tipsy.'

'You were married, Mr Harville?'

'Never. No, no, no. I failed to make an honest woman of his mother. Failed, did I say? I had no intention of marrying her and she was equally unenthusiastic at the prospect of giving herself in matrimony to a mere servant, albeit the butler of a duke. Marriage, no. She had other men at her disposal, a whole flotilla of them, and she picked out the ugliest and richest to be her husband. He died young, fortunate fellow, leaving her but a pittance to live on. That shrewd analyst of marital to-ings and fro-ings, August Strindberg, would have relished their liaison, to judge by the rumours that reached my delighted ears in the safety of the ducal residence. They squabbled in the grand style. They tore a passion to tatters.'

'I recognise that phrase. It's from *Hamlet*.'

'Is it? It must be, if you recognised it. I've used it so often, I've forgotten its origin. Actually, to be honest with you, I thought it was my own clever invention. Well, well. Should I ever feel the need to use it again, I shall be certain to acknowledge its source. *Hamlet*, eh? How shaming.'

'I interrupted your story.'

'You did, indeed, but only for the honourable purpose of improving my education. I am self-taught, Virgil. I was wrenched from school at a tender age and put out into service in order to boost my family's modest income. That was long, long ago. Now *I* am interrupting the story, such as it is.' Derek Harville chuckled. 'It is not an enthralling narrative, to tell the truth. Sufficient to relate that my son, who was exhibiting in childhood every symptom of the dullness that marks his character to this day, regarded me as his benevolent Uncle Derek until he was informed otherwise. It was a role I played convincingly, for the boy was fond of me and seems fond of me still, despite the deception. He would prefer me to be sober and sensible and, I suppose, paternal, but I am afraid I cannot readily assume qualities so very repugnant to me.'

'Your son must have a name. You have not mentioned it.'

'True. He was christened Alexander by his mother and was Alexander Jenkins throughout the years I posed as his uncle. Now he is Alex Harville and the redeeming love of Jesus Christ is virtually his sole topic of conversation. His other passion is money, which he would rather not talk about since he is far too busy amassing it.'

'May I offer you some raisins?'

'Raisins?'

'Yes. I eat raisins whenever I am – what it your quaint English word? – peckish. I am peckish. Give me your hand if you would care for some.'

'Here,' said Derek Harville. 'A modicum will suffice, sufficient Virgil. There is no room in my stomach for more.'

'How is Mr Crozier?'

'How is he? He's crazier, is Crozier, than he was when you met him. He speaks of little else but his impending funeral. He favours a midsummer ceremony at the moment, with the birds twittering in the churchyard trees and the roses in glorious bloom. I have tried to reason with him. I have repeated, and repeated, to him that the Reaper has the last word in these matters. If the Reaper decides it's

141

November, then November it is. Crozier, who has had his own way in everything for most of his useless existence, has somehow convinced himself that he is going to snuff it in June. Next June, perhaps, or the following June, or the June after that, but June it will be. He *knows*, he says. He is also confident that I shan't die before him, as I have been entrusted with the responsibility of comforting the mourners with food and drink once the interment is over and done with. Mourners? Apart from the admirable, tolerant Kitty – accompanied, no doubt, by your good self – and his amused companion, what mourners will there be? If Crozier has his wish, every man, woman and child from the village, and the surrounding villages, will be in attendance. He has issued invitations to the whole neighbourhood. "You *must* come to my funeral. I won't take no for an answer." What an absurd specimen he is.'

'You sounded very like him.'

'It is a gift I have. I might have made a career of mimicry. Crozier is but one of several straw men, imitation men, in my repertoire. He is an impersonator's dream-come-true. His shallowness really does know no depths. I find his company a constant pleasure.'

'Mr Harville, Derek, could you impersonate me?'

'No. Definitely not. I am paying you a compliment when I say that you are not worthy of mockery. I think you are who you are, Mr Virgil Florescu, and no one else. Honesty is not to be mocked, but self-deception is. I draw my inspiration from those who fabricate themselves and I meet plenty of their number. It isn't just the voice I try to capture, it's the temperament, the individual psyche. My victims, and they are myriad, have one characteristic in common – at some stage in their lives they began to perform, to put on a public show. As I did. As I *do*. No, no, you are beyond my imitative powers.'

'I am disappointed.'

'Don't be. You must return to your leaves and I must

push off. I have an appointment shortly with an imposing woman whose working name is Francesca. She insists that her gentlemen callers stay silent while she is at her soothing tasks and I am bound to obey her.'

They rose from the bench.

'Thank you for the raisins. I should have asked you about Romania, shouldn't I? Or are you ticklish on that subject?'

'My English is suddenly woeful. "Ticklish", as in being tickled? I am at a loss.'

'It also means "delicate". Is Romania too delicate a subject for you to discuss with foreigners?'

'I understand you, Derek. Yes, it is a delicate subject. It is a ticklish subject for me, Romania. And I am tickled by it, too.'

That evening, as they sat down to dinner, Virgil told Kitty of his encounter with the man she considered Mephistophelean. He related what Derek Harville had said of her father – '"He's crazier, is Crozier"' – and how he had spoken of his gift for mimicry.

'Did he do Daddy's voice for you?'

'Yes, Kitty. Brilliantly.'

'I found his impersonation too accurate for comfort that day we went to lunch. I couldn't laugh at it. It's wickedly accurate.'

Wicked was a word she had never had occasion to apply to anyone before, but she sensed that Derek Harville was probably wicked. Not wicked wicked, of course, but wicked enough.

'No, Kitty, he is not wicked wicked. He is not of that kind. You should have seen him today in all his finery. He was dressed to kill, as you say. He was wearing a dark-blue suit in some soft material, with a yellow handkerchief in the breast pocket, and a striped silk shirt and a yellow bow tie. His shoes were shining. He had a brown bowler hat

143

and he carried a rolled umbrella. He was the complete dandy, Kitty, from top to toe.'

'That's what Daddy used to be. In his days of glory.'

'I fear I shall be a wallflower, Kitty, a petrified wallflower. I am not a party man.' He smiled. 'What I mean is that I am not a man for parties.'

'You'll meet some interesting people, I promise.'

'I meet interesting people every day – in the park, in the streets, at Mrs Whiteside's. A room of strangers fills me with terror.'

'I'll be with you. I'll hold your hand if necessary. Laura is one of my closest friends. We dropped out of university together. I should love you to meet her. And she's asked me to bring you.'

(She would regret, for years, that she persuaded him to go with her to Laura Clifford's Christmas party. He'd wanted to wait for her at the house, watching nonsense television game shows – to which he had become slightly addicted in a horrified way – or taking a nap on the sofa, or passing useful time with a dictionary. She wished, later, that he had been stubborn with her, mulish, difficult. He had it in his nature to be obstinate, as she was by now aware. He chose to be compliant instead: 'I will come with you, Kitty. I will come along and pretend that I am not desperate to escape.')

'Courage, sweetheart,' she said to him in the rickety lift taking them up to Laura Clifford's top-floor flat. 'You've survived worse ordeals.'

'Have I?'

'Yes. The ones you're secretive about. The ones your modesty won't allow you to mention.'

'You are fanciful, Kitty Crozier. Very, very fanciful.'

'I think not.'

Laura Clifford was on the landing to receive them. She

stared at Virgil for a long moment before kissing and embracing her friend.

'You look wonderful, my old darling. No one would ever guess you'd been in the uterine wars.'

'That was months ago. Laura, let me introduce Virgil. Laura Clifford, Virgil Florescu.'

'Hullo, Virgil.'

'Good evening. It is kind of you to invite me.'

'That's because I have a heart as big as Africa. Isn't it, Kitty?'

'So they say.'

'Follow me if it's intellectual fun you're after. There's champagne, too.'

('I can't forget him,' Laura Clifford would assure her friend when she was given the sad news of Kitty's lover. 'It was his face as he came out of the lift. I gaped at him, I remember. Perhaps my jaw dropped. I thought to myself: all of this man's life is in his face and he's unable to hide it. And then I thought: he is Kitty's man and I am being rude, and that's when I noticed you standing beside him. You introduced us and I said something facetious, as I usually do, and I took you both in, and I didn't speak to him again. I saw him by the window and that was it. Somebody told me he'd left in a terrible state and that you'd gone with him. This is ancient history now, my old darling, as is that bloody Sandor, whom I promised to murder for you and should have done, but I can't forget your Virgil's face that night and don't believe I ever shall.')

Kitty and Virgil edged themselves into the centre of the overcrowded room.

'I don't know anyone here. They must be Laura's recent acquisitions. They weren't around two years ago.'

'Can we stand by the window? I am already feeling suffocated.'

There was a man on the balcony, smoking a cheroot,

who said to Virgil, 'You are not English. From where are you?'

'Europe.'

'Italy? Spain?'

'Neither.'

'Central Europe maybe? Eastern?'

'Eastern.'

'You are from that shit-hole Romania?'

'I am from Romania.'

'You are Romanian?'

'I am Romanian.'

'Nothing to be proud of, being a Romanian.'

'Not now, no.'

'Not now never. I am Hungarian and proud of my country, and I tell you, you Romanian, you have nothing to be proud of.'

'I hear your opinion.'

'You are offensive,' Kitty told the Hungarian, who laughed, tossed the butt of his cheroot down to the street and answered, 'You ain't heard nothin' yet' in an awkward parody of an American accent.

'I think we have heard as much as we can stomach.'

'Have you? I will tell him, Englishwoman, only what he knows. Romanians are thieves and peasants. That's a fact. Their history is blood and shit. They lived in darkness for centuries. Romanian blood isn't pure – it's gypsy blood, and Greek, and Turk. I tell him he is from a bastard race. A race made from rapings and dirty fucks. That is how Romanians came into the world.'

'I hear you.'

'Then hear some more. From where did your kings and princes come? From Germany. A paid-for monarchy, like you pay for potatoes. And your Esperanto language, from where is that? From everywhere.'

'Not everywhere, no.'

'It is from everywhere. From Rome, from Paris, from Athens, from Ankara, from Budapest even.'

'That is still short of everywhere.'

'And what is your culture? Gypsy music, icons, peasant costumes, a poem about a lamb that talks. And what does that lamb say to the shepherd? He says it is better to die than fight. You kill, you stinking Romanians, but you do not fight like men.'

'I am hearing you.'

The Hungarian stepped into the room. 'You are hearing me? I am telling you. We in Hungary, even in the Hungary you stole from us, had a culture, we had aristocrats, while you were all in the mud. We had a language. We had books. You had no language to write for hundreds and hundreds of years. For centuries you had no books.'

'The monks had books, of course. But not the people.'

'The people? The swine. The herd. You call them people, I call them savages. Your writers write in French, don't they?'

'Some. Yes. It is their choice.'

'Our writers write in Hungarian. Yours go to France and become Frenchmen.'

'Not exactly.'

'I tell you they do.'

'I hear.'

'You hear. All you say is you hear. Won't you argue with me? Won't you defend your shit-hole country?'

'No.'

'Why not?'

'Because I am who I am.'

'And who's that? A coward? Yes?'

'I choose not to answer your question.'

'I look at you and I don't see a man. I see a piece of shit from Romania.'

'You see what you see.'

The Hungarian held out his glass for a languid youth to

top up and Virgil, speaking to himself, muttered a few words in Romanian, only one of which – 'Tată' – Kitty understood. Then, almost shrieking 'Excuse me, excuse me, excuse me', he forced a path out of the room and into the hall and on to the landing. Then he scuttled down the stairs.

They lay together, hand in hand, unable to sleep, for most of the night.

'Were you hearing someone else?' she dared to ask. 'When that brute was abusing you?'

'Yes, Kitty, I was. I was hearing him loud and far too clear, and I had to get away from the noise.'

'It's time for breakfast, sweetheart. What would you like?'

He turned to her and smiled. 'Breakfast? Ah, yes, breakfast. I think I would like tea. And some bread. And plenty of jam.'

'I am pleased to be here, Mrs Crozier.'

'And I'm pleased you've come, Mr Florescu. Kitty and I have made a habit of being together at Christmas. I'm not sure what we celebrate, since neither of us is a believer, but celebrate we do, in our quiet way. Perhaps you will encourage us to be a bit rowdier this year. '

'That is a huge perhaps, Mrs Crozier.'

'I am Nelly to you. And I hope you are plain Virgil.'

'Yes, yes. It is kind of you to invite me to your beautiful house.'

'I suppose you shouldn't love a pile of bricks, but this particular pile captured my heart the moment I saw it. I was a girl at the time. All the books I was reading were set in country houses, usually haunted ones, with creaking staircases and hidden doors, and Alder Court, viewed from the safe distance of the road, looked as if it might have a ghost or two inside.'

She had bought it, she said, on an impulse, securing the deal with the agent while she was in a state verging on delirium. She had just inherited her father's bequest to her, after an eternity of legal wrangling, finding herself moderately wealthy for about a week. Her handsome husband – and he was nothing if not handsome – had deserted her for a headachy beauty with a fortune that wasn't moderate, and there was no question as to who would have possession of the twins, Daisy and Kitty. That was Mother's privilege. Naturally. Then she read in a magazine at the dentist's that Alder Court was on the market at a price she could afford and she soon discovered why it was affordable. The house was in a truly terrible condition – there were holes in the roof and cracks down the walls, and several kinds of vermin in the pipes and under the floorboards.

The previous owner had lived there for most of his very long life – in a single room, the kitchen, surrounded by heaps of rotting newspapers dating back to his childhood. It was rumoured in the village that the man, who wasn't a monk but dressed as if he was, had once told someone who told someone else that the world had come to an end without anybody noticing.

'He imagined he was dead, I assume. Anyhow, I'm grateful to him for dying when he did. If he'd lasted a few years longer Alder Court might have been beyond repair. It's a semi-ruin, as it is.'

'I do not see any alders.'

'There aren't any, that's why. Alder Court was built by a Mr Joshua Alder in the seventeen nineties and it belonged to the Alder family until nineteen twenty, when Mr Armageddon moved in with his bundles of newsprint. There never were alder trees here. Only the solitary oak at the bottom of the garden.'

'And the daturas, Nelly.'

'And the daturas, Kitty, as you say. You must return in June, Virgil, when they are in flower. The back of the house will be covered in angels' trumpets.'

'Angels' trumpets? I am ignorant of angels' trumpets. They are flowers?'

'They are, and they're shaped like trumpets when they open. Or bells, if you prefer. Kitty once asked me if she could ring them and I think I had to tell her they weren't really bells but funny trumpets no one else but angels can hear. Did your parents ever stuff your head with lovely nonsense, Virgil?'

'My mother did, yes. But not my father. My father has always been practical. He is a pragmatic man. No, Nelly – no nonsense for Constantin Florescu.'

(Kitty would meet *omul pragmatic*, would have her hand kissed by him, would hear him talk regretfully of the one son who had failed him. 'I can translate his words for you,' Radu Sava would observe, 'but I leave it to you to detect the character of the man behind them. He looks sincere, doesn't he? He is bewailing Virgil's wasted life. He wishes you to understand that he loved his eldest boy, in spite of their differences.'

She would stare at the pink-faced, corpulent survivor and he would smile faintly at her, and she would continue staring at him and he would flinch under her steady gaze.

'You murderer,' she would shout at him, having been assured by Radu Sava that her lover's father spoke no English.)

'Silent trumpets or no, I had to warn my daughters that the datura is poisonous. My warning didn't prevent Daisy from nibbling a leaf one summer afternoon and making herself violently sick. She had to have her stomach pumped. She nearly died, Virgil. The commonsensical *hausfrau* played up like the very devil when she was ten and eleven.'

After dinner that Christmas Eve, as they sat by the fire, Nelly talked of Daisy again – of the acts of devilry that affected, and changed the course of, three lives. She mentioned the Easter of Easters and described its distressing aftermath, with Daisy prey to sudden rages, shrieking and crying and pulling at her hair. It was entirely thanks to these fits of temper, which stopped as soon as Daisy had recovered from the datura poisoning, that she, Nelly, became a schoolteacher. None of the schools in the county would accept the troublesome eleven-year-old, whose bad behaviour threatened to assume the status of legend. The doctors who examined her were agreed that Daisy was quite seriously disturbed, one of them even recommending shock treatment – 'a quick current through the brain'. They were diagnosing madness, but in relatively cosier words: words such as 'unstable', 'upset', 'unbalanced' and – kindest of all – 'capricious'. Daisy was a problem child, that was certain, and likely to remain a problem unless something drastic was done. The drugs she was prescribed caused her to be lethargic, closed-in on herself. She was a breathing nothing. Realising that she preferred her daughter annoyingly alive rather than semi-dead, Nelly threw the pills out with the rubbish and came to a decision.

'We were famous for a while – oh, the shortest of whiles – in nineteen fifty-eight. We had out photograph in the papers – battling mother in the middle and a twin on either side. I was the divorced woman who had asserted her right to educate her children and succeeded where others had failed. I say "succeeded", but my success then was only temporary. I was on trial. I had to prove that I was capable of teaching Daisy and Kitty to a reasonably high standard; but more than that, I had to prove the doctors wrong. They suggested that Daisy should be put away in a special home and I opposed the suggestion. I was teacher and healer combined. What a challenge I'd set myself. I would wake in the night and sweat buckets at the thought of what I'd taken on, and what its outcome might be.'

Yet those were enchanted years, those five years of Daisy's and Kitty's schooling, in retrospect. She had never studied so hard or so diligently: 'I had to, in order to keep a class ahead of my pupils.' As soon as the girls were in bed, she would set out the books she required on the kitchen table and labour by candle-light into the small hours. She often kept herself awake, as Balzac did, by drinking black coffee, but there were many occasions when the stimulant was unnecessary – when the excitement of rediscovery (a Shakespeare sonnet; a fable of La Fontaine; Elizabeth's speech at Tilbury; a mathematical equation that now seemed simple, where once it had been obscure) carried her happily along. Every few months an examiner would appear, unheralded, to check up on their progress – hers as much as Daisy's and Kitty's. He was sceptical about Mrs Crozier's perverse enterprise, he usually declared, but he was willing to concede that Kitty, at least, was doing passably well, despite the absence of other bright students for her to compete with. Daisy's written work was dull, but she was better than Kitty at addition and subtraction. When another examiner, two years on, remarked that Daisy was a 'really old-fashioned young lady', Nelly knew that she had calmed the beast in her daughter and wooed her back to sanity.

'Oh dear, yes. Daisy was an insufferable adolescent, because she was insufferable in the wrong way. She was so sensible. Kitty, I am glad to tell you, Virgil, was already showing signs of going interestingly haywire.'

'What is haywire?'

'Haywire is crazy. She was crazy at university, what with drugs and drink and Freddy. Daisy stayed on here with me, alas, until she whisked Cecil off his feet, or he whisked her off hers – I'm still not sure which one of them did the whisking.'

'I smoked pot with Freddy. That wasn't crazy, Nelly.'

'It was crazy enough to a woman like me. The wildest thing I'd done was marrying Felix. Your education wasn't eccentric, was it, Virgil?'

'It was, in a sense. At *liceu*, I learned there was much I was not intended to learn. I had to believe that the history

152

of my people was lost in continuous darkness until the light of Communism started shining. I didn't believe it. My Uncle Mircea taught me otherwise. It was from him that I heard of Mircea the Old, Vlad Ţepeş, Alexander the Good, Stephen the Great, Peter Rareş and Michael the Brave. They are some of our heroes. They were lost in that darkness when I was a schoolboy. Not now, though. In Romania nowadays it is safe to speak their names. The tide has turned. We are Nationalists as well as Communists now – Communist Nationalists or Nationalist Communists. Whatever. Both are acceptable. As for me, I am neither. I am, I think, unacceptable.'

(He did not add that he was suspicious of heroes, wary of heroics. The heroism he wished to emulate was not that of conquerors or warriors. He was thirteen again and his father was standing over him: 'Where is your spirit, Virgil?' Constantin Florescu flicked through the pages of the book his son was trying to read and stopped at the poem 'Liceu'. 'What kind of a man is it who compares his school to a cemetery? The cemetery of his youth? The cemetery with long corridors? What kind of man, Virgil?' He waited for Constantin Florescu to answer his own question. 'A drunkard. A morbid drunkard. Your school isn't a cemetery, is it?'

'No, Tată,' he said. 'No, Tată, of course not.')

'On this one night of the year, Virgil, I tend to succumb to a fit of piety. Kitty does, too. Would you like to join us?'

'In prayer?' he asked hesitantly.

'Not quite. We mumble the responses.'

'In church, Nelly means. We're going to St Mary's, in the village. We can walk there in ten minutes.'

'I will come with you.'

He sat between Nelly and Kitty in the tiny Norman church. He rose when they rose and smiled as they bellowed out the unfamiliar carols. He was a silent witness, as they were, when the villagers took communion. He heard the

153

vicar ('My mean-spirited bridge partner,' Nelly whispered) remind the congregation that Christ's birth in the lowly stable signified that true goodness was come into the world. Then, as the congregation chanted the Lord's Prayer, a memory surfaced. He and Radu were at the rear of another murmuring congregation, silent witnesses to a crude religious ceremony. The crowd had gathered seconds earlier, as it were spontaneously, to offer respects to the passing Conducător. The moment the presidential limousine slid into view, the young worshippers began to intone

Du-te în pizda mătii
Du-te în pizda mătii

as though the words formed part of the Divine Liturgy.

Du-te în pizda mătii

they recited in unison as the object of their devotions peered at their solemn faces through bullet-proof glass. The Conducător waved to his worshippers, who persisted in advising him to get back into his mother's cunt.

Kitty had taken his hand in hers, he realised. He was beside her in the English church. The chanting was over. There was one last carol to sing.

'We shan't need these,' said Kitty, removing the two hot-water bottles Nelly had put between the sheets. 'We'd have perished from frostbite without them those first winters we lived here. When it was really cold, when the wind came howling down the valley, the three of us slept together, huddled up like eskimos, in Nelly's bed. But you can keep me warm tonight.'

In the poem 'Breaking the Glass', which he spoke to her before they joined Nelly for breakfast on Christmas morning, the soul of a dead man is anxious to be released from the body in which it has been confined and constricted for a lifetime. The dead man's brother goes to the window facing the deathbed and tries to smash it with his fist. The glass doesn't break. He tries again, with a hammer. The glass – ordinary, fragile, everyday glass – remains unbreakable. The dead man's son runs out to the street, looks about him and finds a large stone, which he brings back and hurls at the window, confident of success. The stone bounces off the window, as if it were a rubber ball.

The corpse is washed from head to toe and the cooling water poured on the roots of a tree. The man is buried in his finest clothes, according to ritual. The priest says the final blessing – 'May the earth be light on him' – and the grave-diggers begin their business of covering up the coffin. A cry of anguish, no louder than a whimper, is heard from the grave.

The dead man's family – his brother, his son, his son's wife, his grandchildren, his multitude of cousins – return to the house. Wine is drunk and cakes are eaten. At dusk, the curtains are drawn. The son enters the bedroom where his father died and stands in thought at the window. He touches the stubborn glass with his fingertips. There is a cackle of laughter as the glass shatters into fragments.

'Mumbo-jumbo, Kitty. "Breaking the Glass" is my mumbo-jumbo poem. I think I believe every word of it.'

5

The Time of Afterwards

'Am I speaking to Kitty Crozier? Miss Kitty Crozier?'

'You are. Is that Miss Whiteside?'

'This is she. How did you recognise my voice?'

(Because you separate your syllables, Kitty was tempted to answer. Each one in turn, with emphasis.)

'It's unmistakable.'

'You have quite an ear, I must say. We have only conversed the once, so I am flattered. By the way, I am Mrs Whiteside. I sacrificed my maidenhead in my operatic days, long ago. Mr Whiteside is no more.'

'Is anything the matter, Mrs Whiteside?'

'It is Mr Florescu. The poor lamb is stricken with influenza. He has a temperature.'

'Where is he?'

'Where he ought to be, Miss Crozier. In bed.'

'He's not in hospital?'

'Heavens, no. I am tending him. I will restore him to health, never fear.'

'Yes, but, Mrs Whiteside –'

'The doctor has seen him. He prescribed some medicine,

which I have already collected from the chemist. And I always keep lemons and whiskey within reach, for emergency. Your Virgil is in safe hands.'

'You pronounced his name properly.'

'Of course I did. That's my training coming out. I have no trouble with the sounds of foreign languages.'

'I'll come over later.'

'May I advise you not to? He needs complete rest for a few days. I had to march him back up to his room this morning. I was forced to play the martinet, Miss Crozier, with your obstinate lover. He was determined to go to work, would you believe, even though his face was in a cold sweat and his eyes were dull and his body was shaking. He met his pig-headed match in me, I am pleased to relate. He is sleeping as I speak.'

'You are very kind.'

'I am very fond of him. He has no vanity. This old woman almost envies you his love. No, no – what nonsense. I will keep you informed of his progress.'

'Thank you.'

'Listen, Relu,' he whispered to his brother. 'Mamā is crying.'

'Mamā is crying because she is a woman. Mamā is like a fountain sometimes.'

'No, Relu. These are real tears. Listen.'

'Why listen? I can hear you.'

'She is calling Tatā Titi. She is pleading with him. She is begging him not to put us in danger.'

'Tatā wouldn't do that. Tatā is strong. Tatā is clever. Go to sleep, Virgil.'

That was a night when sleep wouldn't come. Long after his mother's sobbing had subsided he lay awake wondering about the danger ahead. He was fifteen, now, and an increasing disappointment to the respected lawyer who was training his sons in the art of survival. They were to be vigilant, young as they were; they were to follow his example and beware of day-dreaming. They should remember their Roman origins and take pride.

'Are we in danger, Tatã?' he asked at breakfast.

'What silliness is this? Why do you imagine we should be in danger? Have we broken the rules?'

'No, Tatã. No, I am sure not.'

'Then what is this you are saying? Yes?'

'It was an idea,' he responded feebly, not wanting to admit that he had overheard – no, worse than that, had listened in to – his parents' altercation.

'It is no idea worth having, Virgil. Your brother – your younger brother – does not have it.'

Aureliu, his mouth full of bread, nodded in agreement.

'Be off to the cemetery, as your drunken versifier calls it, and learn some wisdom, if you will.'

'Yes, Tatã.'

'You have nothing to be afraid of, Virgil. Nothing in the world.'

'He might believe you, Matilda. Tell him again.'

'I believe you both, Mamã, Tatã,' he said, rising from the table. 'I should not have had my idea.'

'I have made you a clear soup, Virgil. A consommé. Try and sit up, my dear.'

'Yes.'

'Who is wearing a grumpy face tonight? Answer: Domnul Florescu.'

'What, please, is grumpy?'

'Grumpy is bad-tempered. Some people enjoy being invalids, but I suspect you are not one of them. My late husband revelled in his illnesses. The longer they lasted, the happier he was – deep inside, that is. Patrick out-Violetta'd Violetta in *Traviata* when it came to the heart-wrenching cough. Bless him. He would be with me still but for his absent-

158

mindedness. He had his head in the clouds as usual the day a number 39 bus struck him down in Westminster.'

'I am sorry.'

'No sorrier than I am, my dear. Such a waste of a decent life. He was an honest Ulsterman if ever there was one, though it was his airy-fairy streak that appealed to me. Could you manage to sit up a little bit higher? There's an extra pillow to support you.'

'Yes.'

'You look too weak to hold the bowl. Let me feed you the soup a spoonful at a time. Open your mouth.'

He did as she instructed, and drank the hot soup from the spoon. 'No more,' he said, after the second spoonful. 'No more.'

'It will give you strength, my dear.'

'It tastes of meat.'

'Naturally.'

'I have an aversion.'

'Oh, you should have told me. I should have checked with you. I can rustle up a vegetable purée, if you'd prefer it.'

'No, thank you. I have no hunger. Tomorrow, perhaps.'

I am trapped, he thought as Freda Whiteside descended the stairs. I am her prisoner. I am cocooned in her kindliness.

Later that evening she was at his bedside again. She had prepared for him her 'magic concoction' of lemon juice, honey and Irish whiskey, and he was to sip it slowly. 'This will rejuvenate you, my dear,' she promised. 'It's the one and only *bona fide* restorative.'

She wiped his brow with a handkerchief and wished him a restful night. Woe betide if he attempted to leave the house in the morning. Her ears picked up the sound of the faintest football, as an unfortunate rent-dodger had once discovered to his physical cost, and they would be on the

159

alert for any Houdini-like plans he might be harbouring.

'I won't have you going out and catching your death.'

He had to struggle to release himself from the damp sheets. He walked shakily across the room. He grabbed at the door handle and clutched it firmly in order to stay upright. He went out to the landing. Then, with the banister for support, he manoeuvred his aching, tired body towards the bath-room on the floor below.

He was crawling back upstairs when Freda Whiteside surprised him. She set down the tray she was bearing and called out to someone to come to her assistance: this was an emergency, there wasn't a moment to lose, Mr Florescu was in a state of collapse and would someone – a man, not a woman – get here without delay.

'Is that you shouting, Mrs Whiteside?'

'Who is that asking a stupid question? Help me, will you? Light as he is, Mr Florescu is much too heavy for this old woman to carry.'

'Carry me? No one must carry me. I am nearly there.'

'On your hands and knees? That is misplaced martyrdom, my dear. Pick Mr Florescu up, would you, Mr Turner.'

'You want me to lift him?'

'Yes, my dear, I do. Have you met Mr Florescu, Mr Turner?'

'I can't say I have.'

'He keeps strange hours. In fact, he keeps the strangest hours of any tenant I have ever known. You can swap introductions when you have put him in his bed.'

(He would recall that he had felt humiliated; beyond reason, humiliated. The young architect who had borne him aloft and lowered him gently on to the bed to alleviate his distress had performed the task without embarrassment, speedily. Perhaps it was the very ease with which Dudley Turner had transported him – as if he were no weightier than a feather – that inspired his shame. For it was shame he endured in those moments after what Freda Whiteside described as his 'rescue': a shame he would grow ashamed at having experienced and say nothing of to Kitty.)

Dudley Turner, who revealed that he ran five miles every morning and played a fierce game of squash every afternoon to ward off the flabbiness a desk job brought on, wished Mr Florescu a quick recovery and said the office beckoned.

'Goodbye, my dear. You have covered yourself in glory.'

'You do come out with some funny expressions, if you don't mind my saying so, Mrs Whiteside.'

'I don't mind at all. Now get along to your drawing-board, there's a good resident Samaritan.'

'To which tribe do you belong, Virgil?'

'What are you asking me, Dinu?'

'I am asking you, my friend of the miracles, the question all Romanians ask themselves when they stand here.'

'Am I a Dacian or a Roman?'

'Precisely.'

'I am happy to be either, or neither, or both. My father is of the belief – no, the conviction – that we Florescus have Roman blood in our veins. Not the blood of the ordinary Roman soldier, Dinu, but the blood of a senator or a general, perhaps. Or even the blood of the mighty emperor himself. Blood, blood. It is all blood to me.'

'They have no problems with their ancestry,' said Dinu, as a group of Japanese tourists came to a concerted stop in front of Trajan's Column. 'But I am ignorant of their culture and can only surmise.'

Dinu had a story to tell him, if Virgil was in the right mood to hear it. Gregory the Great – the first of the sixteen popes named Gregory and by all accounts the best – was standing one day where they were standing now, admiring the reliefs of the Dacian wars. He was moved by the depiction of the goodness of Trajan and the mercy the emperor displayed towards the barbarians he had conquered. A

Christian mercy, Gregory thought. Then it occurred to him that Trajan was a barbarian too and had ruled over a pagan empire. Gregory was saddened that the soul of such a noble man should be lost and prayed in earnest for the heathen emperor's salvation.

'Were his prayers answered, Dinu?'

'There is doubt in your voice. Yes, they were. According to legend.'

According to legend, Gregory was assured that the soul of Trajan was not beyond redemption. It could and should be saved, if Gregory was prepared to undergo one or two penances. He had a choice between a spell in purgatory – three days of uninterrupted pain and torment – or a life of constant ill-health. Agony *en route* to the next world, or suffering in this.

'And which, according to legend, did he choose?'

'The earthly one. He was unwell from that day forward. He is said to have endured every discomfort without complaint.'

'Someone is approaching us, Dinu. He is waving at you.'

'So he is. He works at the embassy. I dare not trust him. Can you pretend to be Italian?'

'Already my name is Enrico Vitale.'

'Enrico Vitale, Enrico Vitale – I have it.'

For a few tense minutes he was Signor Vitale, speaking to Dinu Psatta and the suspicious Sorin Postelnicu in the language he spoke almost as well as his own. He feigned slight bafflement whenever they broke into Romanian and gave no indication of understanding the insulting comments Postelnicu made about his appearance. He was not, he explained, a friend of Signor Psatta, merely a passing acquaintance, a fellow collector of interesting ruins. 'We were brought together by our admiration for this magnificent column. In Ferrara, my birthplace, there is nothing comparable.'

'I see you have no need of a guidebook.'

'That is true, Signor Post–Signor Post–'

'Postelnicu.'

'Excuse me. Postelnicu. You are observant, Signor Postelnicu. I am a frequent visitor to Rome. I no longer have need of guides. My head is filled to overflowing with the necessary information.'

Sensing that Sorin Postelnicu was poised to test Signor Vitale's historical knowledge, he had the man from Ferrara (why Ferrara? He had only glanced at the city) look at his watch and express amazement that he was still here in the Forum when he ought to be at the railway station meeting his sister (why sister?) off the midday train. Elisabetta (why Elisabetta?) would be desperate with worry if she did not see her beloved Enrico (why Enrico?) waiting at the barrier. 'She is of a highly nervous disposition,' Signor Vitale elaborated, to Virgil Florescu's alarm.

'Goodbye, Signor Psatta. And goodbye, Signor Postelnicu. There, I have completed your name. Postelnicu, yes? I must run. Goodbye.'

But running was impossible with so many people around, and ahead of, him. He walked away as quickly as he could, with Enrico Vitale's anxious sister imploring him to hurry faster.

'It's a rice pudding, Virgil. I've sprinkled the daintiest amount of saffron on top, to add a touch of colour. I haven't gone the whole Turkish hog, with pistachios and currants, as I do normally.'

'You are kind. Thank you.'

'Thanks are unnecessary, my dear. I am enjoying nursing you, in spite of the scowl that is your customary greeting. I want you to eat as much as you can.'

'I will.'

'Please try. The weather is behaving offensively today, if it is any consolation to you. You have heard the wind, surely?'

'I have.'

'Then be thankful, at least, that you aren't out there fighting against it.'

'Yes.'

'With all those other poor souls who have to earn a living. You have your appetite back, I see.'

'The rice is good.'

'It always is when I remember to time it. I didn't think you would appreciate one of my burnt offerings.'

The words 'You are like a mother to me' escaped from him unchecked.

'Should I feel flattered, Virgil? Let me decide. On balance, yes, perhaps I should. I wasn't the motherly type in my younger days, I must admit. I loathed small children with a vengeance. I would have out-Heroded Herod, given the opportunity. No, Virgil, I never welcomed the patter of tiny feet and neither did Patrick, bless his memory. We wanted ourselves to ourselves. But being like a mother to a moody grown-up Romanian is a different matter. I *am* flattered.'

She took from him the dish that he had licked clean, told him he was the ideal son and left.

(He awoke to find her smiling down on him. 'My brave Virgil,' she said.

'Read to me from the book, Mamā.'

'Not Harap Alb again? Not the horrible Smooth-Face and his nasty tricks?'

'No, Mama. The funny Russian soldier.'

'Ivan with the knapsack? You are old enough and clever enough to read about him yourself.'

'I would rather listen to you, Mamā.'

'Is that because you are sick, or lazy, or both?'

'Both,' he replied.

'I will allow you to be lazy just this once. Just this once, remember.'

She sat on the end of his bed and opened the treasured book.

'Are you ready?'

'Yes, Mamā.'

'I swear I shall have a sore throat by the time you are better.'

She began to read, and he was soon absorbed by the story of the drunken old soldier who gave away his army pension of two silver roubles to God and St Peter, believing the shabbily dressed men he met on a bridge to be beggars. God was impressed, though not surprised, by his natural goodness and returned the money to him, saying, 'Learn now, Ivan, that I am God, and can give thee anything thou dost ask of Me; for thou art an honest and a liberal man.'

'What did Ivan ask for, Mamā?'

'Have you forgotten, Virgil?'

'Yes,' he lied.

'No more interruptions, if you please.'

'No, Mamā.'

'You know very well that Ivan asked God to bless his knapsack, as you are about to hear.'

The Almighty, he heard, was amused by Ivan's strange request and blessed the knapsack, bestowing upon the old soldier the power to command what or who should enter it. '"When thou art tired of wandering through the world, Ivan, thou must come and serve at My gate," and Ivan answered, "With pleasure, Lord, but now I must go and see whether something won't drop into my knapsack."

'Then off he went, and walked and walked, until he came at evening to a group of houses he had seen at the beginning of the day on the distant horizon. These were the property of a rich boyar who was close with his money. If Ivan had been any old soldier the boyar would have refused him hospitality, but the wily landowner saw that he was wearing the Imperial uniform and ordered a servant to bring him food and drink. He also offered him a bed for the night, in an empty house where uninvited guests were sometimes permitted to sleep. The grateful soldier ate his fill, and the servant showed him to a room in the empty house and left him there, alone.

'Except that he wasn't alone, as the boyar was well aware. The house was empty of the godly and pious, but not of the wicked and unclean. "He'll pay dearly for his night's rest," said the boyar to himself. "I know there will be work tonight. Either he will get the devils or the devils will get him."'

'What do devils look like, Mamā?'

'You promised not to interrupt. Devils have horns on their heads. And they have tails.'

'Have you ever seen a devil? Face to face?'

'No, Virgil, I haven't. Not face to face. Not with horns and a tail. I haven't seen that sort of devil. In drawings and pictures, yes, but not in the real world. Now, shall I continue? Or is there something else?'

'No, Mamā. Go on.'

'Where was I?'

'With Ivan in the room.'

'So I was.'

Ivan was overcome with tiredness, Virgil heard. After saying his prayers, and using the knapsack as his pillow, the old soldier, fully dressed, fell fast asleep on a comfortable divan. But could he rest? No, not at all. No sooner had he put out the light than the pillow, his knapsack, was whisked away from under him and thrown across the room. Ivan sprang up and lit the candle, and took hold of his sword and searched all over the house, but found nothing. It must have been an earthquake, he decided, that caused his pillow to move.

'It wasn't an earthquake, was it?'

'No, Virgil. Be quiet and listen.'

'Yes, Mamā.'

'It wasn't an earthquake, as Ivan soon discovered. He went back to bed and closed his eyes, determined to sleep. Then, all of a sudden, he started to hear voices – soft at first, but gradually becoming louder. Some miaowed like cats, some grunted like pigs, some croaked like frogs, while others growled like bears. "Aha," thought Ivan, "I realise what this is about. Whoever's there will have to reckon with me, the master." And, rising from the bed, he shouted, "Into the knapsack, good-for-nothings!"

'As if blown by the wind, a horde of devils crowded into the knapsack, one after another. Ivan waited until the very last devil was inside before he gave the knapsack a thorough beating. He laughed as the devils squealed and whimpered with pain.'

'Like this?' Virgil asked, making a squealing noise.

'Probably.'

'Or this?' He pretended to wail, then stopped, remembering he had heard the desolate sound at his grandfather's funeral. He was mimicking real misery, he understood. 'What happens next, Mamã? I swear I won't interrupt any more.'

'Swear?'

'Swear.'

'When he had finished beating the devils, Ivan fastened the neck of the knapsack tightly and placed it beneath his head. Now he really slept. He snored. He carried on snoring until it was nearly daybreak, at which time the demons were supposed to be back with their master Scaraoski. With the approach of dawn, the Chief of Devils grew suspicious that his lackeys hadn't returned and hastened to the boyar's empty house, where he struck the sleeping and snoring Ivan as hard a blow as he could deliver. The old soldier jumped up in a fury and shouted, "Into the knapsack!" and into the knapsack the dumbfounded Scaraoski went, joining the imps who served him.

'"I'll be your judge now, you unclean spirits," Ivan said. "I'll knock the heresy out of you."'

Virgil learned that Ivan was so pleased with what he had done that he stood in the courtyard and woke the boyar and the entire household with his shouting. The servants complained of the confounded Russian – 'Begging your honour's pardon' – who had given them an uncomfortable night, but the boyar himself was pleased and gratified when he was told that Ivan had succeeded, where the local priests had failed, in cleansing the fated house of its devils. Was there anything that Ivan wanted? Well, first of all, Ivan required some stakes with which to finish off his business.

'"I must make them run the gauntlet and beat them, so they remember they have met with Ivan, the servant of God."

'Ivan was presented with a cart full of stakes. He took as many as he needed and tied them together. While he was doing this, word had reached the village that a heaven-sent soldier was in their midst and now the villagers were gathered in the courtyard to watch Ivan chastise the demons.

'Ivan undid the knapsack and removed each devil in turn by his horns and beat him with the stakes.

'"We shall never come back," shrieked the tormented devils, who were covered in weals. And away they fled, with their tails between their legs and the mocking laughter of the peasants pursuing them. The village boys laughed loudest.

'There was only one devil left in the knapsack and that was Scaraoski. Ivan pulled him out by his beard and gave him a specially hard beating, because he was the dirtiest devil of them all. Then Ivan dashed him to the ground, and Scaraoski flew off as fast as a horse-fly . . .'

. . . And there his mother stopped, in the middle of the story. 'Tatã's home,' she said. 'He mustn't catch me reading to a big boy of nine.' She handed him the book. 'Must he?'

'No, Mamã.'

'Tomorrow, perhaps,' she whispered.

The following day his father lifted him out of bed and pronounced him a conquering hero. No son of Constantin

Florescu was going to be defeated by illness. Virgil had fought his first real battle and emerged triumphant.

'Yes, Tată,' he said, wishing himself sick again. 'Yes, Tată.')

He smiled at the notion that his sickness had returned, thirty-three years too late, in a city he had never anticipated visiting. He had been restored to health a day too soon and that promised tomorrow, the tomorrow of Ivan's most extraordinary adventures, became for ever lost to him. The happy Friday of expectation was not to be, thanks to his triumph – the triumph he might have delayed by childish subterfuge, for a morning and afternoon, if he'd had the wit.

'Your surrogate mother is here,' Freda Whiteside sang as she entered. 'Time for your medicine, Virgil.'

Beautiful Kitty Crozier [she read]. I shall see you very soon, but not here. Please do not come here. I shall come to you before the week is over. I am a detestable patient because I have no patience with illness. I try not to hurt the feelings of the good and kind Mrs Freda Whiteside and have to suppress an urge to complain (bellyache) when she is ministering to me. I dislike myself for being so petty and ungrateful.

Confined as I am in this room I wonder even if I am in London. I lie here and travel back in my mind to other places, a complete slave to memory. I am rambling, Kitty. This is of interest to no one except the deranged Virgil Florescu.

Freda W has arrived with her photograph album. It is *bulky*. There are lots, possibly hundreds, of photographs. She is telling me I am her 'captive audience'. She is promising me a 'guided tour' of her past as soon as I have finished writing this letter.

She has passed on your messages. I long to be with you. The day after tomorrow perhaps. Freda W is saying

169

'Scribble, scribble, scribble, Mr Gibbon' and glaring at me. I suppose I must ask her what she means by the remark. I hate not understanding what people are saying to me.

She is opening the album, Kitty, in a pointed manner. I must surrender.

Soon. Very soon.

Your Virgil.

(That same bulky photograph album would be produced when Kitty Crozier visited Freda Whiteside in the late autumn of the following year. She had gone to the house – one of six Victorian survivors on the edge of a concrete estate – to see the room in which her lover had lived briefly. It was occupied by a young New Zealander now.

'He is studying tropical diseases, my dear. That is why those forbidding tomes on beri-beri and malaria and others we know not of are scattered everywhere. Gruesome stuff, yet Mr Mackay is a very cheerful sort with his bright blond hair and big, toothy grin.' She squeezed Kitty's hand. 'There's no trace of Virgil, is there?'

'No, there isn't.'

'Have you seen what you came to see?'

'Yes. Thank you.'

'What were you expecting?'

'I can't say. Oh, I wanted to look at the bed he slept in, I suppose. And the furniture he used. But he isn't here any more.'

'He removed himself completely, my dear. I don't have a single memento of him. Not a matchstick, not a shoelace. It's a rare lodger who doesn't leave something behind, either accidentally or on purpose. But Virgil left nothing. Nothing tangible, that is.'

'You were good to him.'

'That time he was stricken with flu, he told me I was like a mother. Since he made it clear that he loathed being mothered I decided it was not a compliment. Did he ever mention his real mother to you?'

'Yes, he did. He worshipped her. From what he said, she was exceptionally attractive. A classic beauty. Perhaps he was exaggerating. Lots of sons consider their mothers beautiful.'

'Patrick, my husband, considered his a gorgon. He was right. She was. Her mind was as ugly as her face. Let's go downstairs, my dear. This is Mr Mackay's domain, isn't it?'

'Yes.'

'Come along.'

She followed the puffing Freda Whiteside down three flights of stairs, past framed photographs of famous opera singers in costume: Enrico Caruso, Nellie Melba, Beniamino Gigli, Kirsten Flagstad, Amelita Galli-Curci, Jussi Björling, Lotte Lehmann.

'I didn't sing with any of those, my dear. I saw one or two of them, of course: the Flagstand as an over-the-hill Dido and the glorious drunken Swede as Manrico. My father, my beloved father' – she sang the phrase '*O mio babbino caro*' and laughed loudly – 'caught them all in their prime. He's the Henry Fletcher of the autographs. He was so proud of his little Freda when she gave her Nedda at Covent Garden. I did not, needless to say, rise very much higher. I ended up squawking in cattle country. Paddy once suggested, in one of his prankish moods, that I change my name to Lato-Bianco – you had to sound foreign to be anyone in opera in those days – but I lacked the courage. Or cheek, or gall. No, I couldn't pass myself off as Federica Lato-Bianco, the diva from Milano. Paddy dared and dared me to – he thought it the most wonderful wheeze – but I chickened out, abject coward that I was. I stayed plain Freda Fletcher throughout my bumpy career. My Whiteside reincarnation never happened. Come into my parlour, Kitty, and have some tea.'

A plump Persian cat – 'Omar Khayyam minus his balls'

– was curled asleep in a battered armchair near an open fire. 'Off with you, OK,' Freda Whiteside commanded, clapping her hands. 'Make way for our guest, you slothful brute.'

The cat stirred, stretched, scratched an ear with a back paw and flopped on to the carpet.

'Several illustrious and capacious bottoms have made that chair the wreck it is today. I wouldn't part with it if you offered me a Sheraton or a Chippendale. Sink into it, my dear. Let it swallow you up. Lapsang souchong agreeable?'

'Yes. Thank you.'

'And walnut cake?'

'Yes.'

She wanted neither tea nor cake, but found herself incapable of inventing a quick and polite excuse to leave. The necessary lie remained unsaid. She sank into the chair, into the hollow created by the loudest Brünnhilde – 'A voice like a foghorn, my dear, in the middle of the choppy Atlantic' – anyone would remember.

Freda Whiteside picked up the growling cat and went through to the adjacent kitchen, where she began to sing. Kitty listened to a disconnected medley of snatches of arias from operas and oratorios, identifying the more familiar tunes the old woman warbled. The Countess Almaviva languished while she filled the kettle; she summoned the bright seraphim as she set out the china and cutlery; she became a chuckling, contralto Mephistopheles when she mashed up sardines for Omar Khayyam, who howled in accompaniment; she opened the cake tin in the role of Azucena, confining the gypsy's account of her family's complicated lineage to the opening bars ('I've forgotten the rest'); she then decided to know that her Redeemer liveth, and for a finale, merrily pouring hot water into the teapot, she was Don Giovanni and Zerlina by turns, until their words eluded her and she resorted to a series of la-la-la-las and dum-dum-di-dums.

'Come to the table, my dear. Your nose is level with your knees at the moment. Hardly the most comfortable position in which to eat and drink. Will you require a helping hand?'

'I think I have the strength to emerge from the crater unaided.'

The 'guided tour' of Freda Whiteside's past – from the fifty years before her birth in 1919 to the death of her husband in 1968 – took place after tea. 'It isn't often I have a captive audience, my dear. "Captive", of course, is just a figure of speech. This house isn't a prison, although one of my erstwhile tenants used to describe it as Sing-Sing – not a bad joke for a man in insurance. Feel free to go, Kitty. Don't be obliged to stay.'

'I feel like staying.'

'In that case, my dear, you will need fortifying.'

Freda Whiteside filled two tumblers with Irish whiskey – 'Paddy's favourite tipple' – and brought them to the table. 'Cheers, Kitty.'

'Oh, yes, cheers.'

The sepia-coloured dead, captured in stiff or flamboyant poses, were paraded in front of her. Freda Whiteside conveyed, whenever she could, the foibles and idiosyncrasies of this peculiar great-aunt or that mysterious distant cousin; of this crotchety grandmother and that kindly uncle; of the tubercular boy holding a hoop who would be transmogrified into the obese major-general four decades on: 'He's wearing a corset underneath his uniform, which is why his face looks as if it is about to explode.'

Kitty stared at a succession of beards and moustaches, plaits and chignons. The dead, she thought, who were once so contentedly alive. The faces of the various Fletchers and Morlands exuded self-assurance. Any doubts or misgivings they might have possessed in regard to their earthly lot were barely reflected here. The photographers – Mr Burgess of Alton; Mr Reynolds of Lewes – were in the business of recording happy prosperity, it seemed. The Fletchers and

Morlands stood on the steps of their country houses (much more imposing than modest, red-bricked Alder Court) and beamed into the future.

'Our families were well-to-do, my dear, as you can see. They amassed their fortunes in the eighteenth century, in trade. "In trade" marked them out as *arriviste*. To the landed gentry in Hampshire and Sussex my grandfathers were tradesmen, because their money wasn't old enough. Not *nearly* old enough. It was still tainted with work and to work was vulgar. Certain ancient doors never opened for the Fletchers and the Morlands. But that's another story, Kitty – the story the photographs were unable to tell.'

The story of the comely, matronly Adelaide Morland was hidden from the camera, too. She was, in Freda Whiteside's words, 'the biggest beamer in both beaming families', with a smile 'as broad as the Menai Strait'. That was the public side of Freda's mother's mother, who spent twenty-five years in a state of almost perpetual pregnancy. 'Twelve children, eight miscarriages and two stillbirths. The idea of it, Kitty. The sheer, terrible thought of it. Is it any wonder she became moody and foul-tempered? You're looking at the face she put on for the outside world, not the scowl she kept for her children and the servants. My brothers and I called her Granny Grunt. She grunted, my dear, she actually grunted, like some huge unhappy sow, whenever we were pushed into her presence. She's all smiles here, though.'

'Is this baby you?'

'You sound relieved. Yes, that blob is me. Freda Fletcher is born at last.'

'And this must be your christening.'

'It is, indeed. You will notice how the ranks have been depleted. No less than five uncles – three Morlands, two Fletchers – were killed in Flanders. One of them was married. That's his widow lurking behind my mother. What a force of nature Chloe was. The hearts she broke are beyond counting. She was still breaking them when she was mur-

174

dered, in her fifties. A *crime passionnel*, my dear. The love-sick Mr Parker strangled her with a silk stocking. "Quite a stylish exit," her catty mother remarked. "Better than she deserved." I omitted Chloe's mother's comment from the guided tour I gave Virgil, Kitty. I sensed that he might not be amused.'

'"Diverted". That was his word. He always surprised me, Freda. He might have been amused or diverted. I can't say.'

'I played safe. He was in an agitated condition. *Molto agitato*. Flippancy did not seem appropriate.'

'You must have spent most of your childhood by the piano.'

'That's what it looks like, doesn't it, my dear. Yes, my father was a real taskmaster. He was my first and fondest teacher. He ought to have been a professional musician, he had such an ear, but there was safety in soap, and he had to think of his wife and family. He had me singing at a tender age. Nursery rhymes to start with, then one or two Victorian ballads, and after that a little easy Schumann and Schubert. One magical day he took me up to London – in a first-class carriage, among the pin-striped suits – to be seen and heard by the famous voice coach Elsa Latimer. I was terrified as I entered her studio, because she was who she was. "Surprise me," she demanded. I began to sing, but not for long. She brought me to a halt after only a couple of bars. "Where are you going?" she asked as I made for the door and freedom. "Come back and start again. And take a deep breath first, you naughty girl." I did take a breath and I sang, I thought, like a dream, right through to the end, with my father accompanying me. I finished. Profound silence, my dear; a silence to drop pins in. "Once more, please," spoke the oracle. "My pianist will play." Her pianist slowed me down a bit, and I felt frustrated and not so confident. I got through it, though, somehow. "What an improvement!" she cried, banging her stick on the floorboards. "Brava, brava! Now go and sit in the corner while Mr Fletcher and I discuss your future." Which I did and they talked for an eternity. And that is how I became a pupil of Elsa Latimer, on August the fifth nineteen thirty-five. Afterwards my father treated me to a slap-up tea at the Ritz.'

'The Ritz? I met most of my father's wives over tea at the Ritz, as well as the women he didn't get round to marrying.'

'Wives, Kitty? Women? What is this? I should be listening to you.'

'No, Freda. I can't talk about him. I don't want to talk about him.'

'Spoilsport. But I shan't persist. Let's return to little Freda being winsome and pert and *gemütlich*. Here she is, being all three at once, during her début recital in nineteen thirty-eight. She came a bit of a cropper with "The Shepherd on the Rock", and so did the clarinettist, whose throat was dry from nerves, but she found her voice for Hugo Wolf and ended the concert weighed down with roses.'

'Was your teacher pleased with you?'

'Elsa was a perfectionist, my dear, and very hard to please. She was parsimonious with the compliments she paid her students. "Adequate, Freda," was what she said to me that evening, while everyone else, including my father, was telling me I was wonderful. She gave me a peck on the cheek and muttered, "Adequate, Freda. Mistakes galore. Post-mortem tomorrow at eleven." And there was a post-mortem, Kitty. A thoroughgoing dissection.'

'I see you've written "I was adequate" under the photo.'

'Yes. I was adequate then and adequate I more or less remained. Elsa didn't live to catch me being adequate in opera. She died suddenly in December nineteen thirty-nine. Who knows what I might have sung – better than adequately, perhaps – if Hitler hadn't complicated our lives. As it was, I found myself in the Carl Rosa touring company. These are the photographs that brought the flicker of a smile to Virgil's gloomy face. This is me as Ortlinde. She's one of the Valkyries.'

Freda, wearing a horned helmet and a breastplate made of papier mâché, was standing between two substantial women, who were similarly dressed, in front of a cardboard rock.

'That's Mona Randall to the left of me. She got to sing what my lovely Paddy called the "loudmouths" – Brünnhilde, Turandot, Isolde, Aida. Cancer carried her off, the poor darling, in her prime. That rock behind us, Kitty, was pure decoration. It would have crumbled to nothing if one of us had placed so much as a foot on it. We didn't bother with verismo in those days. Virgil lingered over this photograph, my dear. In disbelief, I suspect.'

'Did he?'

'Oh yes. His eyes lit up at the sight of us. I wasn't surprised. We look ridiculous without the music, if you understand me. Paddy was working as a stage-hand when I met him. He was at his happiest on Mozart and Verdi nights, but down in the dumps when it was Wagner. He considered Wagner's music an "almighty pain in the rectum" – his words – and renamed *Götterdämmerung Götterdämmorrhoids*, the disrespectful beast. This is Paddy, with the bloom of youth on him.'

'What a handsome man.'

'Yes, my dear, he was. Handsome was and handsome did before the fool of a man walked under a bus. I had to avoid the 39 route for years. Just seeing the number at a stop distressed me. Enough, enough. Here I am as Nedda in *I Pagliacci*.'

'At Covent Garden?'

'Heavens, no. This was taken in some godforsaken barn, on tour. We trailed *Cav* and *Pag* everywhere. My triumphant appearance at the Royal Opera House was for one night only, never – alas – to be repeated. I was the management's last, desperate choice to stand in for the famous diva

177

who was stricken with laryngitis – seven other well-known Neddas were all Nedda-ing in different parts of the globe and I was the one Nedda who wasn't. There was no time for a rehearsal. I was advised to linger downstage right and let the other members of the cast move me about, which they did. They sang in Italian, I in English, and somehow I survived the absurd experience. My father was in the audience, blinking back tears of pride and joy. I was described as "plucky" and "brave" and "appealing" in the papers, but no one mentioned my voice. The tour's nearly over with, my dear, if you're wilting.'

'Not yet.'

'As I say, I wasn't invited back to Covent Garden. I went to Buenos Aires instead, courtesy of Mona Randall, who had suddenly become a big name out there. "Come and squawk with me" her telegram said. So I left my darling Paddy here and went and squawked in Argentina. Mona could demand anything and anyone she wanted, and she wanted me as Liù in *Turandot* and Musetta in *La Bohème*, two roles for which I was startlingly ill-equipped. Mona was a very forceful Mimi, my dear. But no one seemed to notice how dire I was, especially the critics. I have to confess that I actually came off-stage one night thanking God at the top of my speaking voice that Elsa Latimer was safely dead and buried in her Twickenham grave, and well out of earshot of her promising pupil. "Bit wobbly this evening, the pair of us," Mona said afterwards, blaming the conductor for our wobbles. "The bastard must have had a train to catch or an urgent date to keep with his mistress, to judge by his tempi in the last act. I'll strangle the shit if he does it again." And she would have done if he had, but he didn't. She frightened the daylight out of him, bless her.'

'She looks very noble in this picture.'

'And even larger than usual. This will amuse you, I hope, Kitty. She is carrying excess baggage. I am, too, in all these photos from the South American period. Money, my dear.

178

Tons of paper money. Thousands upon thousands of pesos. I can tell you're mystified. Let me explain. Mona's first words to me when I arrived in Buenos Aires were: "You have to watch these buggers. Do as I do, Freda. Blackmail them. Bleed them, or they'll bleed you." She had sung in opera houses in Argentina and Brazil on the assumption – the perfectly rational assumption – that she would be paid for her services. The trusting Mona had given everything and received nothing, apart from a couple of bouncing cheques. She advised me to insist on cash before each performance and to laugh them to scorn when they told me the banks were closed. "To hear them speak, you would think the banks were never open," she said. "No cash, no show – it's that simple." Hence the excess baggage, Kitty. Night after night, and at quite a few matinées, Mona and I would go on stage with pesos stuffed into our brassières and panties. These were the only safe places on the premises, according to Mona, because the dressers and theatre staff were thieves to a man and a woman. Once, when I was just about to sing as Liù, I got into a panic and peed myself with fright. I could feel all those soggy pesos down below while I belted out my big aria, and it was a real effort to concentrate on the music. I had to put the notes out to dry when I came off.'

Freda Whiteside laughed and Kitty laughed with her.

'End of tour, my dear.' She snapped the album shut. 'I was over there for six months. I came home with a small fortune and delusions of a happy retirement. Then Paddy collided with the bus and there were no more photographs.'

'Thank you, Freda. Thank you for diverting me.'

'My pleasure. I should thank you for being so patient and attentive. Have another whiskey for the road.'

'A little one, please. Otherwise I shall be reeling.'

'He might grow tired of being a missing person, you know. He might come to his senses and return to you.'

'Who?'

179

'Who, my dear? Who else but Virgil?'

Kitty heard herself gasp. She looked into the watery-blue eyes that were fixed on her and said, 'He won't come to his senses. He won't return. He's gone from me.')

She folded Virgil's letter in two and placed it between the pages of the book of Tagore's verses Freddy had given her.

'They were what they were,' Constantin Florescu pronounced, pouring the dregs of the *ţuică* into the glass. 'And what they were was no longer acceptable.'

In the densest silence of his life, Virgil Florescu thought: this is the man I have called Tatā since childhood; this is the man who fathered me – who happily fathered me – with his beautiful young bride five years after; this is a man who has passed among ordinary men, pretending to be ordinary.

This is a man who, knowing what he had done, should have reached for the poison; should have put a gun to his temple or a knife to his heart; should have found some way to cease being a man.

'My intellectual son appears to be lost for words.'

'You had to get drunk to tell me.'

'No, that isn't true. *In vino veritas*, eh? No, Virgil. My tipsiness is coincidental. The secret I have shared with you is not a guilty one. I have no guilt. I have been secretive for reasons of diplomacy. For those alone.'

'Have you told Relu?'

'Yes, I have. I told him what I have told you. I was the model of sobriety.'

'When?'

'Is it important when? When he graduated from the military academy.'

'And?'

'And *what*?'

'What did he say?'

'He said he understood and I believed him. He is my sensible son.'

'And Mamā?'

'Matilda was made aware of the – the *event* by a not-so-chance remark, by common gossip. One of her female friends dropped a heavy hint and your mother picked it up. She was not open to reason after that.'

It was comfort of a kind for him, bleak comfort though it was, this assurance that his beloved mother, his still beloved mother, had deafened her ears to Constantin Florescu's reasonable words. She had not been sullied. She had retreated into her own darkness, but she had not been sullied.

'I was young. I had ideals. I was someone, Virgil, you might try to understand: I was a Romantic. Yes, the dreams I had for my country were Romantic, my clever son. Unity, liberty, purity – those were the things I and my brothers-in-arms wanted for Romania. We even had our national poet Eminescu on our side.'

'He was dead, Tatā.'

'Not his ideas, not his ideals. They were alive. They are alive to this day.'

'You are shouting.'

'Am I?' Constantin Florescu spoke quietly now. 'Forgive me.'

'I think I can forgive you for shouting.'

Because of economy measures the room in which they had eaten countless meals – Tatā at one end of the shining oak table, Mamā at the other – was lit this evening by a single lamp. His father, slumped in the high-backed oak chair that resembled a throne – the heavy, frayed, wine-coloured velvet curtains drawn behind him – looked indeed like some tired old actor playing at being the flawed hero, the unhappy monarch worn down by treachery and intrigue. The setting seemed fit, the sparse lighting apt – except that the tragic king had begun to snore.

181

In this same room, one sunlit morning, he had helped his mother polish the furniture. 'Mamã, why is it that gypsies have no church to pray in?' he had asked and she had smiled at his unusual question.

'You are not supposed to be curious about religion, Virgil. Religion belongs to the past. I can only answer by telling you a story I heard from my Grandmother Monica.'

Then she became annoyingly silent, he recalled, as he sat across from the snoring man who had fathered him.

'The story, Mamã,' he had prompted her.

'It is silly, Virgil. You are not meant to believe it. There used to be a proverb when I was the age you are now.'

'Seven, Mamã. Seven and three-quarters.'

'Yes, yes. We used to say of a man who has spent all his money on food, "He has eaten his credit, like the gypsy his church." Are you with me?'

'You can't eat a church.'

'Of course you can't. Well, I was anxious to know how and why the gypsy had eaten his church, so my grandmother gave me an explanation. A long time ago, she said, the gypsies decided to build a church of their own, which they wanted to stand for ever, until the very end of the world. They held a council to discuss the matter, but they couldn't agree on which material to use. Someone suggested wood, but "Wood rots and does not last as long as the world" someone else put in, and another someone mentioned iron, but "Iron grows rusty and isn't everlasting" yet another someone responded. Then someone had the idea of stone, but someone pointed out that stone breaks, so they threw out that idea too. At last they agreed on cheese, and they built their church – yes, they built their church – with cheese.'

'Which cheese?'

'A hard one, I expect. Anyway, no sooner was the church built than there came a terrible winter, with the snow deep on the ground. There was no food for people to eat. So all the gypsies gathered round the church and ate it – nibble, nibble; bit by bit – until it completely disappeared. And that is why the gypsies have no church to pray in, Virgil. It is a story the peasants handed down and not to be believed.'

'No, Mamā.'

Constantin Florescu stirred, opened an eye and closed it. He farted loudly, but the noise did not waken him. He slept on, and snored.

In the London attic, Virgil Florescu remembered those sounds of bodily contentment, of an old man who had eaten and drunk his fill. An old survivor, with nothing to perturb him but the prospect of his own imminent death. His own decease, in natural circumstances. In a hospital bed, perhaps, with a nurse in attendance; or suddenly, mercifully, without his knowing of it – the quick gathering up of the good and the just.

But no. Let the man who spawned me never die. Let him live on and on, like the Russian soldier with the knapsack who thought he could escape the grave. Let him live to find life itself unendurable.

'There's brightness in your eyes again,' Freda Whiteside remarked. 'Come downstairs and have your supper with me. A mushroom omelette, my dear, and an unburnt rice pudding. I think I'll give you my permission to go to work tomorrow.'

He arrived at her house with a bunch of snowdrops. 'The first flowers of spring, I am told, Kitty.'

'Yes, they are.'

'I have been promoted from litter. I have been moved to Kensington Gardens. I am helping one of the gardeners there. I am happy.'

'Come in.'

She closed the door behind him and said, 'It can't be possible, but you're thinner. You've lost weight, sweetheart. I never imagined you could be thinner.'

'I will disappear soon,' he joked, 'if I lose any more. There will be nothing left of me.'

(Once, caressing his cock, she said softly, 'This doesn't fit the rest of you. It's so fat, Virgil. It's plump. It doesn't really belong.'

And then, afterwards, she would dream one night that the most substantial part of her lover had been separated from his skinny, bumpy body. There it was, complete in itself, moving inside her, slowly, steadily. She called his name and made to stroke his back, but there was no back to stroke, no hair to run her fingers through, no lips to kiss, no eyes looking into her eyes – only the near-darkness of the bedroom, the familiar shapes of a chair and wardrobe. She heard his voice, the voice from nowhere, telling his beautiful Kitty Crozier that he had sent this gift ahead of him by express delivery. He hoped she liked it. 'Oh, I do,' she answered the voice. 'You know I do.' She moaned with pleasure and the voice whispered '*La revedere*' and said it had to be going now, all the way to a mother's grave in Bucharest, and she would awake and see his gaunt face for the briefest instance, and sob again at the cruel loss of him.)

'There's about enough of you left for the time being. Enough to keep me satisfied.'

Later that evening he spoke of his affection for London – 'My unanticipated city' – while she prepared supper. It was even more cosmopolitan than Rome, which he had revisited during his illness, in a state of half-sleep, a slave to memory.

Every race was here, every colour, every language. His eyes and ears were constantly surprised, constantly delighted. Influenza, if that's what it really was, had deprived him of those sights and sounds, causing him to drift back into his past, to the city of wide boulevards from which races, colours, languages were banished.

'I think I wish to stay in London.'

'I hope you wish to stay in London.'

'For the rest of my life, possibly.'
'Then we could grow old together.'
'We could.'
'But – just for the moment, sweetheart – let's eat.'

He predicted, with a smile, that there would be heavy rain in the morning. 'And snow, perhaps. And sleet. And a ferocious south wind.'

It was a Saturday afternoon in March and they were sitting in the garden, enjoying the strangely warm weather.

'The sun is alone in the sky today, but his race against St Theodor isn't over yet.'

'I'm listening.'

'It is one of our legends.'

'I had an idea it might be.'

In this particular legend, Virgil said, God has entrusted the sun with the task of lighting up the earth. The sun enjoys the job to begin with and shines brightly on all the natural wonders below. He is, so to speak, in his element. But then, as the centuries go by, his once pleasant task becomes a burden to him, a daily torture. He finds himself ever more distressed by the wrongs and injustices and evils he is witness to, and attempts to run away. He does this twice a year. In the spring he makes for the south; in the early autumn he edges himself northwards. He is always outwitted – or has been so far – by Nicora, the saint in the north, and Theodor, the saint in the south. They know better than to let him escape.

'He's been joined by a cloud. That means the witches are still at work.'

'Does it?'

'Oh yes, Kitty. Yes, it does. There are nine of them in the sun's carriage, which is driven by nine horses. They use their witchcraft to produce snow and rain and thunderstorms – a thunderstorm is their *pièce de résistance* – to hinder St Theodor's pursuit of them. These witches are old

185

women. What is your word? Hags. Yes, they are hags. Like Dochia, our March witch, who sheds her sheepskin coats at the first glimpse of sunlight and freezes to death just before the arrival of spring.'

Who were the inventors of those ancient, fabulous stories? Did some forgotten individual look up at the sky on a day like today and imagine the sun wishing to avert his gaze from the earth? And did that person convey the conceit to someone else, who then embellished it? Did the legend expand, as a rumour expands, with each new telling? That was how, surely. He liked to think the witches were a medieval addition, and that the idea of the world ending when the sun rises and sets in the same place was another elaboration – by a solitary harbinger of doom, perhaps, anxious to complicate a tale that was altogether too simple.

(She would remember how talkative he was that Saturday. The frequent glint of his Communist tooth offered her evidence enough that he felt relaxed and contented. He was in a communicative mood, wanting to share with her the unwritten literature – 'An oxymoron, yes?' – of his forebears. It pleased him, he said, to realise that the preposterous stories his mother had told him long ago in a voice which was not entirely serious were still lodged somewhere in his mind.

She had to interrupt him once, to ask for a translation. He was in the middle of a story about a peasant who opens his door one morning to confront a stark, wintry landscape. The poor man, blinded by the intense whiteness, is convinced that the world has ended. The earth and sky seem to be one, and there is no sound. He listens, in the hope of hearing a crow or magpie, but the terrifying silence persists. In his fear he mutters '*a venit vremea de apoi*' over and over again. The prophecy in the old legend has been fulfilled, and yes, it is true, *a venit vremea de apoi*.

'What does that mean?'

'It is one of our sayings, Kitty. It means "The time of

afterwards has come". We use it on days when the birds have disappeared, when the trees have no leaves, when the immediate world looks deserted. We would not use it today. Not with the sun beaming down on us.')

In bed that night, before they made love, she told him how lucky she was to have counted ten glimpses of stainless steel. He smiled and said, 'Here is an eleventh for you.'

'It's happened.'

'What has, Daisy?'

'What has what?'

'What has happened?'

'*It* has, silly. *It* has, finally.'

'I'm none the wiser.'

'Aren't you? Aren't you?'

'No, Daisy. Calm yourself and tell me what has happened.'

'Easy for you to be calm. Easy for you to stay calm. It isn't easy for me.'

'I am losing patience with you.'

'Are you really? You're losing patience with me, aren't you? You're a great comfort, I don't think.'

'I want to comfort you, Daisy. I can see how unhappy you are. Now please tell me what has happened.'

'*It* has, silly. The impossible has. The unimaginable.'

'I haven't the imagination to imagine the unimaginable, so will you please tell me what it is.'

There was a long silence, during which Daisy bit her lower lip. 'Him,' she said at last. 'It's him. My husband.'

'Cecil?'

'I don't have any other. Yes, that is his name.'

'Oh, my poor dear Daisy, he isn't dead?'

'Much worse than that. I could put up with him dying. He's left me. The boring bastard's left me.'

Kitty could not say she was surprised, because she wasn't. 'For somebody else?'

'Yes, silly, for somebody else. Some body else. She is half his age. He claims he loves her, the disgusting hypocrite. She's juicier meat is the reason. Young and juicy. If I could get to him with a knife. I'd cut his ugly little thingamajig right off. Snip, snip. That's what he's thinking with. Snip, snip, I'd go.'

Kitty shuddered, hearing the phrase from childhood.

'Snip, bloody snip,' Daisy shouted.

'I'm so sorry, my dear.'

'Not more sorry than I am. Not more sickeningly bloody sorry than I am. I wonder if Gillian has noticed his varicose veins. He has a particularly horrible one bulging out of the back of his leg. I wonder if she strokes it.'

'Shall I make you some tea, Daisy?'

'Shall you make me some tea? No, you bloody shan't. I'm not an invalid, silly. Open his precious drinks cabinet. Pour me a whisky, or gin, or anything.'

'There only seems to be sherry.'

'Sherry will do. Sherry will do me fine. Anything will do me fine.'

'My poor Daisy.'

'He won't be leaving me poor, baby sister. I'll take his money if I take nothing else. I'll pocket his shekels at the very least.'

'Yes, of course.'

'You bet of course. She's six months pregnant, this Gillian creature. She's twenty-three and pregnant by a man who will soon be fifty – that's her happy lot. Good God, Kitty, I've endured his jokes for most of my life. His truly appalling jokes.'

'Yes,' Kitty said quietly, soothingly. 'Yes, you have.'

'I deserve a medal for suffering them. A long-service medal, embossed. What can she see in him? It's as plain as day what he sees in her, but what in hell can she see in him? He's nothing to look at, and his head's full of stocks and shares, and not much besides. He's not what anyone would call cultivated. Is he? Is he?'

'No. Perhaps he isn't.'

'Perhaps? No perhaps about it, silly. He's dull. He used to be dull and dependable, but now he's just dull. He'll bore this Gillian stupid, if she isn't completely stupid already, which she must be. He's in for a mighty surprise when he comes home with his tail between his veiny legs, after Gillian has chucked him over.'

'You haven't mentioned Andrew and Janet, Daisy.'

'No, I haven't. There's my clever-as-ever baby sister. He told *them* face to face. They received the news before their mother did. I got a letter. He sat down with them and broke the news and said he couldn't help himself, he was in love, Gillian had changed his life, he was a different man – all the usual drivel men of his kind come out with when a delicious bit of younger flesh is pushed in their direction. Yes, he had the courage, if that's what it is – the courtesy, Kitty – to speak to them, face to face, but what did his wife get? A snivelling, grovelling, miserable letter – half a page of regrets and apologies with a thank you at the bottom. Thank you, indeed. No words of love for me. Only a thank you.'

'Are they very upset?'

'I suppose they are. A mother's the last person to know what her children are feeling. They're more Trappist than ever is all I can tell you. Andrew says "Oh, Ma" when I manage to catch his eye and Janet stares into space. Which means, I suppose, they're upset. I hope that "yes" is the answer to your question.'

'I'm sure it is.'

'You're the authority, are you?' Daisy shouted. 'When did *you* give birth? You're sure, are you, silly?'

Kitty nodded.

'It isn't as if I've been like you. I've been loyal and faithful. I've been a good wife. I haven't had infatuations like you.

189

I've never allowed myself the luxury. I remember, if you don't, what a fool you made of yourself with that kaftanned creature with the common accent. I have never, but never, been like you.'

'No, Daisy, you haven't.'

'And here you are, at an age when most people are behaving with decorum – yes, that's the correct word, decorum; when most people have attained a bit of decorum, you are behaving – you are behaving –'

'Indecorously?'

'And worse. If you could just see how you look at your daft Romanian park attendant you'd blush to your roots with embarrassment. I've never behaved the way you're behaving. I've always had more sense, more dignity, more bloody self-respect. It's not as if I've been like you. I could understand if I'd been the irresponsible type like you – a clever silly, flitting from man to man with no thought of the consequences – but I have always been responsible. At least I can say I haven't been like you.'

'Yes, dear, at least you can say that.'

'I can and will. I've tried to be as different from you and Nelly as I possibly could, and this is what happens to me. I'm not some kind of Bohemian, am I? I don't deserve this treatment. I don't bloody deserve it.'

'No, Daisy, you don't.'

'He can't even boil an egg. I had to bully him whenever I wanted him to do what I call men's housework. She'll have to bully him, too, if she needs anything done to their love nest. The leopard doesn't change his spots, does he? He is certainly one leopard who won't. You can bet safe money on that.'

(Daisy Hopkins received Cecil's 'snivelling, grovelling, miserable letter' on 26 April 1989 and Kitty visited her the following day. It was to be the first of many comforting visits. She listened with a willed patience to each of Daisy's familiar, much repeated complaints and gave no response when reminded of the numerous infatuations she had enjoyed, including her latest with the 'daft Romanian park attendant'. Cecil, now, was denied his name. 'He', 'him', the 'boring bastard', 'my husband that was' – it was as if the voicing of 'Cecil' was beyond Daisy's powers. Daisy's concern was entirely with Daisy, Kitty discovered. Daisy had been wronged, rejected, and he, the husband that was, had had no reason in the world to reject her, other than simple lust.)

'I wouldn't have him back if he came begging to me. Begging on his hands and knees. Imploring me to forgive him. Not even then would I take him back.'

He sighed when she told him that Cecil had separated from Daisy, to live with a younger woman.

'Cecil is a serious man. He has not done this lightly. He is not cast in the same mould as the diverting Felix. He has not been a wandering husband, of that I am certain. My father was a wanderer, Kitty. He wandered from my mother whenever he had the chance and he found himself plenty of chances. I am sure some woman is with him this very minute.'

It was a custom, in his father's youth, if not *the* custom, among those who had risen above the peasantry to have – how could he say? Which word should he use? – a *free* marriage. Constantin Florescu had been free throughout his marriage to Matilda, free as a migrating bird, just as his father Ovidiu had been free before him. It was said of Ovidiu that he was *un vrai Parisien*, a title reserved for only the most practised wanderers from the marital bed.

'I have broken with the family tradition, I fear. I cannot speak for my brother Relu. He has a wife and children. Perhaps he has taken to wandering, in honour of his Tată.'

('Shall we talk about our previous lovers?' she had asked him early on. 'Or shall we leave them in peace, in the past?'

He had answered, 'Let's get them over with.'

'Who's going first?'

'Will you, Kitty? And try not to be too affectionate, too eloquent.'

There was Freddy, she said, and really there was no one else. He was of average height, with a cascade of blond hair, and his eyes were greenish-grey or greyish-green, depending. He wore beads and colourful clothes, and smoked pot and read Hermann Hesse and Rabindranath Tagore, and talked of universal love and understanding in an entrancing – to her ears, entrancing – Cockney accent. He was like a thousand others, then, except that he wasn't. The sweetness of his disposition was genuine, not assumed. He stole her young heart and she hoped from this distance in time that she had once stolen his.

'You lived with him?'

'Oh yes. In happy disarray. In a damp basement flat with fungi sprouting up through the floorboards. Our magic mushrooms, we called them. We burned incense to cover up the musty smell.'

Their idyllic existence ended with an abruptness neither of them could have anticipated. When Freddy had his beautiful, flowing locks shorn off she failed to see the act of desecration for the portent it was. The almost-bald Freddy said nothing that day of the drastic change that had taken place inside him. The next evening, when she came home from the Italian food shop where she was working, Freddy was gone. He had pinned a note to the kitchen wall. She read that he had seen the light and that he was following it to Ethiopia. It was signed with the letter 'F', under which he had written a couple of 'X's, as kisses. Nothing more.

'I couldn't eat the freshly made tortellini I had brought back for us. I was devastated. I was suicidal. I was convinced I would never recover.'

Months after his departure he wrote her a letter of explanation, or perhaps justification. Yes, justification was the appropriate word. He needed to justify his hasty exit from their relationship. He began by saying that what he had done would strike most people as unjustifiable, but he wasn't a cruel man and she wasn't most people. He had been driven by a force, a higher power, he was unable to resist. His road to Damascus was Marsham Street in London, round the corner from Westminster Abbey. He was strolling past the Missionary Society building when his attention was caught by a photograph in the window of a starving child. Just another familiar starving child, he thought, and then his feet were leading him up the steps, through the door and into the foyer, where he asked a woman sitting by a desk what he could do for that child and others like him. He could do voluntary work, she replied, and handed him a form to fill in, and advised him to go to the recruitment office, which was in a square nearby. She suggested, politely, that he ought to consider stopping off at a barber's on the way.

'That's how I lost Freddy, Virgil – to a photograph. His letter was the last contact I had with him. I don't know if he's alive or dead.'

The verb 'to comfort' and a melancholy Romanian folk song – it was impossible to forget the names of the women in Virgil's life: Alina and Doina. She would ask Radu Sava if he had ever met Alina and Doina, and he would laugh his chesty laugh and say he certainly had, because he was married to Alina, and as for Doina – oh, she would have to meet Doina in the flesh, in order to appreciate her. 'You have the phrase "Seeing is believing". Perhaps you will not believe Doina.'

Virgil had described Doina as 'spirited', but the word seemed inadequate, Kitty would think, in the face of Doina's exuberance.

'I smiled, Kitty, when there was nothing to smile about. Mine was a smiling philosophy. It was very simple. I smiled in public. I dared to look pleased with life, when life was complete shit. I waited in line for bread or meat, and when they passed by, our soldiers or our adorable secret police, I flashed them a smile, as if to say, "Shopping is such a pleasure in Bucharest." I walked with an artificial bounce in my step and smiled until my jaw ached. One day, when we have a true democracy here, I shall welcome every opportunity to parade my unhappiness, but by then I shall be old and weary and toothless, I expect.')

'You don't have any plans to wander, do you, sweetheart?'

'No, Kitty,' he protested. 'No, no, no.'

Daisy flinched as Kitty attempted to embrace her. 'I can't bear to be touched. Not by anyone.'

'Does anyone include your children?'

'They've never been what I call touchers. There's no danger of my being touched by that department.'

'Danger?'

'It's just a word, silly. Just a word. By "danger" I don't mean "danger". Of course I don't.'

'I understand.'

'I should hope so, with your famous intelligence. What are you doing here, anyway?'

'You asked me to come over and keep you company. You phoned me an hour ago.'

'Did I? Perhaps I did. I suppose I did. Well, now that you've arrived, you can make yourself useful.'

'Willingly, Daisy. How?'

I wish I could change you, Kitty thought during the long silence that followed. I wish I could influence you. I wish I could take away your rage. 'How, Daisy?'

'How what?'

'How can I be of use?'

Daisy shook her head slowly. She snorted. She said, 'You can't. No one can. I've been cast aside. Haven't I? By him, for Christ's sake. By the unlikeliest man in the world. What a Lothario. What a Casanova. What an Adonis. What a

Rudolph Valentino. What a heart-breaker. What a Don Juan. What a sight for sore eyes. What a pin-up. What a man in a million. What a charmer. What a Felix Crozier. Yes, what a handsome beast. What a vision. What a glorious vision. What a knight in shining armour. Yes, that's what he is, that's what she thinks he is. That's what.'

Kitty sat with her sister for another hour. Neither spoke. Then she rose, blew Daisy a kiss and let herself out of the quiet house.

Of all the stories he told her in those last months, none was stranger – the stranger for being true – than the one he remembered that warm Wednesday evening. He was at the stove, frying fillets of lemon sole for their supper, when he remarked that he had met a fat man that afternoon while he was working – 'Hoeing, to be precise' – in the park. He wouldn't be telling her about a fat man if the fat man hadn't talked to him. 'In a high-pitched voice, Kitty, a very high-pitched voice, like a castrato.'

The voice had startled him, and the man had smiled and said, 'I'm a bit of a freak of nature, nothing more. Don't be scared of me. When I answer the telephone at home I'm always mistaken for my wife. Dora and I have learnt to enjoy the confusion.'

The man had introduced himself as David, and he as Virgil, anglicised, and the two of them had chatted. David bred goats 'for purposes of yoghurt', which was produced by Dora and her team of willing ladies on their farm in the Midlands.

'And I revealed that I am Romanian and lucky to be in London and doubly lucky to be in love with an English-woman. He accepted a handful of raisins and waddled away – "waddled" is a good word, isn't it? – with three of the white roses he had stopped to admire.'

The man's incongruous voice, the eerie sound of it, had stayed with him for the rest of the afternoon. It was reminding him of something, but he couldn't imagine what. He had no castrati among his friends – not yet, anyway. He was perplexed.

'It wasn't until I reached the bottom of Exhibition Road that the penny dropped, as you say. It was the memory of a memory that was plaguing me. It was my mother who had heard a voice like the fat man's. When she was a girl, on a visit to the capital with her father.'

(The voice she heard, in June 1932, in the baking-hot city, belonged to the driver of the carriage the young Matilda and her Tată were driving in. They had picked up the *trăsură*, the droshky, at the Gare du Nord, and Matilda had stared in wonder at the sleek and shiny horse, and the impossibly tall man who was brushing its coat with gentle strokes. He was dressed in a black velvet robe and wore a fetching white cap. And his skin, she saw, was as soft as a woman's, as delicate as any fine lady's.

His hips were womanly, too – the ample hips of a plump matron. He had a man's slender shape down to his waist, but then his body expanded alarmingly. She stared at this phenomenon, who caught her stare and wished her good-day and lifted her into the cab. On hearing the driver speak she giggled, for the strange noise that came from his mouth seemed to belong to his soft skin and his big hips, rather than the manly parts of him. She gazed into his sad brown eyes and her fit of giggling subsided. She blushed with shame at her rudeness. She did not giggle again.

The droshky set off, with a horde of the station's sooty urchins in pursuit. Matilda's father took several small coins out of the 'beggar bag' he always carried in Bucharest and tossed them into the street. The children scrabbled after the money, shrieking and swearing and cursing the miser, the *zgîrcit*, who had not thrown notes.

Soon their cries died away and for a while Matilda was serenaded by the steady clip-clop of the horse's hoofs. She wanted to ask her father why the driver's voice was so funny, but knew that now was not the time for such a question. Ştefan Popescu, sensing her curiosity, patted her hand and whispered, 'Later.'

She learned, in the evening, at the dining-table of their relatives, the Anghelescu family, that the driver of the *trăsură* was of Russian origin and a member of a peculiar – some would say crazy; Victor Anghelescu would certainly say crazy – religious sect. To put it in a nutshell: they believed, these escaped Russians, that Christ had returned to the earth in the form of the Czar who never was, Peter the Third, who was supposed to have been murdered on the instructions of his wife, Catherine the Great. These Russians, who called themselves *Skoptzi*, maintained that Peter did not die and were convinced that he wanders from country to country, the humblest of nomads, waiting to come again in his appointed role as the Redeemer. When he is ready, he will ring the huge bell in Moscow Cathedral and the faithful will gather near him for ever.

'Yes,' said the impatient Matilda. 'Yes, but why? You haven't explained why the man speaks like a woman and has no hair on his face.'

Her father and the Anghelescus – Victor, Ana and their son George – laughed at Matilda's outburst. The more they laughed, the more irritated and bewildered she became. Why were they laughing? They should tell her.

But they were silent. They were annoyingly silent. They were smiling conspiratorially.

'Why?'

Victor looked at Ştefan and Ştefan looked at Victor, and at last it was decided that Victor would provide the explanation.

'Your driver, Matilda, is a eunuch.'

The word was new to her, without meaning. 'A eunuch? What is a eunuch?'

George, who was a month older than Matilda and already shaving, sniggered at his cousin's innocence.

'The *Skoptzi*,' Victor resumed, 'are eunuchs. The men, that is, not their wives. They marry before they become eunuchs. They have two children, so that there will be a new generation of *Skoptzi* and then they' – he looked at Ştefan, who was grinning broadly – 'and then they are parted from their manhood. With a knife. Or scissors, maybe. No, I think with a knife. It must be very, very painful. Will that do, Matilda? Does that answer you?'

Matilda thanked her uncle, although she was still confused, and Victor, who was red in the face, said that what he needed was a strong drink. It was not every day he was required to talk about eunuchs to his thirteen-year-old niece.

'Remember, Matilda, such people are fanatics.'

'Our driver was polite.'

'Even so, even so. Deep down inside he is a fanatic.'

'But he isn't deep down inside,' said George. 'He has lost the two things that make him deep.'

Then there was laughter again. Ana clapped her hands as cue for the maid to clear the plates and bring in the apricot pudding. She had had enough of eunuchs. She said so in French, to save the maid embarrassment.)

'My poor Māmică didn't discover what the knife removed until she was married. My father supplied the details. Anyway, the *Skoptzi* have all gone now, with their terrible self-defiling faith. They've disappeared, or died out. Come and see if I have cooked the fish correctly.'

She stood behind him, her arms around his waist. 'They look fine.' She kissed the back of his neck and gave him her grateful thanks for not being a fanatical disciple of Peter the Third.

'He would be crowing if he knew, wouldn't he? Our father who art not destined for heaven is who I mean. How many wives has he left in the lurch? He has probably stopped counting. If he knew what has happened to me he'd crow his head off – cockadoodle-do – the awful old lecher.'

'I think you will find, Daisy, that some of his wives left *him*.'

'They could have spared themselves the effort. They should have given him a wide berth at first sight.'

'You haven't mentioned him in ages.'

'No time like the present, then. Now that my mind's in shreds.'

('Now that my mind's in shreds' – the dramatic phrase, like the other dramatic phrases Daisy Hopkins coined that summer, was spoken flatly, despite its desperate import. 'My life's in tatters' and 'My little world's in ruins' and 'This house isn't a home, it's a prison' were dull statements of fact, it seemed, not sad revelations. Kitty Crozier listened to her in dismay.)

'The Trappists are cooking lunch today, God help us. They nagged me, would you believe, into letting them do it.'

'A nagging Trappist must be something of a novelty.'

'They're not Trappists any more when they nag me. That's when I wish they really were.'

'There's a very pleasant aroma wafting out of the kitchen.'

'I shan't be eating much. I've lost any appetite I had, thanks to him.'

'Cecil,' Kitty almost whispered.

'Him. I have an awful suspicion that Janet is making what I call a complicated sauce.'

'Oh, dear.' Kitty smiled, relishing the long-established, but now unexpected, Daisy-ism. 'That will never do.'

'Your tongue will stay stuck in your cheeks one day.'

'I hope not.'

'Let's go and find out what the chefs are up to. They've been in there the whole morning. Try and pretend everything is fine, even if it isn't.'

'We may not to have to pretend. I'm sure we won't have to.'

'You sound confident.'

The meal began with watercress soup.

'This is very good. Who made it?'

'I did, Auntie Kitty. I have to own up. It isn't too chilled, is it?'

'It's lovely, Janet.'

'It's not something I would ever make myself.'

'But do you like it, Mum?'

'Like it? Yes. Yes, I suppose I do.'

'We cooked this together,' Andrew said as he started to carve the roasted leg of lamb. 'A joint effort.'

'That could be one of *his* awful jokes. "A joint effort" is the sort of stupid thing *he* says.'

'Sorry, Ma.'

'You're forgiven.'

'There's a simple mint sauce to go with it.'

'Thank the Lord.'

'Nothing fancy, Ma. Except for the rosemary and the garlic.'

'The rosemary and the garlic,' Daisy repeated. 'The rosemary and the garlic. I see.'

'We found the recipe in your Cordon Bleu book.'

'I've never used it. I glanced at it once or twice, but I've never really used it. *He* gave it to me some Christmases ago. I don't know why.'

'Sorry, Ma.'

'You're forgiven.'

'Will you have a little?'

'No, Andrew. I will have a lot. Give me a lot. Give me an extra large helping. I'm hungry all of a sudden. I'm ravenous.'

Daisy ate everything – lamb, potatoes, peas – in a fury, Kitty thought. She appeared to be annoyed with the food her children set before her. She glowered at the meat and vegetables.

'I dispatched that lot pretty quickly,' she declared, banging her fork on the empty plate. 'I'll have some more as

soon as you slowcoaches are ready for me. My name's
Oliver Twist today.'

'Can you wait a moment, Mum?'

'Can I? Yes. Yes, I suppose I can.'

'It isn't like you to eat so much so fast.'

'You're right. It isn't. I'm usually a dainty eater. Dainty
old Daisy. Table manners personified. I'll have some more
of the Cordon Bleu lamb whenever you are ready.'

Daisy ate more lamb, in the same furious way, and said
yes, and yes again, when Janet offered her a slice of pear
tart with ginger ice-cream. Then she stood up and
announced that she was stuffed full and needed to lie down,
but not on the bed she used to share, God help her, with
him. It was the guests' room for her. That was where she
took what rest she could get, which wasn't a great deal,
not with matters as they were at present.

'We'll walk the Baskervilles, Mum.'

'The dogs? Yes, you walk the dogs. Perhaps your aunt
will go with you. If she's in a dog-walking mood.'

'I think I am, Daisy. I'll go with them. That was a splendid
lunch they gave us.'

'Was it? Yes, it was, I suppose. To give the chefs their
due, it was. They have hidden talents. And that's all the
praise they'll be receiving from me. We don't want the
Trappists feeling too pleased with themselves.'

'No, Ma.'

As Buster and Bruiser pulled Janet and Andrew towards
the park, Kitty quickened her pace to stay alongside them.

'It's a shame Virgil couldn't eat with us,' said Janet. 'He's
working, isn't he?'

'Yes, he is,' Kitty lied. The truth was that Daisy had
ordered her not to bring him. 'We don't want your
Romanian casting his gloomy pall over the proceedings.'

'I can still hear him laughing, Auntie. He made such a
wonderful noise.'

'He still does. Sometimes.'

'Are you happy with him?'

'Yes, Janet. Yes, I am.'

'Mum thinks you aren't. She doesn't understand how you can be. But then, she's no expert on happiness these days.'

'Poor Daisy.'

'Dad's happy. He's in some kind of seventh heaven. He does his best to look solemn and serious when I visit him, but it's only show. His eyes keep giving him away.'

Inside the park, once the dogs were set free and Andrew was running after them, Janet said: 'Andrew doesn't come with me. He's disgusted with Dad. He stormed out in a rage when Dad broke the news to us. He swears he'll never speak to him again. But I can't do that. I wouldn't do that.'

'No, of course not.'

'He's going to have another daughter. Gillian – that's her name, Auntie – went for a test and they're going to have a girl. Andrew hates him for starting a new family.'

'And do you?'

'I can't hate him. Or her. I ought to hate them, but I can't. I think Mum thinks I'm a bit pathetic.'

'Can you talk about her? What's your impression of her?'

'She smiles at me all the time. She dresses in mauve. What else? She has a squeaky voice. And she's seven years older than me and five and a half years older than Andrew. Which means she's young, Auntie.'

'Yes, she is.'

'She works in the City. Dad says she's very high-powered. And she's making him happy. That's all I know.'

They joined Andrew, who was stretched out on the grass, a panting dog on either side of him.

'I wish I could get inside Ma's head. I wish I knew how to help her.' He sat up. 'I wish she would just cry. If she could break down and cry then I could put my arms round her and show her what I feel. But the only thing she does is glare and there's no getting near her. I wish Ma would just bloody well cry, Aunt Kitty.'

That, Kitty felt unable to disclose, had been her own constant wish and still was. She could not remember when Daisy had last shed tears, whether of joy or sorrow. 'Be patient,' she advised her unhappy nephew. 'Try and be patient with poor Daisy.'

(It was foolish advice, she realised even as she spoke. There was no point in his being patient with his impatient mother. On the evidence of the past, he would wait in vain for Daisy's display of helplessness. Her 'splendidly average' son would have to make do with Daisy's love at arm's length. It seemed unlikely that he would ever find himself embraced by it.)

'Some people are better at crying than others, Andrew. I'm the Crozier cry-baby. Don't expect Daisy to change character overnight. She decided, long ago, that crying is a useless activity.'

Dear Kitty [she read]. You are no doubt aware that your irresponsible father has a birthday in the offing. Although he is now talking of being READY TO MEET MY MAKER (an encounter I shall not be privileged to witness, alas), he behaves with the demented coyness of a superannuated movie glamourpuss when invited to reveal his exact age.

Please descend upon us a second time, if you can muster the requisite courage. I scoured Green Park yesterday in search of the haunted Virgil and was disappointed not to find him. May I ask, impertinently, if you are together? Is he employed somewhere? I hope it is possible for him to accompany you.

Trusting that lunch on the twenty-fifth will be convenient and in joyful anticipation of a repeat performance of the monkey's bum ritual, I am,

Yours most sincerely,
Derek Harville.

'Are you in the mood for more diversion, sweetheart?'

'Always.'

'Daddy has entered his mystical phase, according to Mephistopheles.'

'You shouldn't call him that,' Virgil snapped. 'He does not merit such a description. I have met the Devil, Kitty. Believe me. He comes in many disguises and none of them resembles Mr Derek Harville. No, no. Derek is a mere imp, I assure you. He must not be judged by the devilish glint in his eyes. You really must not judge him so.'

'He's no match for your father?' The question leapt from her tongue, as though it needed to ask itself.

She was about to apologise for her crass insensitivity when he replied: 'Derek is indeed no match for my father. No match at all. Constantin Florescu is streets ahead of him. Boulevards ahead of him. Avenues and squares and motorways ahead of him. One day I will make it clear to you how much ahead of him Constantin Florescu is. But not yet, Kitty. Not quite yet.'

The treasured book of his childhood had the unappealing, uninviting title *Opere Complete*. The Complete Works. It was from the Complete Works of Ion Creangã that his mother read to him, satisfying his early craving for the mysterious and the magical.

There was one story, however, she did not finish reading. He was nine years old and able to read for himself, but because he was ill in bed with a fever his *Mãmicã* decided to spoil him. The tale he wanted to hear was the strangest and silliest in the collection. It concerns a Russian soldier, much in love with meat and vodka, who is retired from the regiment he has served since boyhood. He is sent off with only his rifle, his sword, his knapsack and two shining silver roubles. 'Ivan Turbincã', 'Knapsack Ivan', recounts his wild and comic adventures on earth, in paradise and in purgatory – and then on earth again, where Ivan is doomed to roam for ever.

'But my father came home before Ivan even got to heaven and that was the end of Mamā's bedside readings.'

'For your brother as well?'

'Oh, yes. Relu was too sensible, even at the age of six, for tall stories. He favoured the real. "That couldn't happen," he kept saying. "That's stupid." No, the fantastic was not to Relu's taste. And probably still isn't.'

(The kindly Radu Sava would take her to meet Major Aureliu Florescu. The Major would kiss her hand and welcome her to his modest apartment. He would inform her that Aureliu was not a common name in his beautiful country, and offer her tea and biscuits, or coffee and biscuits, whichever she desired.

The Major was barrel-chested, with broad shoulders. His pink face was running to fat. 'You are looking to see Virgil in me. You will not find him. We are not alike. We were never alike. We sprang from the loins of the same mother and have the same father, but there is no likeness between us.'

'No.'

'Almost from birth, apparently. You will permit me to present my daughters? All five of them. Diana and I obeyed the orders from above and swelled the ranks of Romanians. I had hoped that one of them, at least one of them, might have been a boy, but I was thwarted in my plans.'

The girls entered the room as if on cue, the youngest leading the procession. Each gave Kitty a quick curtsey before stating her name and age: 'Elena, three'; 'Grete, five'; 'Cornelia, seven'; 'Nicoleta, nine'; 'Livia, twelve.' Each had her brown hair tied with a red ribbon and each wore a navy blue velvet dress that ended just below the knees. White socks covered their ankles. Their black shoes had gold buckles.

To Kitty, who was trying hard not to receive them in the manner of visiting royalty, the Florescu girls seemed like relics from her own childhood. She could imagine Magda

Esterhazy-Williams cooing approval: 'They are five little Dresden shepherdesses. They must be the most elegant young ladies – *très, très chic* – in Bucharest. Oh, they are lovely, lovely.'

Poor Elena, poor Grete, poor Cornelia, poor Nicoleta, poor Livia, she thought as her eyes passed from one apprehensive child to another – I want to untie those ribbons; I want to free you from those ludicrous clothes; how I want you to stop simpering and preening yourselves.

She asked Radu to ask Aureliu if his daughters ever wore jeans.

'Diana is worried by tomboys. She loves grooming her pretty chicks and they love being groomed. Jeans are for tomboys and Americans.'

An impossibly pretty woman – a larger Dresden shepherdess, with false eyelashes – appeared in the doorway. She honoured Kitty with a sad smile. 'I am the wife of Aureliu. I am Diana. Your refreshments are prepared. Please to follow me into the dining-room.'

Kitty would remember with what dignity Radu Sava responded to Diana's observation that he was, perhaps, not in good health. 'You are right. I am not as well as I ought to be. We medics are notorious for not taking care of ourselves. I seldom heed the advice I give my patients.'

He might have answered her with justified bitterness, reminding the pert Diana and her slightly embarrassed husband of the gruesome facts that they surely knew – that he, one of the most respected surgeons in Romania, had been declared insane by a committee of selected experts and removed to an asylum, where he was treated with drugs that robbed him of energy and fed on stale bread and watery soup. He and his fellow 'lunatics' had been left to starve to death when news reached the remote country town of the revolution in the capital. The superintendent and his staff had given each of the inmates a last injection before they disappeared into the wintry night. 'It is good of you to express concern for me. I shall never enjoy the kind of robust health Major Florescu enjoys. These biscuits are delicious.'

'I made them to my mother's recipe. I ration myself to one and one only. A woman of my age has to keep a close watch on her shape.'

'Your children are very quiet, Doamnă Florescu. I don't hear a sound from them.'

'That is true, Domnişoară Kitty. That is as it should be. They are respectful of their elders. The walls are thin and their voices carry. Today they must be silent. We have told them who you are: a friend – not the wife, of course – a close friend of their uncle. Their peculiar uncle. Livia has some memories of him, but not the others.'

'They will laugh and play when you have gone,' Aureliu Florescu assured her. 'When I have said the little I have to say concerning my brother.'

The little he had to say, after his wife had left the room with a pitying smile aimed at Kitty, contained no revelations. Virgil, she heard, was a natural outcast, a man out of tune with the times. 'He was not a sportsman. If he had boxed or played football his life would have been easier. He lived too much inside his head.')

'Is this the prelude to another story? Tell me about the Russian soldier, then.'

The dirtiest of all the devils, the fiendish Scaraoski, was running away from his joyful tormentor when she stopped the car in front of Derek Harville's Tudor cottage.

'Happy birthday, Daddy.'

'Thank you, my dearest darling. Where are the years going? Where have the years gone?'

'A fondness for rhetorical questions is one of the more irritating characteristics your father has assumed since you were here last summer. Be prepared for a plethora of them this afternoon. Monkey's bums at the ready, if you please, Crozier.'

'Have you a monkey's bum for me, Kitty darling? I shall quite understand if you haven't.'

'Of course I have. I always have.'

'That's my daughter.'

They kissed twice, and then she hugged him.

'Welcome back, Virgil. I scoured Green Park in search of you a couple of Wednesdays ago. I fell to wondering, I confess, if you had fled the country.'

'I am in another park. I am working in Kensington Gardens.'

'Virgil's a gardener now.'

'Kitty exaggerates, Derek. I plant the bulbs and seeds as instructed and I pull out the flowers when they are dying. You are a true gardener. I am a novice.'

'Your flattery does you proud. And so does your modesty.'

'You remember Virgil, don't you, Daddy?'

'Ah, yes. The Albanian.'

'Romanian.'

'Same neck of the woods. I hope he's treating you well.'

'Ask him.'

'No, no. No necessity, I'm sure.'

'Absolutely no necessity, Crozier. I'm afraid we shall have to be housebound today. Crozier's Maker, as you can hear, is in a skittish mood regarding the weather. Or must we suppose the thunder and lightning are some kind of celestial tribute to the grand old man on his – I hesitate to risk a number – on his *umpteenth* birthday?'

'You may mock, Derek.'

'May I? That's gracious of you. May I also fetch the champagne and open it?'

'Permission granted.'

Derek Harville walked backwards out of the room.

'What a sarcastic so-and-so Derek is. Picks me up on

every word I utter.' Felix Crozier put a thumb to his nose and twiddled his fingers at his companion. 'That elegant package you're holding, my dearest darling – it isn't for me, is it?'

'Yes, Daddy. It is.'

'I hope you haven't spent money you can't afford.'

'I haven't.'

'Because your terrible father doesn't deserve expensive presents.' He tore off the wrapping paper with a child's eagerness. 'It's a tie, Kitty. A lovely silk tie. Italian, I see. Very discreet, very tasteful. You should not have bought it, but you did, and I am deeply touched. Thank you. Another monkey's bum is in order, I think, while that wretched Derek is in the kitchen.'

They kissed again, in the way he had taught her to kiss that far-off Easter, by the monkey house.

'Unhand her, Crozier, and clear the newspapers from the table.'

'Allow me.'

'You are courteous, Virgil. Toss them in the empty *jardinière, s'il vous plaît.*'

'Look what Kitty has given me, Derek. Isn't this the loveliest tie?'

'Loveliest? It's certainly becoming.'

'Only five years ago it would have been the ideal present for me. I was still a touch vain then. I admit it, I admit it. The ageing peacock still cared about his appearance, more fool he. But he has changed since his return to England. I mean *I* have changed since my return. I'm not vain any more. I am even a bit of a country bumpkin. I hardly dress up at all. Except for church, that is. I like to be presentable in church. Not ostentatious, oh no. Not that I was ever really ostentatious in my dress – just smart. I shall wear your lovely tie to Evensong this week, Kitty darling. That's a promise.'

'You never used to be a regular church-goer.'

'True, my darling, true. I led a life devoted to Mammon, and to Mammon alone, as you know all too well. I wish I could somehow compensate for my wrongdoings, but time is no longer on my side. Sitting in that Norman church –'

'Saxon, Crozier. It's Saxon.'

'Sitting in that ancient church, where so many have sat before me, I feel – oh, what do I feel? – I feel humbled. Yes, that's what I feel. And uplifted, too. Humbled and uplifted.'

'How very affecting, Crozier. Take a glass.'

'Bless you, Derek.'

'What was that work you used, Virgil? *Noroc*, wasn't it?'

'Yes.'

'Let's wish the birthday boy masses of *noroc*.'

'*Noroc*, Daddy.'

'*Noroc*, Felix.'

'Thank you, thank you. It may surprise you, Kitty, but if Daisy walked in right now, guns blazing, I would find it in my heart to be polite to her. I honestly believe I really would. What's more, I believe I could forgive her for those incredibly nasty phone calls and letters she bombarded me with.'

'But would she forgive you, Crozier? Has it not occurred to you that Kitty's termagant twin may not have achieved the state of grace her absent parent has attained – with the minimum of anguish – in his dotage?'

'I said guns blazing, Derek, and guns blazing is what I meant. What news of her, Kitty darling?'

'Nothing out of the ordinary. Nothing unusual.'

('He's not like our ghastly father, is he?' Daisy had remarked to her sister the night before her wedding. 'No one could describe Cecil as a handsome beast. I must be the only girl who has ever given him a second look. It stands to reason that I'm not infatuated with him. Besides, I'm not the type for infatuations. He's dependable, is Cecil. I want some safety, Kitty, and Cecil has safety written all over him.')

'You haven't revealed my whereabouts?'

'No, Daddy. Of course not. Consider yourself safe from Daisy's blazing guns.'

'Well, my darling, as I say, I have it in my heart to forgive and be forgiven. And how is your splendid mother?'

'Nelly's still splendid. She's off on one of her Egyptian jaunts. She sent me a postcard from the Sudan last month, with the cryptic news that she is thriving.'

'The Sudan, Kitty? My word – the Sudan. Just fancy – the Sudan. Not a place for a single woman of any age, let alone Eleanor's, the Sudan, I should imagine. I hope, for her sake, she's wearing sensible headgear. The Sudanese sun must be pretty fierce, what with the amount of sand there is. I once posed with a camel, Kitty darling. Not in the Sudan, naturally. No, this brute came from the Bronx Zoo. I had to stand alongside him – I presume he was a him; I didn't explore below – dressed in a white tropical suit and my, did the creature stink. He yawned an awful lot, I remember, and when a camel yawns it shows its yellow teeth and fouls the air with its rancid breath. Yet in the photograph, which is in one of my albums upstairs, the camel and I come across as the best of old friends – the master and his trusted steed, as it were. Not a hint of stink. But then, the camera can't capture a smell, can it?'

'The thunder's getting nearer. We shall be eating wild salmon, Virgil, as a mark of respect to your feelings. There will be no blood on our plates today.'

'You are kind, Derek.'

'I read an article just this morning about the man with the unpronounceable name who runs your country. How do you pronounce it?'

'Please do not be offended, but I would prefer not to say it. His is a name I never speak. I call him the Conducător. The Leader.'

211

'As you please, in that case. It seems that he is destroying villages and building himself a monumental palace.'

'He is, yes. He is.'

'I assume he is short in stature. The worst tyrants tend to be small. They resent having to look up at their fellow men.'

'They do. This one certainly does. When the French president, who is immensely tall, visited Romania, his height caused problems for our respectful photographers. He stood way, way above our Leader. He towered over him. The photographer who reflected this obvious fact would lose his job, even be certified insane, perhaps, since what is obvious to the man who has eyes to see is not obvious to the Conducător and the people who keep him in power. When the photographs of the two smiling presidents appeared, one was distinctly smaller than the other. The Frenchman had undergone a severe cropping – is that the term? – and was now two or three inches shorter than his host. They say the camera never lies and maybe it doesn't. But the person behind it does – when he has to; when his life is dependent on the lie itself.'

At Derek Harville's request, and to Felix Crozier's annoyance, Virgil described the Conducător's other 'endearing foibles'. He mentioned the insensible bears and the fearless hunter shooting – and sometimes missing – them at close range; Comrade Corbul, the black Labrador, riding in lone state down the Street of Victories; the gargantuan, ghost-written speeches, delivered with a robot's attention to nuance; the books of those same speeches, in a multitude of languages, attracting nothing but dust in a bookshop in the capital from which all other books are banished; the tasters of wine and food, employed to eat the presidential meat and drink the presidential claret before each and every meal – 'There might be a poisoner in the building. The tasters perform this daily ritual to protect the Conducător and his consort. It is of no importance if they foam at the mouth and die. That's their duty.'

'The notion of poisoning Crozier, with a dash of ratsbane in the beef stew or the *poulet à l'estragon*, has not lost its appeal for me. Did the tasters apply for the job, Virgil? Did they supply references from other demented, but satisfied, employers?'

'Oh, that is – that is – that is – that is *felicitous*.'

(Her lover shouted the word he had struggled to find. Virgil's triumphant '*felicitous*' was the prelude to an out-pouring of laughter that followed a now familiar course. He spluttered to begin with and tried to say 'felicitous', but could not get beyond the second syllable. A sound from somewhere deep in his throat rose steadily higher and higher and ended, eventually, in a gasp for breath. Then he sighed and said 'felicitous' quietly.

'That was his last outburst,' she would tell Dinu Psatta in Paris. 'I never heard him laugh like that again.')

'Are you finished, Virgil?'

'Yes. Yes, I am.'

'You are the perfect audience, the ideal listener. My witti-cisms usually fall with a thud on the none too responsive ears of Crozier, who is slow to appreciate the pearls I cast before him. But you are generous with your laughter and I am grateful to you.'

'I used to be frightened of thunderstorms, Kitty darling. I was a real cowardy-custard. I crawled under tables and hid in wardrobes. I turned to instant jelly as soon as a storm started. Not any more, though. I'm not hiding, am I?'

'No, you aren't hiding, you brave soul. You are courage incarnate. We are drawing inspiration from your heroic presence among us.'

'Mock on, Derek. Mock on. I need my lunch. I'm starv-ing. And so is Kitty's friend, if I am any judge of appearances.'

'He has a name, Crozier. Call him Virgil.'

213

'I am only peckish, Felix. I do not starve in England.'

'You're too thin, young man. Peckish, indeed. Even in my heyday, when I was svelte, I had a healthy appetite. Peckishness is for women. You could do with fleshing out.'

'Could I?'

'Yes, you could. You're lost inside those clothes. That jacket is several sizes too big for you. I'm not the snappy dresser I once was, I admit, but at least everything I wear fits me. Nothing fits you, young man. Your shoes, yes, but nothing else. I'm surprised Kitty allows you out of the house.'

'Don't be surprised, Daddy.'

'Where on earth do you get them?'

'My clothes, Felix?'

'Exactly.'

'In shops. You have such shops here that sell – what is the word? – cast-offs. I wear cast-offs. I am happy to wear things other people have worn.'

('I love to hold a book that has passed from hand to hand. I feel a kinship with the readers who were there before me. It's as if I am communing with them when I turn the pages.'

The feeling had come to him first in early childhood, he told her, and had never deserted him. The thought of his great-grandparents reading the story of Harap Alb by candle-light from the selfsame book his mother had just left at his bedside was strangely exhilarating. 'They were dead, Kitty, but I felt they were with me. In spirit.'

The copy of George Herbert's *Poems*, which he was to buy at a stall on the Left Bank and which she would take out of the Galeries Lafayette bag when she knew he was gone from her life, had been the property of a Mr Cedric Tiverley, who had acquired it on 19 September 1895, as his yellowed *ex libris* testified. 'I am passing Mr Tiverley's precious book on to you. It is not a cast-off, like the clothes I wore that so upset the stylish Felix. Mr Tiverley died, I think, and then it set off on its travels. Now it is travelling from me to you, with love.')

'Each to his own, of course, but I wouldn't be happy in somebody else's cast-offs. There's no way of knowing who that somebody else is or was, is there? He might be the world's worst scoundrel. And then there's the matter of somebody else's body odour. However much you boil his shirts or clean his trousers, his smell is always present, however faint. I presume you draw the line at underpants?'

'Me? Yes, Felix. I draw the line.'

'Let us draw a line under you, Crozier, and go in and eat. The sooner your mouth is occupied with food, the better the day will be for Kitty and Virgil, and your embarrassed factotum.'

'I meant no offence, Derek.'

'All is made clear. That was ingratiating charm you were exhibiting. How imperceptive of me.'

'I am not offended, Derek. I am truly not offended.'

After lunch, Felix Crozier talked of his impending death. Soon, too soon, he would be in a place where there was no cucumber mousse, no salmon, no mayonnaise, no Jersey potatoes, no gooseberry fool, no Sauvignon Blanc, no Armagnac – no, not one of the delicacies his good but mocking friend Derek had set before them. It was his profound hope that Derek would continue to treat himself to these modest luxuries when the subject of his mockery was six feet underground. Did he have Derek's promise, Derek's solemn word, that this would be the case?

'You are drunk, Crozier. You are as drunk as a maudlin skunk.'

'Not maudlin, Derek. Heaven forfend. I am merry. I am a little merry, as an old man deserves to be on his birthday.'

On the journey back to London he finished telling her the 'half-told story' of Ivan, the soldier who – unlike Felix, if Felix was to be believed – cannot abide the idea of dying.

215

God has granted him a glimpse of Paradise, where he was
bored, and he has been to Hell, too, which was more to
his taste, but overall he prefers the known world of rivers
and forests, of firelit taverns, of whores and vodka. When
Death comes to see him he decides he must outwit her –

'Her, Virgil? Is Death a woman?'

'In the folk tales, yes, because my ancestors – in their
wisdom, or lack of it – regarded Death as God's hand-
maiden, doing his bidding. Sometimes she seems capricious
– striking down the young and healthy, snatching the new-
born baby from its grieving mother – but to the old and
weary she is a welcome guest. Not to Ivan, though. He is
determined to cheat her. He wants what you call the last
laugh.'

When he was a boy, reading and rereading 'Ivan Tur-
bincă', reading it so often that he knew whole passages by
heart, he was most amused, most excited, by Ivan's cleverest
trick, the ultimate *coup de main*. Ivan has been commanded
by his exasperated God to quit fooling – 'Creangă did not
write "quit fooling", Kitty. I heard "quit fooling" in a
movie' – to quit fooling with Death, who has complained
to Him about Ivan's mad behaviour. God releases Death
from Ivan's knapsack and warns the soldier, who was once
kind and compassionate, that enough is enough. Ever since
God blessed the knapsack, giving it supernatural powers,
Ivan has got above himself and now must rue his fate. It is
Ivan's turn to die; it cannot be avoided. Ivan is contrite and
beseeches God, with tears in his eyes, to grant him three
days in which to cleanse his soul and make his own coffin.
God answers his final prayer, deprives him of his knapsack
and instructs Death to take Ivan away after three days.

With his two silver roubles Ivan buys wood, cords,
hinges, nails, a pair of rings and a strong chain, and starts
to construct his 'everlasting house'. On the fourth day, while
he is standing back and admiring his work, and thinking
of the earth that will cover his beautiful little house, Death

appears behind him and asks if he is ready. He smiles at her. Yes, he is ready.

Death is relieved to hear this and suggests that he get into the coffin immediately. There is no time to lose, she says. She had people to visit who were waiting for their passports.

It is then that Ivan performs the cleverest of his clever tricks. He gets into the coffin and lies face downwards. Death is mildly irritated by his silliness and tells him to lie in the proper position for a corpse, so he moves on to his side, letting his feet hang out. Death is beginning to be annoyed and reminds him that she is in a hurry. Will he please behave like a sensible corpse? Ivan turns on his other side, with his head dangling and his feet still hanging out, and Death responds with words that are music to him. She calls him a fool and orders him to get up from the coffin. She will show him the correct position for eternal rest.

Ivan watches with feigned humility as Death demonstrates what ought to be obvious to him. She lies down in the coffin with her face uppermost, her feet stretched out, her hands on her breast and her eyes closed – Death herself pretending to be dead. '"Look, Ivan, this is how you do it."'

'He slams the lid on her. Is that what happens?'

'Yes, Kitty.'

And that's what amused him, that moment in the story when Ivan becomes the man who coffins Death. It seemed a wonderful joke to a boy of nine recovering from influenza. Years later, in *liceu*, it seemed a wonderful notion, too, when he was reminded of Ivan's tiny, short-lived triumph by a line of John Donne's: 'Death, thou shalt die.'

The bold and confident Ivan has forgotten, or overlooked, the bargain he has struck with God. He lifts up the coffin and carries it to the river and throws it into the fast-flowing water, wishing it a swift voyage to Hell. The Apostle Peter, witnessing this unprecedented scene from above, draws

God's attention to Ivan's arrogance. ' "He said well, Lord, who said 'Give them an inch and they will take a mile'." '

God releases Death from the coffin so that she might revenge herself upon her captor. When she stands before the old soldier he is petrified. She speaks to him for the very last time. He listens in silence as she scolds him for his obstinacy and for trying even God's boundless patience to its limits. From now on, she says, he will long to die; he will drag himself in her footsteps, begging her to take his soul. God has commanded her to ignore Ivan, and to let him live on and on and on, so that he will learn that life can be insufferable.

Death abandons him to life with the words: 'As long as light and earth exist the wind will not put out the fire.' And Ivan's fire, fuelled by brandy and strong spirits, will never be extinguished. Death has turned a blind eye on him and he will live for centuries, trying not to go mad with boredom.

'Because I was young, Kitty, I did not understand that the silly story has a tragic ending. How could I? I had no idea what boredom was. And what was so terrible about being alive for ever? Being dead was far, far worse, I thought. I am afraid I have been telling you too many stories.'

'You can't tell me too many.'

'These last weeks I have been – which is the best word I can use? – *garrulous*. Yes, that is the best one. I have been garrulous. Forgive me.'

'There's nothing to forgive.'

'You are sure?'

'Yes, sweetheart.' She patted his knee. 'Yes, I am.'

'I have been confused. Is that what I mean to say? They have been crowding out my brain, these stories. I have needed to share them with you.'

'I know you have.'

(He is giving me his childhood: the realisation came to

218

her, she would recall, on a roundabout in Purley. He is giving me the stories that brightened his childhood.

It struck her, then, that this might be his parting gift to her. Her hands tightened on the wheel.)

' "I presume you draw the line at underpants?" ' she asked as she undressed him that evening. 'Or is my presumption false?'

'No, Kitty. I do draw the line at underpants. You must believe me, even if your sceptical father doesn't.'

Dear Kitty [she read]. I have never had much cause to write to you before, apart from Christmas cards and the odd thank-you letter. Here goes.

This is a mammoth task for yours truly. Business correspondence has never been a problem, as you can no doubt imagine, but I am not writing to you about stocks and shares and high finance in general. I almost wish I was (or is it were? You are the grammarian, so please excuse any basic howlers!). It would certainly be easier.

Let me begin by saying that I have always admired you. I like your independent spirit. You are the chalk to Daisy's cheese. You have a quiet strength of character. It is not my intention to flatter you, although flattery is nothing less than you deserve. I feel this is the truth I am writing.

On with the mammoth task. I have left Daisy for another woman. You know this already. I want to take this opportunity to explain why, if I can, not being the sort of person who finds it easy to deal in words with matters of the heart. I am in love. It is as simple (and as complicated!) as that. The amazing fact is that Gillian loves me in return. She is young enough to be my daughter, just about. You will not be surprised to learn that I was the subject (object?) of much sniggering in the Exchange when our affair started. That's over now. The sniggering. Everyone can see that I am seriously smitten

219

and now sowing my last crop of wild oats. I am going to be a father again, which you also know.

If you have made it this far, please continue. The hardest part is yet to come. For me, the ham-fisted writer. Bear with me. I have left Daisy in the proverbial lurch, but I mean to see that her nest is properly feathered. She will not be short of money. She may even find herself with too much for her needs. Money isn't everything, they say (I have never met anyone who says that and really means it, but 'they' exist), though Daisy won't be averse to it, all the same. She enjoys her few creature comforts. I will ensure (and insure!) that she goes on enjoying them. That is the least I can do for her. I can afford to be generous in this regard, if no other.

I am a bit in knots now. There *is* another way in which I can show generosity, and that is by harbouring no bitterness or rancour *vis-à-vis* our long marriage. Daisy and I had the absolute minimum of squabbles. We were reasonably happy together, it seems to me, and when there were any dark clouds above us they soon passed quickly. From the very beginning, before the kids came along, Daisy insisted on running the household like a captain runs a ship. Her First Mate seldom complained. In actual fact he (I!) was quite satisfied with the arrangement. I might have gone on being quite satisfied with it if I hadn't fallen in love.

Did I ever think I would be writing these words one day? And to you? Only nine months ago, not in a million years. Let me claim in my defence that I was frightened to begin with. I was scared out of my wits. I am not a vain man, though I say so myself, but I took to staring in every available mirror in order to see what she sees in me. I saw plain Cecil Hopkins and nobody else. A case of 'In the eye of the beholder', I suppose. I was the Frog transformed into the Prince, except it was the Frog who was staring back at me.

Please persevere. I want you of all people to understand the situation (alias mess!). I tried my level best to put Gillian off, but to no avail. I only caved in and decided to take the proverbial plunge when Daisy returned from her trip to India. That was the turning point. That was the crunch. I was hoping Daisy would surprise me, Kitty. I was hoping (against hope?) that she would come back to me a new woman, full of new-found enthusiasm. I reasoned, during her absence, while I was holding my feelings for Gillian in check, that the experience of India might change Daisy for good and all. I was hoping to find her brimming with excitement, with lots of interesting and amusing anecdotes to pass on. I almost hoped she would be sporting a sari as she came through customs! Fond hope. She was even more like the old Daisy than ever, if that doesn't strike you as double Dutch. She was Daisy in spades. My every question was answered with a complaint. When I asked her to describe the sights and smells of India, she embarked on a diatribe about sacred cows' poop (shit to the rest of us!). I laughed and was duly reprimanded. She was serious. It is her (considered?) opinion that India stinks. As you have no doubt heard, *ad nauseam*.

I am skating on thin ice here and may very well sink. If there was a moment (decisive? deciding?) when I thought 'Gillian, it's you now, I'm sorry I've kept you waiting' it was when Daisy got on her high moral horse regarding your poor long dead grandfather. It dawned on me that I had spent twenty years of married life ignoring (or putting up with, or laughing at, but with no smile on my face) Daisy's intolerant views on other people's behaviour. I was accustomed to listening with half an ear, and sometimes with no ear at all (logic?). But when she let rip on sad Mr McGregor's cowardice(!) I told her to shut up. I told her I had heard enough.

If anyone should be accused of cowardice it's me. On

the day I moved myself out of Richmond and into Clerkenwell I wrote Daisy a letter. (I wasn't such a coward with the kids. I poured my heart out to them.) It was a short letter (not like this endless screed!) giving the bare facts. A stronger man would have told his wife to her face that he was leaving her, but not me, I'm afraid. It wasn't so much that I lacked courage. What scared me is that I would end up pitying her and put the damper (or is it dampener?) on any future happiness. I have pitied her for years. Pity is a demeaning thing to feel for another person, especially someone so close to you. I have been torn apart with pity for Daisy at times. I can't help myself. Perhaps I knew I wouldn't have been able to help myself when I chose not to tell her in the flesh. I am more of a coward than the tea planter. And that's the awful truth!

Be patient a little longer. The mammoth task is nearing completion. Thank you, Kitty, for reading this far (if you have! But somehow I know you have) and for your kindness to the Hopkins family while it lasted. I want to express my esteem for you for the way you handle your sister. You never allow yourself to become her whipping boy (ought to be whipping girl, but she's not in the dictionary!) and I have to admire (so do the kids) the good humour you always display when Daisy is throwing her casual insults at you. The kids and I think you are really remarkable. And remarkably tolerant.

Janet is bearing up under the strain of her parents' separation and I am sure she will survive the once-in-a-lifetime (definitely!) experience. Andrew isn't speaking to me. I appreciate what he is going through. He loves his mother deeply. His love shows in his embarrassment. Since Daisy is incapable of being embarrassed herself, Andrew assumes the responsibility instead. Hence his blushes and groans . . .

I hear from Janet that you and the intriguing Virgil remain happy together. Give him a message from me.

Next year Gillian and I (and the new arrival, touch wood) are planning a holiday in Crete. It is my ambition to meet and chat to a Socrates, to add him to the Homer and Virgil I have already 'scalped'! I would wager a large amount of money that Virgil's command of the English language is more secure than mine. How can I say that Gillian has lightened my dull life, and not just in the bedroom, which is entirely our business? I can't, adequately. I am more at home with the beautiful abstraction that is mathematics than I am with words.

Let us keep in touch.

With kind wishes, Kitty, and with love,

Cecil.

('Stay with me a while, Virgil. Your father wishes to give you a history lesson.'

'What kind of history lesson?'

'The kind, my cultivated son, you did not receive in *liceu*. In the cemetery, as your gloomy poet called it. This will be a lesson from life. The life I have lived.'

'It is a lesson in survival, then.'

'Partly. Fetch yourself a glass and drink some of this excellent *ţuică*, Eduard's wife, Pia, has made.'

'Her *ţuică* is too powerful for me. I do not have your constitution, Tată.'

'I am the ox and you are the fawn. That is apt, is it not?'

'Have you forgotten the lesson?'

'No, no. I should not have said I am the ox. I am the elephant, who does not forget. Sit down. You are restless, as ever. Sit down, Virgil.'

'If you please.'

'Permit me to collect my thoughts. I wish to talk to you about a Romania – *the* Romania – you were born too late for.'

'You have talked a thousand times about your glorious youth. This is a history I know too well.'

'You are wrong. This is a history of which you are ignorant. How many Jews have you met?'

'Not many. We do not have *many* Jews to meet. There is a brilliant scholar, Marcel Antip, here in the city. Professor Costea hosted a reception for him once, after his lecture on my majestic namesake. He is a delightful, modest man.'

'Did you speak to him?'

'Yes, I did. I said little. I was – and am – in awe of him. I listened to him and learned much.'

'Does he have freckles on his face?'

'Freckles? I did not see any.'

'I remember lots of freckles. Freckles, freckles, freckles. And red hair.'

'This is going to be a Jewish history lesson, is it?'

'You listened to him – this – this –'

'Marcel Antip.'

'You listened to him. Now listen to me. Did Matilda ever tell you the tale of the bowl of soup and the boiled cockerel?'

'No.'

'You sound certain.'

'I am. Every story Mamã told me is – is *engraved* on my memory.'

'You remain your mother's son. I do not have her flair, her knack, but I will do my best to piece it together for you. I heard it first when I was a small boy – long, long ago. I was a devout Christian child and believed it to be true.'

'I am listening.'

'Good. That is all I am asking of you. The story begins on the night of Christ's resurrection, with a group of Jews gathered round a dinner table. A large tureen of soup, with a boiled cock-bird inside it, is brought in and put down in front of them. They start to discuss the resurrection. Did it really happen? Was it a miracle? Was it an illusion? They cannot make up their minds. Then one of them, a doubting Thomas, says in a loud, vulgar voice that if such a thing as

Christ being resurrected were possible then they might as well expect the cock inside the tureen to return to life. No sooner has he spoken than the cock, with a mighty crow, leaps up, flapping his wings and sprinkling them all over with soup. And that is how the Jew came by his freckles.'

'Which I did not see on Marcel Antip's face.'

'No? I saw them on hundreds of faces, because there were many, too many, Jews in our country when I was young. You could not move out of your door in the Bucovina without seeing a Jew with the fur of a red fox on his hat. And talking of red fox fur, we had a Jewess installed in her own special villa near the royal palace – Madame Lupescu, the mistress of Carol the Second, our apology for a king. She was his du Barry, his Pompadour, his pet she-wolf. He ruled us with the bitch Lupescu's consent. There was no other conniving Jewess behind no other European throne. That was our unique privilege.'

'I am still listening.'

'They were everywhere. They owned everything. In the cities, they had banks and stores and buildings to let, and in the towns and villages they ran the shops that supplied the materials our women craved – silks and velvets and organdie. Even the poorest of them – *not* many – had enough money to run a tavern, where they served the peasants watered-down drinks. Not like this *ţuică*. This is the pure stuff.'

'Is that the end of the lesson?'

'No. No, my fidgety son, it is not. I promised you a history lesson from life and I will keep my promise. Most, if not all, of my brothers-in-arms are dead and I may be the very last survivor. The one last witness. Be attentive. The horse's mouth is about to open for you.'

'Tată, you are getting drunk.'

'I was drunk on my wedding night, Virgil. I have rarely been more than slightly inebriated since. A drunkard does not stay in office. A drunkard is not entrusted with impor-

225

tant information. A drunkard becomes an outcast, like that wretched poet you worship so much. Are you prepared to pay attention?'

'If you wish.'

'I wish you would. The horse's mouth will soon have to be bridled again. It may be the only one left. On the night of January the twenty-second nineteen forty-one – there, my boy, I have given you the exact date – I was involved in an event that could not be averted. It was destined to happen. It was on the cards. It was fated. That was what we believed, my brothers-in-arms and I – my young, handsome, idealistic brothers-in-arms. We were the legionaries of the Archangel Michael. We had the future of Romania in our minds and hearts, a future that had no place for the freckled scum from Russia and Poland who were everywhere in our country. Our united country was not even a century old, and here it was infected already by usurers and pawn-brokers. They were everywhere. They owned everything.'

'You are repeating yourself.'

'Of course I am. I want to impress upon you, in your ignorance, just how many of them there were, with their greasy locks and gabardines and hissing voices. You have me to thank, and my brave brothers-in-arms, for the fact that their numbers were reduced. If they had all been modest scholars we would not have done what we felt – what we felt passionately – we had to do. We would have left them to their harmless studies. But those people were not modest. They were not modest when they were go-betweens for the boyars: modest men do not demand money from the starving peasants. No, no. They bowed and scraped and pretended to be humble, and a vile pretence it was. Modesty does not make a man wealthy. They were bleeding us. They were bleeding us weak. And that is why we bled them.'

'Bled?'

'Yes. In the slaughterhouse, on the night of January the twenty-second nineteen forty-one, when I was a young,

Christian patriot. My brothers-in-arms and I rounded them up, as many as we could find, two hundred or more, and forced them – squealing like the pigs they do not eat – into the slaughterhouse, where we killed them the way they kill their cattle. They bled. And as they bled we sang the hymns, the Christian hymns, their vast scattered tribe despises. We sang of Our Lord rising from the dead and of His birth in the stable. It was for us a mystical occasion. And now I want you to understand that I feel no shame or guilt. I was caught up in an act of Christian brotherhood, or retribution. And I survived. I am here to tell the tale. My brothers were shot – by the army, Virgil – but I disappeared. I disappeared and I came back, then I disappeared again. It is a gift I have. It is a necessary gift, Virgil. Just think of it! The Russians themselves would have executed me for doing what I believed was my Christian duty. The stinking Russians, who exterminated millions of the chosen race. We had no extermination camps in Romania. Not one. Not a single one. We had a few *events*, that was all. Stop squirming. I am not shit under your shoe. I am your father. The history lesson is over. What had to be done was done. They were what they were. And what they were was no longer acceptable.')

'Talk to me, sweetheart.'

He laid his head on her breast and talked to her.

When she awoke each morning he was there beside her, sleeping lightly.

This guest-house, which was called Braeview, had a gong outside the dining-room. Mrs McFarland, the owner, had warned Mr and Mrs Florescu that she was in the habit of banging it vigorously on the dot of eight, to summon her laggards down to breakfast. She banged it now, with the promised vigour. 'It's the only serious exercise I get.'

Mr and Mrs Florescu's short honeymoon in Scotland was almost at an end.

'The gong has sounded, Virgil. Tea and marmalade await the newly-weds.'

'The mature newly-weds. The doddering newly-weds.'

The table Mrs McFarland chose for them offered a panoramic view of the usually visible brae, but a September mist was shrouding it at present, which she hoped would clear before too long.

'I see no marmalade.'

'I can fetch you marmalade, Mr Florescu, if that's your desire. May I invite you to be a wee bit adventurous and try something different? I make my own jams and there's one I'm especially proud of, I have to confess.'

'I shall try it. Thank you.'

They ordered porridge and scrambled eggs, and when they had finished eating Mrs McFarland brought them a pot of her special jam.

'Taste it.' She spooned a glistening, dark-red dollop on to his plate. 'Let me have your verdict.'

'It is exquisite, I should say. It is truly delicious.'

'Can you identify the fruit?'

'I am not sure. It is a berry of some kind.'

'It is, indeed. Wild raspberry, to be precise. We have wild raspberries in Scotland. This was made with last year's crop.'

'Oh, it is exquisite. You are kind, Mrs McFarland. It is simply exquisite.'

'Are those tears in your eyes, Mr Florescu? I've received my fair share of compliments for the wild raspberry jam, but no one has ever wept over it before.'

'It is bringing to me a memory.'

'Not a happy one, by the looks of it.'

'A happy one. Yes, yes. A happy one.'

'That's good. Will you still be requiring marmalade?'

'No. No, thank you.'

'Then I'll leave you in peace.'

They ate in silence.

'Is it such a happy memory? Is it, Virgil?'

'When I was a boy –' he began and smiled. 'I always seem to be saying that these days. I apologise for the predictable beginning.'

When he was a boy, he said, his mother often tantalised him with visions of fragile pastries and richly scented sweets and chocolates in a vanished *cofetărie* she had visited during far-off summer holidays. It had seemed to her a fairy-tale place, but it was real enough and famous throughout the Balkans. The shop belonged to a Greek family named Kalinzachis in the town of Sinaia, a popular resort where the king had a residence. Matilda Popescu's favourite delicacy was a preserve of wild raspberries from the Carpathians. The fruit was sometimes difficult to find, because the *zmeure salbatice* were loved by the mountain bears, who risked being shot by hunters in order to feast on them.

'It was a happy memory for *Mămică*. From the time when her life was carefree.'

(On their pretend honeymoon, she discovered a new aspect of Virgil's character. For an avowed lover of cities he was surprisingly knowledgeable about birds that live mostly in the countryside. The sore-throated laugh that sounded as if it were mocking them as they picnicked in a field on the edge of a pine forest belonged to a disappearing jay, he informed her with obvious pleasure. 'It looks pinkish when it is still and rather plump, but when it is in the air it shows the blue and black stripes on its wings. It has a white bottom also. Do you see the beautiful stripes?' The jay let out a final scream before vanishing into the trees.

'You must accept my word that those are migrant red-breasted flycatchers passing over us, eating as they go,' he said to her three days later. 'Yes, I am sure that is what they are. The black-and-white tails are distinctive. We are very lucky, very fortunate, they are flying so close to earth. They are enjoying their last Scottish meal, I should imagine.'

How, she wondered, tickling him, had Mr Florescu

acquired his ornithological expertise? He giggled and begged her to stop. There was a simple explanation, if she would kindly remove her roving hands.

'When I began to learn English in earnest I needed books, any books, as many books as I could find. I had an English Grammar, and an out-of-date phrase book and some newspaper articles. I had a comic book with silly words like "Bam" and "Wham" and "Zap" and "Zonk". It was too soon for Shakespeare and Keats, far too soon, but I managed to read a novel by P. G. Wodehouse without realising, alas, that it was supposed to be humorous. I was desperate for English sentences to unravel and put back together. Then, one wonderful morning a school-friend gave me a book his father had picked up on a train – abandoned, he assumed, by that rarest of creatures, a tourist. It was called *A Guide to the Birds of Europe*. I read it, reread it and studied the photographs, and lo and behold, I was an expert. If the book had been *A Guide to the Fish of Europe* instead, or *A Guide to the Trees of Europe*, or any other such guide, I would be dazzling you with a different kind of expertise. I am, perhaps, not quite so clever, Kitty. My knowledge is accidental.'

In Edinburgh, at the start of the holiday, after Kitty had shown him the imposing stone house in the New Town in which Nelly had been born and raised, a sudden strong wind nearly blew them along the crescent. They turned into a side street and entered a wine bar. While they waited for a table Virgil spoke a poem by Montale to her – 'His only Edinburgh poem, as far as I can tell' – and translated 'Vento sulla Mezzaluna' into 'approximate English'. She would remember the image of the preacher on the crescent who asked the poet 'Do you know where God is?', received an unexpected answer and was lifted up by the whirling wind into a darkness above the city. 'I should like to meet a fire-and-brimstone preacher, Kitty. And see him carried off like that. Is Scotland still the place for him?')

That evening, strolling back to Braeview, they were brought to a halt by the eerie sound of a woman singing to the accompaniment of a harmonium. They saw, through the open window of a room lit by an oil lamp, that the woman was old and toothless, and playing the instrument herself. They strained to catch the words she was wailing, but could only make out the repeated phrase 'And love will waste my body'. Sensing that she was being watched, she turned her head and took her hands from the keys, and screeched what they assumed, from her expression, was an obscenity. They resumed their stroll and the woman her wailing.

'"And love will waste my body",' Virgil whispered.

'Not yet, sweetheart.'

The next day, as they were leaving, Mrs McFarland presented them with two jars of her wild raspberry jam. 'I shall always think of you as the gentleman who wept with joy when he tasted it. It was joy, wasn't it?'

'Yes. Thank you. It was.'

'Godspeed, Mr and Mrs Florescu.'

That Christmas they followed the progress of the revolution in Romania on a television set Nelly had hired for Virgil's benefit.

'These must be troubling days for you.'

'Very troubling, from such a distance, yes. I am finding it somewhat unbelievable. Too good to be true, perhaps. At the moment, Nelly, it is far too good to be true. But I may be wrong. I hope most fervently that I am wrong.'

(The Conducător, protected against the fierce December cold in a heavy greatcoat and lambskin hat, stands on the balcony of the Central Committee building and waves to the working people who have just been assembled in the square below. He has come to convince them that all is well, despite the rumblings from distant Timişoara. He has plans to better their lives, with promises of food, of higher wages, of the inevitable 'improved conditions'. The droning old man anticipates applause, but suddenly there is booing and yelling from the back of the crowd. Someone shouts 'Timişoara!' The sounds of disrespect and discontent are taken up by others and soon there is scarcely anyone who is silent. The Conducător, who has always been assured by his advisers that the ordinary citizens of Romania love him as a father, is startled by this unaffectionate display. He mumbles the word '*aceasta*' before speech deserts him. His expression changes from incomprehension to amazement to something like terror. His burly bodyguard warns him that the crowd is moving nearer and the voice of his unseen consort is heard, ordering the man to be quiet ... and the picture of the terrified leader is blacked out; the direct transmission terminated.)

'It is pleasing to me to see fear in his eyes. So the cunning fox is finally trapped. It is a pleasing spectacle.' He smiled and added: 'There are other foxes, though. Masses of them. Some have gone to earth already, I should not wonder.'

On the morning of Christmas Eve, when it seemed that Romania had been liberated from tyranny, Virgil – who had stayed awake the entire night – rose from the kitchen table and announced that he needed to take a solitary, thought-collecting walk. 'I have too many ideas and not enough intelligence.'

He kissed Kitty's hair and closed the kitchen door quietly behind him. His feet scrunched the gravel on the driveway.

'Now we can deal with trivial matters,' Nelly said. 'Until Virgil returns. I mean comparatively trivial matters, like your rejected sister's state of mind. I am concerned for her, Kitty, as I haven't been for years. She is behaving rather as she behaved after Felix – there's a trivial subject – abandoned us for his heart-throb with the headaches. I was shocked when I saw her last week. I was so shocked, in fact, that I suggested she come here with the children. Thank

232

God she declined. Tantrums *à la* Daisy *and* the Romanian revolution – no, no, I couldn't have coped.'

'I had a rambling letter from Cecil. He loves this young woman. I can't believe he ever loved Daisy as deeply.'

'As deeply as she loved him? Let's be more serious than trivial for a moment. What distresses me about Daisy is that I find it impossible to sustain a conversation with her. I dread saying even perfectly simple things in her presence. She asked me yet again why I visit Egypt so often and I was unable to tell her the truth. It's my undying fascination with the Valley of the Kings, I said. I'm still keeping Omar a secret from her, because I don't want to give her another reason for reproving me.'

'I give her plenty of scope for disapproval, Nelly. Virgil does, too. It's a pity she and Daddy can't compare notes. The one thing that unites them is their contempt for my "daft Romanian park attendant". That's a fairly recent Daisy-ism, if you didn't recognise the tone.'

'I despair of her. I hate to play Cassandra, but I predict she might go to pieces once Cecil's girlfriend has had their baby. When is it due?'

'February. Late February.'

'We shall batten down the hatches in February then. Be on Daisy alert, Kitty. Be prepared for disaster.'

Virgil came back in the early afternoon. 'I have walked miles, but my thoughts are no clearer. I should like to accompany you to church tonight.'

'Of course you may. No need to ask.'

'I should like to hear Christian hymns in the appropriate setting.'

'The vicar will be pleased to see you again. You must be hungry and thirsty. Would you care for a beer while I rustle up some onion tart and salad?'

'You are kind, Nelly. Yes, I should like a beer.'

'Kitty is glued – as we say – to the television. It really does seem that your country will soon be free.'

233

'It does seem so, yes. I will join her. I too will be glued.'
He smiled. '"Glued to the television" is good. It is a new
turn of phrase for me.'

('He is the Emperor's personal poet, Kitty,' said Virgil,
identifying the fat man in a black cloak who was being
jostled by the crowd. 'No, not a poet. He is a versifier. He
was a poet when he wrote for his own pleasure. Then he
began to evacuate – yes, "evacuate" is the *mot juste* – hundreds and hundreds of wretched verses in praise of the
nation's saviour, and hundreds and hundreds more of an
even worse wretchedness, and his talent – his small, but
genuine talent – bade him a last goodbye. That's him, the
unstoppable Adrian. You remember my telling you the
Securitate visited upon me a silent thug called Adrian, along
with the vacuous expert on Emily Dickinson? That was a
literary joke for my amusement. The name Adrian is not
associated with wordlessness. Ha, ha, ha. Ho, ho, ho. They
have brains as well as muscle, our resourceful secret
policemen. And women.'

A second poet – 'He is honourable. He has courage' –
appeared on the screen. 'He is not lost for words. He has
been unable to speak for several months.' An actor – 'Our
Romeo, our Hamlet' – stood beside him. Virgil could identify most of the people crammed inside the television studio
the revolutionaries had seized. 'Radu is not there. Radu
should be there. I wonder where is Radu.')

She held his hand throughout the midnight service.
Prayers were said for the sick, the bereaved, the lonely, and
for the martyrs and victors of the Romanian revolution.

They drank whisky on their return. The previous year,
Kitty and Virgil had danced to Nelly's records of Fred
Astaire, the dapper idol of her girlhood, and Virgil had
surprised them both by singing, or growling, 'Black Mountain Blues': 'I am not a jazz fiend, as are many of my friends,
Radu in particular, yet I do love Bessie Smith. I found this
easy to learn.'

234

'Black Mountain people are bad as they can be
Black Mountain people are bad as they can be
They uses gunpowder just to sweeten their tea,'

he sang, in an impossible American accent, which only made
him sound more Romanian than he did when speaking.

'I'm bound for Black Mountain
Me and my razor and guns
I'm gonna shoot him as he stands still
And cut him as he runs,'

he growled, with his eyes shut tight for concentration.

They had applauded him and demanded an encore, but
he had laughed, saying 'That is the beginning and end of
my repertoire. There is nothing else I can sing.'

Now they sat round the kitchen table, talking quietly.

'I fear very much those students, those martyrs, have died
fruitless deaths. I fear they have died in vain. It may be that
they were simply murdered.'

'Perhaps your fear is unfounded, Virgil.'

'Perhaps.'

(Radu and Alina Sava would take her to the bleak cemetery in the northern part of Bucharest where the murdered
students and schoolchildren were buried. She would read
the messages on the obelisks that marked their graves – 'My
dear parents and brothers, please forgive me for leaving you
when I was only thirteen. Octavian Burcioaila – "Tavi"' –
and gaze at the bright and confident faces that stared out of
the photographs. Beyond the burial ground were apartment
blocks resembling beehives. 'Buzzing with misery,' Alina
would comment. 'The families in those beehives must often
wish they were over here.')

'That is convenient. That is very convenient,' Virgil muttered when they heard, late on Christmas Day, that Nicolae
and Elena Ceauşescu had been shot dead by a firing squad
after a brief trial in a makeshift court at the army barracks

in Tirgoviste. 'Oh, that is *perfectly* convenient. Neat and tidy and – what is your expression? – shipshape. The square pegs have been adjusted to fit inside the round holes and everything is hunky-dory. Except that it isn't. Comrade Iniquity and his iniquitous wife have been released. They have been set free. They should have lived. They deserved to live. They did nothing to deserve this quick kindness.'

'They look peevish,' Nelly remarked, when the Ceauşescus were shown sitting on a bench, haughtily refusing to answer their inquisitors. 'They look like a peevish elderly couple. They look like Punch and Judy.'

'They do. A pair of terrible puppets. Punch and Judy is indeed apropos.'

The bulletin ended with a picture of the corpses.

'Is that real blood on his face, do you imagine? Two rag dolls, thrown to the ground. Two crumpled marionettes. That's all they look like now.'

'Will you be going home, Virgil?'

'I am not sure. I shall wait until I receive word from my few close friends. I am in no hurry.

'I must unglue myself from this,' he said, as the camera revealed a smiling woman holding up the Romanian flag with a hole where the Communist insignia had been. 'My eyes and ears and brain are tired. I am all of a sudden exhausted.'

'Goodbye, Nelly.'

'*Au revoir*, if you don't mind, Virgil. *Au revoir*, please.'

'We say *la revedere.*'

'In that case, I shall say it too. *La revedere.* Come back in the spring, come back in the summer, but come back. You still haven't seen my datura in flower.'

'The angels' trumpets?'

'The very same.'

'I shall bring him, Nelly.'

Nelly spread out her arms and held Kitty and Virgil in a single, long embrace.

'Happy New Year, beautiful Kitty Crozier.'

'Happy New year, sweetheart. Happy New Decade.'

'I shall be staying for breakfast. I shall be staying for tea and the dregs of the wild raspberry jam.'

'That's hours and hours in the future. We must think up ways of occupying ourselves till then.'

'Kitty, this is Virgil. Thank God you are there. I am calling you from the airport. I will be again in England soon. Oh, my English is failing me today. There is something in the post for you. You will get it, I hope, tomorrow. I must fly, in every sense. I love you.'

The 'something in the post' was a poem: '*A venit vremea de apoi.*'

He sent her a card from Bucharest, with a reproduction of *Magic Bird* by Brâncuşi: 'Beautiful Kitty, I shall be with you. I want to be with you. Your V.'

A second card came from Paris four months later, of Brâncuşi's *Adam and Eve*: 'I am getting nearer to you. There is only the Channel between us. I shall be on your doorstep soon. I am thought-collecting meanwhile and not good company for you. With my love. Your V.'

There were three more cards, each inscribed 'Kitty Love. Your V', of the same Brâncuşi sculpture: *The Bird in Space.*

Kitty had her sister to think of while she waited, with a desperately willed patience, for Virgil's return. The birth of Cecil's and Gillian's daughter, Lucy, reduced Daisy to numbness and silence. An occasional slow nod was the sole indication that she understood what Janet and Andrew, Kitty and Nelly were trying to say to her.

Then Dinu Psatta arrived, on a drizzly January day, bringing the news she wanted not to hear.

'You might solve a mystery for me, Mr Psatta. If you can.'

'Mystery? Which mystery?'

'Virgil never told me how he escaped from Romania. Do you know how?'

'Yes. The Dunārea. You say the River Danube. He crossed the River Danube.'

'In a boat?'

'No, no. With body.'

'He swam?' She pretended to swim – her arms beating a way through imaginary water. 'Virgil swam across the Danube?'

'Yes, yes. From Turnu Severin. God was with him. Many others were shot. Many were caught and shot. Virgil survive.'

Epilogue: The Names in the Dark

A life in a shopping bag.

('I have ownership of his burnt remains,' Dinu Psatta had said.

'Ashes.'

'Thank you. Ashes. I have his ashes in a black casket. I have not brought the casket with me. I could perhaps send it?'

'No. I don't want Virgil's ashes. No.'

'Then, I am thinking, if his mother's modest grave could be found and the casket put inside the problem will be solved.'

'That sounds like the ideal solution.'

'Thank you. Then I will pursue the matter.')

The copy of *Miorița* was inscribed 'Popescu Matilda Aprilie 1932'. She took out the broken-backed edition of Marcus Aurelius's *Meditations* and placed it carefully on her work table. There was a third book: *Poems of George Herbert*, a recent addition to his portable library. Its pages were stained with tea or coffee and annotated with innumerable pencilled comments.

Virgil had attached to each of the five poems his own rendering into English prose.

She opened the letter, cautiously, with a paper knife. It ran to twelve, closely written pages. She felt sick with apprehension as she began to read. Nothing it contained could be worse, she reasoned, than what she already knew. Virgil was dead. Virgil had killed himself. Virgil was finally gone from her.

Her hands were trembling, even so.

The first page was dated 10 January 1991.

For many years, Kitty, there was a photograph in the living-room of the Florescu apartment in Bucharest. It was in a mahogany frame and it showed my parents happily dancing the hora on the night of their wedding. It stood alone on the top of a cabinet. My mother dusted it every morning and often I caught her kissing the glass. Because it stayed in the same position, it signified permanence and security to me. Then the photograph and the frame disappeared. I was seventeen. The dance is over, I thought, seeing the empty space. One of them has decided that the dance is over.

I guessed it was my mother. I dared to ask her why the photograph had been removed. She said she had grown tired of it. She was no longer the pretty and carefree girl in the picture and the Constantin who had captured her heart was a changed man now. She said something I did not understand and because I made no sense of it I kept it in my memory. She said the photograph reproached her. And then she laughed and told me to forget the stupid remark.

I am trying to write in my best and clearest English, Kitty.

My mother's decline was slow and gradual, not dramatic. Meals were cooked when required, the furniture was dusted and polished, beds were made and unmade, our clothes were washed and ironed, everything was as normal. She prayed to her God, as she had always prayed, when there was no one about. But I would sometimes hear her sighing and muttering to herself while she performed her daily tasks and wonder why she was in the grip of what sounded like sadness. I would go to her in the kitchen or in the dining-room or wherever she was and take her hands in mine and invite her to share her worries with me. The only worries she had, she answered, were Romanian worries, the worries we all had in such a country at such a time, the worries that would not go away. We would embrace and she would stroke my hair and advise me to tend to my studies, for they would be my salvation.

I tended to my studies and persevered with the complex language I am writing in, and she was pleased with my progress. I left the Florescu apartment in my early twenties and lived the precarious life of a student and a teacher. She seemed to be more and more unhappy with each visit I paid. My father, the man I was still calling my father, told me he had heard her talking to her dead relations, chatting to them as if they were at tea together, in a voice as high and as irritating as a bird's.

Kitty, I think I have come to understand at long last why Matilda Florescu felt reproached by the photograph and why she feared to go on looking at her partner in the dance. On the day she took it from the cabinet and threw it out with the garbage – for photograph and frame vanished without trace – she had learned of Constantin Florescu's role in the historical event, the 'mystical occasion' that happened before her marriage. Her bridegroom, the happy bridegroom in the photograph, was a man who had butchered his fellow men and women, who had slit human throats as though they belonged to beasts.

That, I believe, was the dreadful knowledge my mother

241

could not share with me. That was her worry beyond all worries.

She let out a howl of misery and listened to the silence that followed it.

Then she picked up the phone. 'Nelly, I have some bad news, some really bad news. Virgil's dead. He died in Paris a few days ago. He took his life.'

'Be brave, my brave girl. Do you want me there?'

'No. I do and I don't, actually, but I'll settle for don't. I'll be in touch.'

'Of course you will. Now that Daisy's her sensible self again I can give you my full attention.'

'As you've always given me.'

'That's true.'

11 January 1991

You were always too considerate to say so, Kitty, but you must have wondered often if I was in my right mind. You were such a patient and attentive listener when – it was a frequent when – I was in a story-telling mood. I have to plead in my defence that I could not stop myself. The stories insisted on being told. They are my curious heritage, which I needed to pass on to you in some small measure.

As the Hungarian it was my misfortune to encounter in London rudely – but correctly – observed, we had no books in Romania for several centuries. (We had no Romania for several centuries.) Our poets had tongues but no tongue. Their words wandered from mouth to mouth and the resting-place, the sanctuary, that is the printed page was as remote to them as the stars they glorified in their verses. Their names are not recorded. Their names are in the dark, like those of the humble soldiers in my mightier namesake's mighty epic.

('What a perverse student Virgil was,' the blind Teodor Costea would say to her as they sat on the balcony of his house in Constanţa. 'And what a brilliant one also. His classmates wrote of the anguish of Dido and the rescue of Anchises from the flames of Troy – the big set-pieces, you might call them – but Virgil chose to deal, I seem to remember, with the plight of the Arcadian fisherman, one of the hundreds, or indeed thousands, killed by King Turnus. He has a name, does he not?'

'Menoetës.'

'That is the man. Will you permit me to smoke my pipe?'

'Please do.'

'We Romanians are walking chimneys, as you have probably noticed.'

'I have.'

'The smell of my tobacco is not so pungent when there is a breeze coming from the sea. Is the wine to your taste?'

'It certainly is.'

'Have you cast an eye over the Roman ruins?'

'Yes, I have.'

'And were there discarded tins and bottles and cigarette packets to spoil the view?'

'I'm afraid there were.'

'It is upsetting, this cavalier way people have with trash. An international custom, I hear. Blindness has a few compensations. Did you pause in front of the statue of the great Ovidius and pay him his deserved respects?'

'Yes, I did.'

'He was exiled to this region. This is where he wrote his *Tristia*. I still had my sight when I moved here with my late wife. Had I some romantic notion of being closer in spirit to my hero? I think I had. For me, Miss Crozier, Ovid is the sublime one. His language is like the finest champagne, which – diligent Romanian academic that I am – I have very rarely drunk. He has such wit, such lightness. I attempted, when I was much younger, to translate the *Metamorphoses*, but I abandoned the effort. It is a crime, a sin, to remove Ovid from his own words. I have him in my head now and when I am

243

unoccupied or incapable of sleep I speak his lines to myself. It is a daily ritual for me, a cleansing of the mental system. Take more wine, dear lady. Be generous with yourself. I keep a moderately well-stocked cellar.'

'You are kind, Professor Costea.'

'Virgil was not kind to you when he did that senseless thing. He was cruel to you. He was cruel to me. He was cruel to all of us. I loved him as a son. My old and worn-out eyes have a single use left to them, and that is to weep. You will excuse me?'

'Yes. Yes.'

'He was a gentle soul.'

'He was.'

'In this society designed for the comfort of brutes. He ought not to have done what he did. It was an act of cruelty.'

She would not be able to tell Teodor Costea that Virgil had regarded his suicide as an act of atonement.

'He should have heeded Marcus Aurelius, whom he did not study in Greek. The Emperor warns against impulses that are wrong. Virgil succumbed to a wrong impulse. Have you begun to forgive him?'

'I wish I could have persuaded him that his being a good man was enough. I shall never forgive him for not letting me have the chance to do that. He took himself off when I might have been most helpful to him. He was thought-collecting, he said. That was how he put it.'

'Poor Miss Crozier. It is a sign of the truly good among us that they find themselves wanting in goodness. It pains me that his last act will stand as a contradiction to the rest of his life. But there. When Domnul Sava returns from the hospital we will go to a restaurant I patronise. We will eat freshly caught fish and perhaps – with the assistance of a little more wine – I shall recite some lines of Ovid for you.')

Kitty, I was telling you the stories and speaking the poems because I wanted you to have a few memories of me that

244

cannot be obliterated by the action I have decided upon. This I realise now, in retrospect. Only weeks ago I was intending to see you in London with the idea of 'twisting your arm' into joining me on a long visit to my 'sad country full of humour'. By the way, the silent Adrian is selling perfume behind a counter in one of the new shops that have opened for business since the fake revolution, while the voluble Adrian is our representative in Strasbourg, when he is not waxing rhetorical in our selectively televised parliament. The situation is exceedingly humorous.

The expert on Emily Dickinson was one of the many secret policemen who were rounded up and shot. He was never in America, as I had suspected. His Emily Dickinson and Robert Frost performance was created specifically for Virgil Florescu. The smooth-faced master of disguise and dissimulation had other performances for other offenders. I imagine him discussing Beethoven with a musician, or Saint Teresa of Avila with a religious, or our great Brâncuşi with a sculptor. On with the motley! Variety is the spice of a policeman's life! In the Conducător's Romania it was insufficient just to 'put the frighteners on' a man or woman with opinions of their own. The questioners had to have some fun, some diversion. We invented a theatre of the absurd, after all. 'Are we in agreement that *The Column of the Infinite* is the most serene work by Brâncuşi, rising as it does to the very heavens? Or do you prefer his early *Sleep*, with the sleeping head still entrapped in marble? And are you shitting your pants yet?'

(I picked up 'put the frighteners on' in London, in a pub at Gospel Oak. The raciest expressions can be acquired over a glass of beer. 'They put the frighteners on him and he squealed' was what I heard.)

I have been deprived of the pleasure of bumping into Corneliu on a busy street and saying to him:

'I never hear the word "escape"
Without a quicker blood,
A sudden expectation,
A flying attitude!'

and relishing his reaction. Would he have replied 'Written in or around 1859 and published in 1891', like the expert he once was?

I have spoken to the silent Adrian however. He told me the price of a small bottle of Eau Sauvage. He was very polite, obsequious indeed. He appeared not to recognise me. He has the ideal voice for a salesman – soft, silky, persuasive.

'When this Romanian, his name is Dinu, gave me the news, I surprised myself by not being surprised. I was calm. I talked to him. He answered a question Virgil never answered, except in riddles. When I heard how Virgil escaped I laughed, because the idea of his swimming the Danube seemed incredible. Comical, even. I opened some wine and we chatted. He came back yesterday evening with a shopping bag containing three books, five poems and a very long letter. I cooked a simple meal, which he enjoyed. He thanked me and left. I phoned you after reading the first page of the letter. I quite literally didn't have the stomach to read on because I was retching so much. I've just finished the second page and the third is beckoning. I'm gabbling, Nelly.'

'Gabble on.'

'I can't. That's it. That's it, for the moment. I can't say any more.'

'I'll be here when you can.'

12 January 1991

Kitty, during those first happy weeks after we met in London – in the park, not the hospital, of course – I would relive my escape from Romania while spiking and

246

disposing of the leaves and litter. I told you I had ways and means of escaping and that is what I told everyone else, including the diverting Derek Harville, who is neither Mephistophelean nor devilish. You know now that Constantin Florescu is streets, boulevards, avenues, squares and motorways ahead of him in devilishness. Streams and rivers and oceans too.

I swam the Danube, at its narrowest point I believe, but it was wide enough. I was expecting the guards' lights to pick me out. I was expecting to be arrested and beaten up or shot with a marksman's bullet. But I reached the farther side. I slept my first sleep of liberty in a field in Yugoslavia, with the morning sun slowly drying me. I travelled at night for safety, resting in woods and forests in the daytime. I lived on bitter-tasting berries and herbs, and I drank running water . . .

('Typical, typical, typical,' Doina Rangu would exclaim, clapping her hands. 'It was typical of Virgil to choose a route no one else had taken. Virgil loved making life difficult for himself. There was a man working for the Red Cross just a few kilometres from the border, and Virgil – *typically* – contrived not to meet him. Why make contact with a man who can supply you with food and shelter, and ease your path across the country, when there is the exciting alternative of eating grass and sleeping under bushes, like a hermit? Oh, Kitty, Virgil had a genius for difficulty.')

. . . Until the day I drank strong beer and ate grey bread and orange-coloured cheese. These were the gifts – the benison, to use your lovely old word – of a farm-hand named Branko who invited me to share his lunch. He offered me salami too, which I had to decline. We communicated in mime show and in babyish French. His generosity warmed me and stirred me with hope. I felt honoured in his presence.

That is how I escaped. Swimming the Danube at dead

of night sounds like the action of a hero, but I am not heroic and I did not want anyone to consider me so. You would do it if you had to. Hundreds did it. That is why I spoke of ways and means. Ordinary ways. Simple-minded means.

I was reliving my journey of escape because it led me to you, via Split, and Ancona and Rome, and thanks to an obliging woman named Pamela who allowed me to marry her and become quasi-British. Everything seemed to fit into place, taking on a strange logic, when you wrote your address for me on the scrap of chocolate paper. How often I looked at that Lindt wrapper and counted myself blessed.

For I could not begin to believe in such a vast sprawling city as London – Bucharest is minute by comparison – I would meet again, and speak to, the beautiful woman I had wheeled on my porter's trolley from the operating theatre to the ward. I had neglected my duties for many minutes that day, Kitty, while I sat by your bed and watched you. And when I came back the next morning and saw that your bed was occupied by another I was sad but philosophical. I had prepared a little speech to say to you, but it had to go unsaid.

Kitty, you were my best hope. There were many times with you, in and out of the untidy bedroom we made untidier, when I thought: Yes, I am free. She is giving me my real freedom. She is liberating me from him, the man who sired me when he should have been dead, the man I had called – with all the shades of meaning children employ – my father. Kitty, you must know that I called him 'Tată' for the last time on the evening of his confession. The word became filth in my mouth from then on.

But you could not and cannot give me that real freedom because he took it from me with his boasting. He took it from me with the history lesson no son in the whole

248

wide unhappy world should ever have to listen to. I think
sometimes (no, I think of it with unbearable frequency)
of his making love to the young and innocent Matilda
Popescu with the blood of children on his hands. And I
am the product of their love-making. I am their first-born
child.

I have some claret to drink, which a good friend has
brought me. I must stop writing for today.

'Nelly?'

'No, this isn't Nelly. It's Daisy.'

'Hullo.'

'Is that all you can say? No "Lovely to hear you, Daisy"?
Not after all your sister's been through?'

'I'm sorry.'

'You promised to ring me on Sunday.'

'Did I? I must have forgotten.'

'Obviously.'

'The truth is that I'm working on a very difficult manuscript at present. It has masses of cross-references. The
author keeps jumping from one subject to another. I am
finding it very hard to keep pace with him. He's presented
me with quite a challenge, Daisy.'

'Excuses, excuses.'

'No, my dear. This isn't an excuse. How are you?'

'I thought you'd never ask. In actual fact, I'm on top of
the world, to coin a phrase. Can you guess why?'

'Surprise me.'

'It's to do with him.'

'Cecil?'

'Him. The one and only. He's agreed to the deal. He has
coughed up with everything my solicitor demanded. There
wasn't a peep of protest out of him, apparently.'

'I'm glad it's settled.'

'Not half as glad as I am. Now I can say I am finally
shot of him.'

249

'Yes.'

'And look forward to a new life.'

'Yes.'

'And start afresh. I shall be giving the male of the species a very wide berth from now on, I can tell you.'

'Yes.'

'I'm wasting my breath, aren't I? There *are* other words than "yes", you know.'

'I'm not in a talkative mood.'

'So I gather.'

'I have to get back to work, Daisy.'

'Work, work. My clever silly sister and her work. I'll go and talk to the dogs instead. They can't be less interested than you.'

13 January 1991

Kitty, did I ever mention a friend called Dinu Psatta? Radu I talked of I remember, but perhaps not Dinu. His parents named him after our great concert pianist Dinu Lipatti, who died very young. Dinu is also a musical man. He publishes music here in Paris, but before that he was in the embassy in Rome. He led a quietly dangerous life there, helping people who had escaped. We met in the Eternal City in clandestine fashion, in churches mostly. He says he has become a Roman Catholic as a result of those furtive meetings, to the accompaniment of Palestrina and Lassus.

I hope he will befriend you. I hope you will befriend him. He is a believer in everyday miracles. The accidents of fate that aided me on my journey through Yugoslavia he sees as miraculous events, preordained from Above. He will tell you this with his wry smile, but I am sure he is sincere. I know him to be sincere.

Kitty, I have discovered your poet George Herbert. I did not read him in *liceu* when I was reading John Donne. That was my loss. I have been studying him and learning his words ever since I came upon a very old copy of his *Poems* – dated 1895 – on a Left Bank bookstall. It was owned by a Mr Cedric Tiverley, who must have been a discerning gentleman. I am passing Mr Tiverley's book on to you. It is not a cast-off, like the clothes I wore that so upset the stylish Felix. Mr Tiverley died, I think, and then it set off on its travels. Now it is travelling from me to you, with love.

Kitty, it is a wonder to me that these marvels of wit and intellect were on the printed page two hundred years before my country (but we had no country, as such) had a written literature. What a fortunate English boy I would have been in 1633, in 1733, in 1833, to have sat in school with a book of Herbert's poems on my desk. (I am forgetting that I might have been a poor English boy in 1633, in 1733 and 1833, who had had no schooling.) In Moldavia or Wallachia I would have been listening to an elder speaking *Miorița*, the oldest ballad in our language – the ballad that did not find a resting place until the 1850s. And perhaps I would have added a line to it, a new conceit, a flourish of my own, as others have added their special conceits and flourishes, century after century. The poem, truly, of a people.

The man who sired me said on the evening of his revelations that our national poet, Mihai Eminescu, would have been 'on the side' of the butchers. 'He was dead, Tatā,' I told him – and that was the last time I called him Tatā, you must know, Kitty. 'His ideas are alive to this day,' he thundered. He apologised for shouting. I accepted his apology. I could accept his apology for shouting.

Eminescu, Kitty, was a man of his time, and the time was ferociously nationalistic. He blamed the Jews for all the troubles that beset our young uniting country. He is, nevertheless, our Keats. He is our first great poet on the printed page. He is our first literary name out of the dark.

I think I once spoke for you a poem by George Bacovia,

complete with approximate translation. It is he, of all our poets, I have most loved and envied. I cannot envy him his life, which he spent on the rack of depression, but I am jealous to this day of his finest work. There is a poem, Kitty, about a town bathed in autumn twilight. The sky has turned everything violet. Two poplar trees, appearing in silhouette, seem to the poet like a couple of apostles in violet surplices. His urban poetry is filled with such startling visions.

George Vasiliu (that was his real name) worked for a period as a government clerk, though he had no faith in politics. He left it to others to welcome the various glorious futures that became grim history in his lifetime. He drank to keep despair at a distance, but the drink only brought it closer.

I remember that when I was thirteen the man who sired me came into the room where I was reading and snatched the book of Bacovia from my hands. He flicked through its pages and stopped at the poem 'Liceu'. 'What kind of a man is it who compares his school to a cemetery? The cemetery of his youth?' he asked. I was silent. I waited for him to provide the answer. 'A drunkard. A morbid drunkard.'

Constantin Florescu did not appreciate Bacovia's irony. He had seen the sad Visiliu shuffling about the city supported by his wife and was confident in the judgement that such a wreck of humanity could produce nothing but 'morbid' verse. The idea that inside the wreck there existed an artist of the rarest delicacy and subtlety could not occur to one who was and is a stranger to those qualities.

I have finished thought-collecting for another day.

'Is that Mrs Florescu? Pamela Florescu?'

'It's been a long time since anyone called me that. Yes, this is she.'

'I have some news of your husband.'

'My husband? Husband in word, not deed. I allowed him a chaste kiss in the registrar's office and then it was curtains matrimonially speaking. Who am I talking to?'

'My name is Kitty Crozier. I'm a friend of Virgil.'

'A friend friend, may I enquire, or someone more intimate?'

'Someone more intimate.'

'He's never mentioned you. He had nothing of any consequence to tell me, he wrote in his last letter, sending me yet another change of address. I always suspected him of being a dark horse.'

'Really?'

'So what's the news?'

'He's dead.'

'Dead? Virgil Florescu dead?'

'Yes.'

'They haven't murdered him, have they? He didn't go home and get himself murdered?'

'No. No. He died in Paris.'

'Were you with him? May I call you Kitty?'

'Yes, Pamela. No, I wasn't with him. I wish I had been.'

'I bet you do. How did he die, Kitty?'

'His heart gave in. He'd had problems with his heart.'

'He wasn't fat, was he? I didn't have to see him with his clothes off to know he wasn't carrying any surplus flesh. What doctors describe as a murmur, was it?'

'Probably.'

'What a waste. He was still quite young, wasn't he?'

'Forty-four.'

'That's young these days. Have you had the funeral?'

'Yes.'

'Did you give him a nice send-off?'

'It was very quiet.'

'And what have you done with him? Has he been buried or cremated?'

'Cremated. It was what he preferred. The ashes are going to Romania.'

'I'm sorry, Kitty. For him and for you.'

'Thanks.'

'Bear up.'

'I'll try.'

'I suppose I could offer myself for marriage again. But I shouldn't imagine there's much demand any more, would you. Those countries are free now, aren't they?'

'Yes, they are.'

'Not as free as us, but freer than they were.'

'Yes, Pamela.'

'Well, thank you for letting me know. And, as I say, try to bear up.'

'I will. Goodbye.'

'Goodbye, Kitty. God bless.'

14 January 1991

Kitty, I received my unwanted history lesson the year before I made my escape. I told no one about Constantin Florescu's involvement in the 'mystical occasion' – except for Radu, that is. Radu said, 'Sons do not have to emulate their fathers. You must live as well as you can.'

My 'aversion' began the moment I left the Florescu apartment. My body sent the message to my brain that I could no longer eat meat. It was easy not to be carnivorous in Romania at that time. Steak, lamb and pork were luxuries. Chicken too. I had vegetables (not many), and rice (a little), and apples to nourish and sustain me.

'You must live as well as you can' – Radu's advice made a kind of sense. I went on with my teaching and then I wrote the poem that caused the authorities to take a particular interest in the writings of Virgil Florescu. Corneliu paid me his first visit.

('We knew we had arrived, Kitty, when we became aware of the bugging device above our heads. They were listening

254

in on our every conversation. What is that funny poem in *Alice in Wonderland*?'

'Oh, "Jabberwocky".'

'Yes, yes. Virgil tormented our hidden listeners – we hope tormented – with "Jabberwocky". He and I would sit in silence and then he would recite "Jabberwocky". Night after night he recited it – softly, loudly, fast, slow. But always seriously. That was the beauty of the joke for us. He spoke the "Jabberwocky" poem as if it was very serious, very sombre and serious.'

'Tell Kitty about the bean feast, Radu.'

'The bean feast, yes. Doina is referring to a mad evening when she cooked for us all the beans she could find.'

'In a tomato and onion sauce of my own invention.'

'She cooked this mountain of beans in a big pot, and Virgil and I gorged ourselves eating them. We washed them down with beer.'

'I insisted they eat them up, Kitty. So that everything went according to my brilliant plan.'

'Which it did. Doina said not a word that evening, which was a terrible strain for her. And a relief for us.'

'Ignore his sarcasm, Kitty. The opening salvo came at nine fifteen, with a tremendous blast from Virgil. We vowed we would not laugh, and oh, it was an agony for us keeping a straight face. We were determined they would hear nothing but the farts, which went on and on and on, I am pleased to remember.'

'Our thoughts were in our arses, Kitty. And our glad tidings to those who were preying on us.')

And soon there was the orchestrated business with my mother's precious carpet and its cheap replacement, which Radu and I emptied our bladders on.

I believed I was simply running away from a dictator and his minions. It is with shame I record that the 'mystical occasion' was not foremost in my thoughts. I believed in a future for Virgil Florescu and the loved and loving friends who would one day taste freedom. I was fleeing a country ruled over by a man of consummate mediocrity, a man smaller in soul than he was in height. I was leaving a city in which that pygmy's dog Comrade Corbul was better fed and better housed and better groomed than the majority of its human occupants.

(Kitty, did you read or see that many people raided his villa and stole the tins of food that were flown in for Comrade Corbul? They filled their hungry bellies with the meat. They fed themselves to bursting.)

I was escaping from a banal farce, Kitty, in which the Conducător and his vicious little spouse were the leading players. We – his and her underlings – were required to assume supporting roles, with our positions neatly chalked on-stage. We were meant to remain on our marks and speak the lines that were scripted for us. But there were those, and I was one of them, who found the lines unspeakable. I lacked the late Corneliu's aplomb. I wanted to live a natural, ordinary life but that was denied me. The farce demanded actors and I was reluctant to perform.

(The diverting Derek would understand this. He has recreated himself, as he admitted the day he surprised me in Green Park. He has done this of his own volition, not at the whim of a despot.)

So, as I journeyed towards Italy, with these ideas of freedom crowding inside my head, the significance of the 'mystical occasion' had still not completely 'sunk in', as you say. It was not until I lay ill in the kind Freda Whiteside's attic that the horror struck me, as it strikes me now, you must know, Kitty.

'Felix Crozier speaking.'
'Hullo, Daddy.'
'Kitty, my dearest darling, what an unexpected pleasure. How was your Christmas?'

'I spent it with Nelly, as usual. Daisy joined us, with Janet and Andrew.'

'The grandchildren I've never had the privilege of meeting. Your twin has recovered, I take it.'

'Yes, she has. She's happy, too. Cecil has given her a great deal of money and the house in Richmond as well.'

'My, my. It's amazing what a chap will pay to free himself from a woman on the warpath. I expect he would have parted with the crown jewels, if he'd had them.'

'Daddy, is Derek there?'

'Mr Mockery, you mean. I'm a martyr to his tongue, my dearest. It's Crozier this and Crozier that the livelong day.'

'Is he there, Daddy?'

'Yes, he's here, thinking up his next put-down. Honing it to perfection.'

'I should like a word with him.'

'With Derek?'

'With Derek.'

'What on earth have you got to say to him that you can't say to me?'

'It's a cookery matter.'

'Ah. Ah, yes, that is rather his department. I'm as useless as the Pope's balls, I have to admit, where cuisine is concerned. My skill lies in polishing off the delicious concoctions the master-chef provides. Whatever faults Crozier has, failing to appreciate Derek's food is not among them. We ate wood pigeon this evening, my darling, in a port-wine gravy, with a celeriac *dauphinoise* on the side. And then a caramel orange tart for dessert. My waist is a thing of the distant past, only to be glimpsed in the photograph album upstairs. But do I miss it? No, I do not. I won't let vanity get in the way of my appetite any more.'

'I should like a quick word with Derek.'

'You're asking for the impossible. No one has a quick word with Derek, unless it's a word in edgeways you have in mind. He might grant you one of those.'

257

'A word with Derek.'

'If you insist.'

She heard her father calling Derek to the phone. 'It's my daughter. The sweet one, of course. She wants a quick word with you.'

'Good evening, Kitty.'

'Hullo, Derek. Is Daddy in earshot?'

'Yes.'

'I've told him I'm ringing on a cookery matter.'

'I am at your service.'

'But I'm not ringing you about cookery. I don't want Daddy to know what I have to tell you.'

'Carry on.'

'Derek, Virgil is dead.'

'Mayonnaise, Kitty, has driven finer cooks than I am to despair.'

'Thank you. He killed himself.'

'The ingredients should be at room temperature. For a generous half-pint you require two egg yolks, two table-spoons of white wine vinegar and three of olive oil.'

'In Paris.'

'I am of the Dijon mustard persuasion myself. Add the tiniest amount, along with the salt and white pepper.'

'Ten days ago.'

'And please use a balloon whisk for beating in the oil. The spoon and the spatula have brought grief to many a talented chef. And while I am on the subject, lemon juice could be substituted for the vinegar. A lemon-flavoured mayonnaise is the perfect accompaniment to asparagus.'

'He was cremated. There was no funeral, at his request.'

'The monstrous duke for whom I once slaved and skiv-vied expressed a preference for the dreadful bottled muck. It contains milk and cornflour and is cooked. Cooking may-onnaise is a contradiction in terms.'

'He left a note. It was an open-and-shut case.'

'Why don't I write down the recipe for you? With all the possible variations?'

'A friend has Virgil's ashes. He is sending them to Romania.'

'I wish you every success in advance. You can't go wrong with a balloon whisk.'

'That's it, Derek.'

'The recipe will be in tomorrow's post. Crozier is signalling that he has something else to charm your ear with. Goodbye, Kitty.'

'Goodbye.'

'Here he is.'

'Kitty, my dearest darling, please forgive me. I was wittering on about my waistline, or rather the lack of it, and I clean forgot to ask you how you are. How are you?'

'I'm fine, Daddy.'

'I'm glad. Is that Romanian fellow still abroad?'

'Virgil. Yes, he's still abroad. He keeps in touch.'

'I should hope so. Now make sure you follow Derek's instructions. His mayonnaise is second to none.'

'I'll follow them.'

'That's my girl. Good night, my dearest darling. Lots of monkey's bums to you.'

'Good night, Daddy.'

15 January 1991

Kitty, you see their photographs in the newspapers from time to time. I am thinking of the plump old survivors, cornered in Brazil or the Argentine and put on trial. But they are everywhere, and there are some whose photographs you will never see. That courteous gentleman walking his dog. The spruce and boyish figure on the tennis court. The kindly grandfather, pulling funny faces to amuse the sons or daughters of his son or daughter.

Constantin Florescu – my brother informed me – is worshipped by his grandchildren.

('Radu, I think I have to see him. Can you arrange a meeting?'

'Are you sure of this, Kitty?'

'It's a gut feeling. I need to take a look at him and to hear his voice.'

'He speaks no English. I should have to interpret for you. And for him as well if you wish to address him.'

The meeting would be arranged. It would be an honour for Constantin Florescu to be introduced to the English-woman who had loved his unhappy Virgil.

Radu would come to the lobby of the once opulent hotel and draw her discreet attention to the Sicilians who were discussing business with a government official. 'We have the Mafia with us now. We have truly arrived, Kitty.'

They would walk in the summer sunshine through the Lipscani market, past stalls selling cakes and rissoles and mass-produced icons and nylon underwear, and Radu would stop and show her a plaque commemorating the journalism – 'Not the serene poetry' – of Mihai Eminescu. 'His noble schemes for our young country.'

They would step over bags of stinking refuse in the court-yard and climb the decrepit stairs to the apartment where Constantin Florescu lived alone. A cleaning woman with a mop in hand would lead them into his presence.

Constantin Florescu, *omul pragmatic*, would rise from the chair in which he had been reading the morning's news, and come towards her and kiss her hand. 'I am honoured. I am deeply honoured.'

'Good day to you.'

'Sit down, please. The maid will fetch tea or coffee.'

Radu would decline the offer, and the pink-faced, corpu-lent survivor would return to his chair and let out a long, weary sigh before he began to speak to her.

'This was a handsome apartment once, when my wife was alive and my boys were small. Alas, I have had to dispose of the antique furniture, some of it from France,

Matilda and I inherited from our families. The velvet curtains remain, but they are frayed and faded, and do not merit close inspection. We have lived through hard times. You have seen something of our city already?'

'Yes, I have.'

'Then you will be aware, perhaps, of the grandeur it enjoyed. Our boulevards, our parks, our Parisian buildings. In the years between the wars we had more restaurants in Bucharest than any other city in Europe.'

'Virgil,' she would say. 'Virgil.'

'He is the one son who has failed me. His brother has risen high in the ranks of the army, and commands respect and admiration. But Virgil wasted the life I gave him. I loved him. I love him, you must understand, in spite of our differences.'

'I can translate the words for you,' Radu would observe, 'but I leave it to you to detect the character of the man behind them.'

She would stare at the father of her lover and he would smile faintly, and she would continue staring at him and he would flinch under her steady gaze.

'You murderer,' she would shout at him. And then she would turn to Radu. 'I am a coward, aren't I? What is the Romanian word?'

'You have a choice, Kitty. There is *ucigaş* and *asasin*.'

She would get up from the chair in which she had felt imprisoned and go to Constantin Florescu, and look down on him, and spit out: '*Ucigaş. Asasin.*'

There would be a silence, and then he would say to Radu: 'The Englishwoman is too neat, too tidy, in her accusation. Tell her the English have made heroes of the Dresden bombers. Tell her she is as ignorant of history as my foolish elder son. Tell her to get out of my sight.'

He would follow them to the landing. 'The Jews were what they were, Englishwoman.'

She hugged Radu in the courtyard. 'It smells much

261

sweeter down here, doesn't it? Let me buy you a seriously strong drink for arranging that unforgettable meeting.')

His five Roman Romanian granddaughters.

'You are Roman Romanians.' That is what he told Aureliu and me when we were little. 'You must always be conscious that you have Roman blood in your veins.'

I asked him, years later, how he knew. He replied by advising me to examine my reflection in a mirror. The refinement of my features was evidence of my Romanness. Was my nose a peasant's nose, a gypsy's nose? Was it not similar to the noses on Roman coins? 'Blood makes distinctions, my son. Blood indicates who we are. A man may be silent, but his blood will speak.'

I hear him, Kitty. I hear him.

He never talked of the Roman soldiers, the peasantry, the names in the dark. It was Trajan, Trajan, Trajan, the conqueror of Decebalus and his Dacian hordes who was on his lips. We Florescus were descendants of Trajan – not Nero, not Caligula, not Commodus. Not the men who fashioned terror. Not the men who killed for sport.

It is one of the worst sadnesses of history that Marcus Aurelius sired Commodus. It should have been the other way around.

I tried to persuade you, when I was still full of secrets, that your father, your father who admits – vainly – to being terrible is not so terrible. If I had the power, I would sanctify him for his shallow stylishness, his facile metaphysics. St Felix, the saint of (relatively) harmless selfishness. St Felix, the breaker of hearts that have the capacity to mend. St Felix, the father who would have irritated me beyond endurance if I had been his son. His grateful son, Kitty. I would welcome a father who lamented his jowls, who showed me his guilty affection with kisses that resembled the bums of monkeys.

Daisy also should count her blessings.

'Kitty.'

'Nelly.'

'Am I expected?'

'Soon, I think. Quite soon.'

'My holdall is packed.'

'I'll phone.'

'I'm here.'

16 January 1991

Kitty, I want to write about Cerberus, the dog with three
heads who guards the entrance to Hades. My feeble poem
merely hints at his resourcefulness. His six eyes and ears
have ensured his eternal survival. The entrance to Hades
cannot be demolished; it is a permanent fixture, and the
gifts, the talents, of Cerberus will always be employed.

Constantin Florescu has those gifts, the necessary gifts for
survival. He tried to pass them on to me. Why did I resist?
Why did I feel that being watchful, constantly (or Con-
stantinly) watchful, was a bad, a degrading way to live?
These are perhaps rhetorical questions, even though I asked
them of myself more times than I can remember. Being
watchful means being suspicious – suspicious of friends, of
lovers, of every decent gesture, of every act of kindness.

Cerberus will growl when he has to growl, will roll
over and offer his tummy for tickling, will bark at those
who are out of favour and pant for those the state
approves of, and because he has six eyes and six ears he
is never short of the latest information. The Conducātor
growled and barked and panted, and had his tummy
tickled when Gheorghiu-Dej was the master, and when
the master died he bided his time until he and his bitch
could take command of Hades. And having gained control, the Cerberus-that-was called for his Cerberuses-in-
waiting to gather at the gates, and with what fleetness,
Kitty, they appeared. With what stealth. With what deep,
dark cunning.

(We will excuse the 'Baskervilles' from these scrictures, and the Dobermann I encountered in Yugoslavia, and Comrade Corbul, that bemedalled innocent.)

The man who sired me – the father of Aureliu – has been a Cerberus for sixty years. He is ever watchful. He is ever suspicious. His six Roman Romanian eyes and ears will not fail him. Here he is, Kitty, at the gates. Throw him a bone.

'Kitty, it is Dinu. Dinu Psatta.'

'Hullo.'

'I feel I broke the news badly for you. It was a big problem for me. Virgil did not make things easy. Your trout was wonderful to eat. I hope, please, you will come to Paris.'

'I will.'

'I omitted to mention one tiny fact. Virgil broke a pane of glass in the window of his room before he died. He was remembering the Orthodox faith of his mother, I think. He was letting his soul, at least, go free.'

17 January 1991

The photograph is on the top of the cabinet. The Oltenian carpet is on the floor. My mother's box of treasures is on her dressing-table. Tată is at his desk in the government building, sifting through his papers, keeping the *status quo* in place, as it is his lawyer's business to do.

And I am happy to be ill in bed, because I am alone with my *Mămică*, who is reading to me the silly story of the old Russian soldier who thought he could outwit Death.

The curse of nostalgia, Kitty.

3/ ii/ '91

Dear Kitty:

Herewith the recipe for mayonnaise, as promised.

I am saddened by your news, but I am not surprised. Virgil was a man of some considerable grace. I have chanced upon the right word, for once. He was a man of grace. I have a happy memory of eating raisins with him in Green Park.

And he was so appreciative of my jokes. A licensed jester could not have played to a more responsive audience.

I send you my sympathy.

That living monument to human folly, your father, is demanding his lunch. This may be the moment for the ratsbane.

Yours ever, Derek H.

18 January 1991

Kitty, you can now purchase 'bodice rippers' in Bucharest. These tales of 'unbridled passion' and 'steaming lust' were banned in the days of the Conducãtor. His First Lady objected to them on the grounds that no one but she could experience such transports of the flesh. Hers was the only pussy in Romania permitted to mew with pleasure.

There are game shows on the television now, but they are not as diverting as the ones I used to watch with you.

('Oh, it is felicitous. It is irresistible. Come and look, Kitty.'

A female contestant was guessing the selling price of a dishwasher, a double bed, an ornamental table and a reproduction of Van Gogh's *Sunflowers* in a gilt frame, and whenever her guess was correct she was the tearful recipient of sustained applause and cheering.

'She is weeping, Kitty. And the congregation is overjoyed for her. This is a religious ceremony, with Money as the object of worship. It is delightful for me to behold.')

And the palace the Conducãtor had built to celebrate his earthly power and glory stands deserted in the putrid

265

heart of the city he almost razed for eternity. It is said that rats scuttle across its imitation marble floors.

In the stateliest of the state bedrooms – rumour has it – the ghostly sound of a ghostly pussy's mew of pleasure can be heard at dead of night.

'Hold me, Nelly.'

'There. There.'

'We must keep Virgil's death a secret from Daisy. I'll say he disappeared, when and if I have the strength to face her.'

'Be brave, Kitty.'

'Perhaps I *was* infatuated. Perhaps I am the silly creature she insists I am. I'm beginning to wish that I'd never seen him in the hospital and that I'd taken a taxi to the Ritz that day instead of walking through the park.'

'Think of him. Think of the burden of guilt he was carrying, Kitty. He was beyond rescue. Weep your fill.'

19 January 1991

Kitty, there are people in Romania today who are known as the 'nostalgics'. They are the men and women, mostly old, who waited in line hour after hour for stale bread and unsightly cuts of meat. The bread is no longer stale and the meat pleases the eye, and both are expensive. The poor 'nostalgics' have nothing to wait for now. They, truly, are cursed by nostalgia.

(She would see a stooped 'nostalgic' place a bunch of tired lilies on the nondescript grave of Nicolae and Elena Ceauşescu, and Alina would say, 'My heart aches for the deluded soul. I shall offer her a little money, but she might be too proud to accept it.'

The woman would not be too proud. She would peer at the note before stuffing it into the pocket of her cardigan. 'You miss them too, gentle lady?'

'We miss them, yes. They will always be in our thoughts.'

'Life is not the same without them.'

That evening Doina would remark, as they sat down to eat, 'Are you sure you lasted two whole years with Virgil? Are you sure, Kitty?'

'Of course I'm sure.'

'Do you hear her, Alina?'

'I do.'

'We lasted what – two weeks, two months? He was the worst kind of lover, was he not, Alina?'

'The very worst.'

'And what kind is that?'

'Are you saying you do not know?'

'I think I am.'

'He was a mother's boy. We loved him, we loved him very much, but dear God in heaven, he was a mother's boy through and through. When I sleep with a man the bed contains him, me and no other. I make that understood in advance now, thanks to Virgil.'

'Matilda came into my bed also, Kitty, and I did not welcome her.'

'I wasn't bothered. I wasn't bothered by Matilda. She never really bothered me at all.')

And Constantin Florescu thrives. The ancient has a brand-new entrance to guard. There is life – as you say in England, Kitty – in the old dog yet.

'Laura?'

'Is it you, Kitty?'

'Yes, it is. I've been a lousy friend to you lately.'

'There are ways of compensating for your lousiness. Restaurant ways.'

'Message received. Oh, Laura.'

'What's the matter, lousy friend?'

'He's dead.'

'The Romanian?'

'He took his life.'

'Kitty. Kitty.'

'You remember him?'

'I can't forget him. It was his face as he came out of the lift. I gaped at him, I remember. Perhaps my jaw dropped. I thought to myself: all of this man's life is in his face and he's unable to hide it. And then I thought: he is Kitty's man and I am being rude, and that's when I noticed you standing beside him. That face, Kitty, that face of his.'

20 January 1991

Kitty, there is a village museum in Bucharest. What is not savage in our history is enshrined there. The beautiful wooden huts and churches, with their roofs of mud and straw, were constructed by a host of names in the dark.

('Radu, he blamed himself for what he did to you.'

'I helped many to escape. Blame, blame. We will forget blame. We will brush blame to one side. That rug, Kitty, is it not a marvellous object? Virgil was in awe of it. Those birds, those trees – is it not marvellous? We will dispense with blame.')

The life that transcends savagery. The life that crafts bowls and spoons and everyday utensils. The life that is touched with the holiness of the useful.

'Kitty?'
'Yes.'
'It's Cecil.'
'Hullo.'
'How's Daisy?'
'She appears to be very satisfied with your settlement.'
'That's a relief.'
'Let's hope she stays satisfied.'
'Let's hope. Touch wood. Daisy's not consistent.'
'True.'
'Kitty, I'm ringing you to say I've met a Socrates.'
'A Socrates?'
'A real live Socrates. An illiterate Socrates, in Corfu. In

Kalami, to be pedantic. I've just been there with Gilly and the babe for a winter break. Yes, a Socrates of very few words, but the genuine article.'

'A Socrates, Cecil?'

'Homer Bradley? Your Virgil? Do you catch my classical drift?'

'I catch it.'

'Tell Virgil I've bagged him at last, won't you? A real live, garlic-breathing Socrates.'

21 January 1991

Kitty, I have been wanting and wanting to write a poem. The title is intact. It is 'The Names in the Dark'.

The stubborn words will not budge. I feel them as stones inside me.

('There is a fresh pane of glass in the window, Kitty.'

'I'm a grieving idiot. There's nothing of him here. There was nothing of him in the rooms in London. What have I been searching for?'

'Go to Romania. You will meet Radu and Alina and Doina, and the magnificent Teodor Costea, if he is still alive. I will put you in touch with them. You will find there traces, at least, of him.'

They would leave Virgil's last address, on rue L'Agent Bailly, and Dinu would take her to a restaurant near the Bastille, where they would eat roast lamb and drink 'an ocean' of Burgundy.

They would return to his elegant apartment on rue de Dunkerque and drink more wine and listen to Dinu's own 'mightier namesake' playing Bach, and then they would stumble into bed, laughing, and attempt to make love, and fail, and Dinu would say, 'I am so unsinful, Kitty, that I bore my father-confessor to drowsiness. A description of our tumultuous struggle will perhaps awaken him' and they would laugh again and sleep, entwined, and rise in the morning perfectly content with each other's company.)

Kitty, this evening I telephoned the man who sired me. The number rang and rang. I thought: He has outwitted me. He has died a peaceful death.

Then I heard his voice, his familiar rasping voice. It had been my intention to wish him a happy anniversary but I did not have the heart or stomach to do it. 'Who is there? Who is there?' he shouted and I slammed down the receiver.

Fifty years ago today the man who was yet to sire me put on his green shirt of the Legion of the Archangel Michael and tied a bag of pure Romanian soil around his neck and wore it like a sacred medallion.

And he sang, as he went to the slaughter, the hymns of his childhood. He sang of Mary and Jesus as he bled them as their kind bleed cattle.

I hear them. I hear them.

And he and his brothers-in-arms consigned their names to the huge darkness of history.

I am not leaving a bloody mess behind. I have a piece of rope to hand.

I am erasing the life he gave me. It is the least I can do on this day of days.

Post Scriptum: Forgive me, Kitty. I am to blame for Radu's ordeal in the institution. I hope he also forgives me.

('I realise my opinions have never counted for anything with you, Kitty, but for what it's worth I think your new Romanian is a distinct improvement on the other one. He wears sensible clothes. He doesn't look as if he had the worries of the world on his shoulders. And he doesn't laugh like a madman either.')

Another Life, another task to distract her.

The Life that was to release her from her trance of grief

was scarcely more than a monograph – a short character study, simply written, running to a hundred and twenty pages. Its subject was Wilhelm Friedemann Bach, the eldest son of the great Johann Sebastian, a man desperate to escape from his father's shadow. She learned that he was an accomplished composer at an early age, the pleasant harmonies coming easily and naturally to him, in the fecund manner the music-lovers of Leipzig expected of a Bach. Yet Wilhelm Friedemann grew disenchanted with the facility with which he was able to write for the orchestra, the keyboard and the cathedral choir, and took to experimenting. His ambition was to create a new sound, a sound distinguishable from Johann Sebastian's, a sound that would be recognised as his and his alone. But his father's shadow lengthened and darkened with each new composition and Wilhelm Friedemann sought relief from his frustrations in drink. Alcohol mellowed him, dulled his demons, and in his final years he was one of the familiar sights of unrespectable Berlin – an amiable drunkard, shuffling from tavern to tavern in old and shabby clothes, his once tormented nature apparently at rest.

By the end of the book she was moved to tears of pity and deep commiseration. She went out to her garden and let the rain fall on her. And as she stood there, she saw Virgil coming across the lawn, his Communist tooth gleaming in the dimness.

Five Poems

by Virgil Florescu
newly translated by Kitty Crozier and Dinu Psatta

Stainless Steel

The archaeologist opens the glass case
And brings out, like a conjuror, a shining object.
He is aglow with scholarly excitement
As he stands before his devoted pupils
Who are waiting impatiently for him to speak.
He is their favourite elucidator of mysteries.

He invites them to pass the bright little beauty
From hand to respectful hand, with care.
They are amazed, bewildered, awe-struck, speechless.
They have not looked quite so confused, he tells them,
Since the day he produced the Bronze-Age kettle,
Battered and rusted beyond recognition.

Would they believe the object was once a tooth
In somebody's mouth, a thousand years past?
A fabricated tooth, from the age of Stainless Steel,
Guaranteed free from corrosion, and unbreakable?
Its owner was *homo sovieticus*, a man or woman
    unsung
Of whom this little beauty is the only trace.

It is my tooth the students are examining.
And now the words of the dentist are almost echoed
By the astute professor of archaeology.
I hear him saying to my anxious mother, on edge at my
    side,
That the tooth will see me through the longest life
And even after. Worms will find it indigestible
And the fiercest fire concede surrender.

Cerberus

He has only one head in the photograph,
The usual allotment of eyes and ears,
A solitary nose he is proud to call Roman
And a thin-lipped mouth that looks like a scar.
He would seem to be ordinary.

His other heads are temporarily invisible.
He has the gift of making them vanish
Whenever his master recommends concealment.
Heads Two and Three are always camera-shy:
A pair of shrinking violets.

Three heads are better than one in his profession.
It's a risky business, guarding the gates of hell.
You need exceptional qualifications
And he's exceptionally qualified – this beast
Seen here in the guise of a man.

I am the son of Mister Trinity-Head,
The human Cerberus, the beast in a suit.
He tried to teach me his canine tricks –
Licking the devil's hand; barking the devil welcome.
I was a hopeless student.

He's an old beast now, the three-headed survivor
With a single cunning brain. While he sleeps
Four eyes stay open, and four ears pick up
The faintest footfall. The devil rests secure
With such a restless guardian.

The Fisher of Perch

I told the recruiting officer
I was living a quiet life
Here in Arcadia.
This is a place, I said,
Where nothing much occurs
Of any significance
Between birth and death.
History of the bloody kind's
Unknown to us.

He patted his gleaming sword
And strode into my humble hut
Near the brooks of Lerna.
I watched as his cold eyes noted
My few necessities –
My pots and pans, my bed of straw,
And the garb I wasn't wearing.

The brooks are bursting with spotted perch
And I'm a fisherman, I babbled,
With work to do, with mouths to fill.
Besides, I don't know what your war's about.
That's when he laughed. Oh poor Menoetës,
Ask Jupiter, ask Juno, question all the gods,
Ask every Trojan who came through the flames
And then ask Prince Aeneas. Don't ask me.

And so I didn't. I went off to fight,
Losing my peace of mind that brisk spring day.
I shared his ignorance until my death
Some several battles later.
No less a hero than the great King Turnus
Dispatched me with a swift and savage jab.
I tasted fish before my gullet flowed.

Breaking the Glass

Free me, the voice inside the body whispered.
Free me, I beg of you. Let me be released.
I've served my sentence. Set me free at last.

The dead man's brother could not hear the cries.
He smiled to think a soul was hidden somewhere
Within the mass of flesh, bent on escape.

Please break the glass, the feeble voice insisted.
Do as I plead. The window's right behind you.
Waste no more time. Proceed without delay.

The brother made a fist and hit the glass.
It stayed unbroken and his hand unbloodied.
He told his nephew, then, to fetch a stone.

The stench is foul in here, the voice complained.
Please set me free to breathe the cool fresh air.
The glass is fragile. Smash it. Smash it now.

The corpse's son hurled the rough piece of brick
Straight at the window, but the brick bounced off
As though it had a spring in it, like rubber.

Please try again, the tired voice entreated.
Take pity on me. Show a little mercy.
I've suffered long and hard in this dark place.

The brother and his family washed the body,
Then poured the cooling water round a tree.
The dead man's soul would drink it on its travels.

'And may the earth be light on him', the priest intoned,
And from the coffin came an anguished gasp –
His soul's last sound before eternal silence.

That night the dead man's son stood at the window
And stroked the stubborn glass. His gentle touch
Did what the fist and stone had failed to do.

A cackling laugh rose from the shattered fragments.

The Time of Afterwards

is when
no one hungers
no one thirsts

is when
no one craves peace
no one covets war

is when
there is a lasting silence

is when
no one hears that silence

is when
there will be no when
or now
or then

The time of afterwards
will be no one's time

will be no time at all